COME THE FEAR

The Richard Nottingham Historical Series
by Chris Nickson

THE BROKEN TOKEN
COLD CRUEL WINTER ★
THE CONSTANT LOVERS ★
COME THE FEAR ★

★ *available from Severn House*

COME THE FEAR

A Richard Nottingham Novel

Chris Nickson

CRÈME de la CRIME

This first world edition published 2012
in Great Britain and the USA by
Crème de la Crime, an imprint of
SEVERN HOUSE PUBLISHERS LTD.

British Library Cataloguing in Publication Data

Nickson, Chris.
  Come the fear.
  1. Nottingham, Richard (Fictitious character)–Fiction.
  2. Leeds (England)–History–18th century–Fiction.
  3. Detective and mystery stories.
  I. Title
  823.9'2-dc23

ISBN-13: 978-1-78029-030-0 (cased)

All Severn House titles are printed on acid-free paper.

Severn House Publishers support The Forest Stewardship Council [FSC],
the leading international forest certification organisation. All our titles that
are printed on Greenpeace-approved FSC-certified paper carry the FSC logo.

MIX
Paper from
responsible sources
FSC® C018575

Typeset by Palimpsest Book Production Ltd.,
Falkirk, Stirlingshire, Scotland.
Printed and bound in Great Britain by
MPG Books Ltd., Bodmin, Cornwall.

For Ray Nickson (1914–2001)
and
Betty Nickson (1919–2008)
I hope they would have liked this.

Oh my lord, how she bleeds.
Out and come her heart's thick blood out and then come the fear.
Lucy Wan, traditional, Child Ballad 51

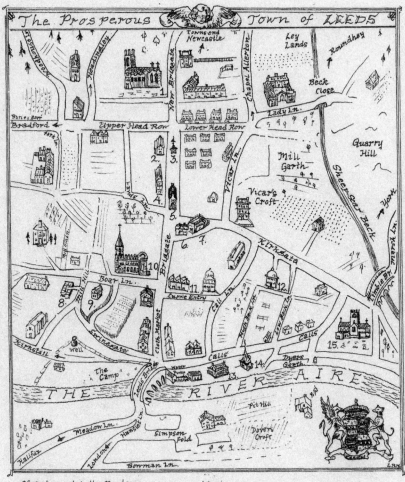

The Prosperous Town of LEEDS

Of Interest to the Reader:

1. St. John's Church
2. The Talbot
3. Market Cross
4. The Ship
5. Moot Hall
6. The White Swan
7. Gaol
8. Shaw Well
9. Davidsons House
10. Holy Trinity Church
11. Old Kings Arms
12. White Cloth Hall
13. Tunstall & Jackson
14. House Fire
15. Leeds Parish Church

One

It was the last day of March and the sun had risen bright and pale. There was a crispness in the early morning air; Richard Nottingham felt it cold against his face as he walked and it cut sharply through the old wool of his breeches, a reminder that spring hadn't fully arrived yet.

Last night there'd been a large full moon that hung low over Leeds. He'd stood at the window and watched its light spread across the fields.

It had been a damp, chill winter, a time of aches and pains, agues and rheums. He'd felt enough of them himself with sniffles and coughs that hadn't wanted to leave. Now, though, there was new life in the air, and not before time. In the city the last of the season's understanding and compassion had been scraped dry. Tempers frayed quickly and violence fired all too readily in words and fists.

He crossed Timble Bridge, seeing the light shining like sparks on the water and feeling the strange clarity of the air, his boots clattering flatly over the old wood, before walking slowly up Kirkgate towards the jail. He glanced at the churchyard as he passed, and his eye rested on the headstone for his older daughter, Rose, buried a year before. Loved in death as she was cherished in life, it read. Last month, once the earth had finally settled enough, it had finally been put in place. He'd knelt at the graveside and traced each single letter, feeling the clear marks of the chisel and thinking of the girl who'd grown so fast, and had been barely married when the fever took her away. In time the inscription would wear and weather to nothing and the stone might split or crack. But by then he'd be long dead, along with Mary and Emily and all who might have held the girl in their heads and hearts. By then she'd just be another fading, forgotten entry in the parish register.

He shook his head to clear the memories and strode on. It was still early enough for the air to smell fresh, before the night soil was thrown out and the ripe press of humanity filled the streets. All around him Leeds was coming alive, servants chattering quietly in the yards, and behind the closed shutters of big houses, the smoke of kitchen fires pillowing up into the blue sky, the soft sounds of grumbling and laughter. The poor were coming from their tenement yards for another day of work. On Briggate the weavers would be starting to set up their trestles for the cloth market, laying out their finished lengths of wool and warming their bones with a hot Brigg End Shot breakfast of roasted beef and ale.

Nottingham opened the door and walked into the jail. Rob Lister was sitting at the desk completing the last of the night report. He looked weary, and his red hair stood out wildly from his scalp where he'd run a hand through it.

'Anything?'

'Nothing much, boss.'

So far 1733 had been an uneventful year, and as Constable of the City of Leeds, Richard Nottingham was grateful. There had been the usual robberies and killings, rapes and fights. The poor suffered while the wealth of the rich grew until all that anchored some of them to earth was the weight of their purses. But that was how the world had always been, the way it would remain until the end. The crimes had been easily resolved, the product of drink, rage or desperation that would leave men to hang or spend years transported across the ocean. It had been normal business.

'Go home and sleep,' he said, though Lister seemed in no hurry to stir. He knew the boy would wait, glancing eagerly out of the window, his eyes searching for Nottingham's younger daughter Emily, as she walked to her position as an assistant teacher at the dame school. They'd been courting for half a year, and Nottingham approved of the match. He liked the lad, he was quick and clever, and in his short time as a Constable's man he'd learned the fine difference that separated law and justice. He'd changed, grown deeper into his skin.

Finally Rob smiled and dashed out into the sunshine. He'd barely been gone a moment when the door opened again and John Sedgwick, the deputy constable walked in laughing.

'I thought he was going to run right through me to catch up with your lass.'

'Come on, John, you remember what young love's like,' Nottingham said with a smile.

'Was always young lust with me,' the deputy snorted, taking off his battered tricorn hat and tossing it on the bench against the wall. He looked drawn, his face pale, ringed and deeply shaded under the eyes, but that was hardly surprising, Nottingham reflected. In February his woman had given birth to a pair of girls. One had died before the day was through, but the other was healthy enough, growing and hungry and keeping them sleepless.

'Go down and keep an eye on the market,' Nottingham told him. 'We had that cutpurse there a fortnight ago, we don't need any more of that.'

'Yes, boss.' He poured a mug of small beer from the jug on the desk and drank. 'By the way, someone was telling me there's a new pimp in the city.'

'Another one?' Nottingham asked in quiet exasperation.

Sedgwick nodded. Since Amos Worthy had died the previous autumn, too many others had scuttled into Leeds, eager to establish themselves and their girls and become king of the trade.

'Do you have a name for him?' Nottingham asked.

'Joshua Davidson.'

The Constable sighed.

'I'll find him later and have a talk.'

In his time Worthy had been untouchable, supplying girls and loans to the city's merchants and members of the Corporation in return for their protection. He was violent and unscrupulous, yet he and Nottingham had enjoyed a strange relationship, a mix of hatred and curious affection.

The new pretenders didn't have his power and the Constable was determined they'd never get the chance to take his place. Whenever one surfaced, trailing his whores like treasure, Nottingham would talk to him. Men were going to buy prostitutes; that was simply the way of the world and no laws or punishments would ever change it. But he'd give his warning; with the first trouble, the slightest complaint or whisper, the pimp would be gone, banished from the city.

So far there had been no problems. The men kept an uneasy, watchful truce while the girls befriended and helped each other.

As sure as tomorrow, though, it would change. Sooner or later the violence would begin and then they'd have to spill blood to keep order. But the longer the inevitable waited, the happier he was.

'Anything after the market, boss?'

'Just look around. You know what to do.'

John Sedgwick walked down Briggate at his usual lope, greeting some of the weavers with smiles. The merchants stood together in small groups in the middle of the street, some in their finery and best powdered periwigs, some subdued, and the Quakers apart in their plain coats. But all of them gave off the distinctive smell of money, he thought. He watched as they passed idle time until the bell rang and the earnest business of Leeds began.

Thousands of pounds changed hands at every Tuesday and Saturday market as coloured cloth was bought, ready to be finished then shipped to Spain or Italy or America, anywhere the merchants could sell it at a profit. It had gone on for centuries, first on Leeds Bridge and now here. It had become the biggest in England, they said, so large they'd built a grand hall for the white cloth sales, as imposing and beautiful as any church. Trade had made wealthy men of the merchants, with money to spend to insulate themselves behind thick walls in large houses. They ran the Corporation and ruled the city.

Trestles lined the road all the way to the bridge over the Aire, and the deputy moved his gaze from side to side, eyes wary for pickpockets or the cutpurse who'd struck before. He stopped by the river, feeling the sun beginning to warm his face, and leaned against the parapet, watching the water flow.

He was tired to his marrow. Isabell was a bonny babe, but Christ, did she cry. He doubted he'd had a full night's sleep since she'd been born. She'd come out screaming, as if she hadn't wanted to leave Lizzie's womb, and sometimes it seemed as if she'd barely stopped since. At least she was alive, better than her sister, stillborn and quickly put in the ground.

James, the son from his marriage, left by his wife when she vanished with a soldier, had never been like that. He'd been a tender baby, quiet, pliable. But having a little sister had changed him. He'd been used to all their attention, and now he didn't have it the boy had turned wilder, sometimes gone all day and rarely heeding what they told him. Even the belt had little effect. It was one more thing to tear at his soul. But Lizzie was blossoming with it all, motherhood shining from her face even when she had precious little rest.

He started back up the street after the chimes had rung, long legs carrying him quickly, fascinated as ever by all the dealing done in whispers, the brief handshakes, the swift folding of a cloth to be moved to a warehouse. The bargain made, the merchant would move on, flitting from clothier to clothier like a bee at the flowers.

He stood and watched for a while, knowing he was seeing riches far beyond anything he'd own, and that the weavers would have little of it. Enough for more wool and to feed their families, to keep them working on the next cloth and the next. Most of the money would stay in the merchants' strongrooms.

Finally he moved away, cutting through to the Calls to begin a circuit of the city, picking his way through the rubbish and the stink and listening to the raw, urgent voices of the poor.

'I can walk you home once you've finished today,' Lister offered. Emily smiled. She was dawdling outside the school, and he was making the most of their brief morning time together.

Finally she nodded her agreement, and he grinned.

'You make sure you get enough sleep, though,' she told him. 'You know Papa, he won't be happy if you're too tired to work tonight.'

'I will,' he promised, holding up his palms in surrender. Rest would be no problem. As soon as he reached home he'd fall into his bed. The night had been so quiet that the hours had dragged like creaking ghosts; it had been all he could manage to stay awake.

He stood looking at her, filled with joy at the laughter in her eyes, the gentle curve of her mouth. He could trace her face in his sleep, feeling the soft down on her skin against his fingertips, the taste of her lips from their kisses.

'I need to go in,' she said. He nodded, reached out and stroked her hand for a moment.

'I'll be waiting for you this afternoon,' Rob said, then turned before glancing back to see her vanishing through the door.

He made his way back down Briggate, easing through the crowds of servants and mistresses that moved between the trestles and the buildings until he reached the house a short way up from the bridge. The ground floor was his father's business, filled with a large, cluttered desk, the printing press for the *Leeds Mercury* and bundles of paper. The dark smell of ink seemed to seep from the walls; he could still smell it after climbing the stairs, as if it had become a part of the building.

The rooms were empty, his mother out, his father busy somewhere, the servants working down in the kitchen. He closed his door, struggled out of his clothes and lay on the bed. He didn't even care that the sun was shining full in through the window.

The Constable finished his daily report for the mayor, pushed the fringe out of his eyes, and strolled up to the Moot Hall where the business of Leeds was done. The building stood firm as a castle, right in the middle of Briggate, the Shambles on either side, filled with the hard iron tang of blood from the butchers' shops, carcasses hanging in the windows, stray dogs clamouring and snapping for offal.

He walked through the thick wooden doors and up the stairs where the air smelled of polish, beeswax and leather. The deep Turkey carpet muffled his footfalls and the voices behind the walls seemed muted and respectful. At the end of the corridor he rapped on a door, waited and then entered.

John Douglas lowered his quill when Nottingham came in and pulled down on his long waistcoat. As the Constable sat he reached for his clay pipe and a tinder, lighting the tobacco and puffing it to life.

'That's better,' he said with satisfaction, sitting back and watching the smoke rise towards the high ceiling. 'I've been here since six and I'll be here while six tonight. Never let them kid you it's a sinecure, Richard.'

Nottingham smiled. Douglas had started his year in office in September, a man ill-suited for formality. He was in his early fifties, hair stubbled and grey under his wig, body thin as a sword blade; he wore a good suit carelessly, his stock roughly tied at the throat. He looked tired, diminished by the power that should have raised him. The skin sagged under his eyes and his mouth drooped downward in a frown. There was an air of exquisite sadness.

He was a merchant, a man with his coffers full, but he'd started life humbly enough, apprenticed to a draper, all his parents could afford. He'd worked his way up through intelligence and ambition, but he remembered his past.

'You're better off as Constable, believe me.'

'Just not as rich.'

Douglas laughed. 'Aye, maybe,' he agreed. 'Much crime yesterday?'

'Precious little.' He laid the paper on the desk. 'Maybe they're all enjoying spring.'

'It'll change,' the mayor said. 'You know that.'

Nottingham liked Douglas. He was the first in office to treat the Constable as an equal and his sense of ceremony was ramshackle. For all his complaints he seemed to enjoy the work, just not the pomp that came tied to it.

'True,' he admitted wryly, 'but let's pray they're in no rush, eh?'

He ambled slowly back to the jail, savouring the mild warmth of the sun on his skin. All around him people seemed happy, smiling, glad to be out in the weather. But he couldn't help feeling their joy was a brittle one, and could so easily be shattered into fragments.

Maybe he'd done this job too long, he thought as he settled back at his desk. Seeing so much sorrow and pain, it became hard to look beyond that for the good, and for the tiny, simple pleasures of life.

He spent the morning immersed in small jobs, sorting through old papers and cleaning. By the time he finished he felt a small satisfaction and the bell at the Parish Church was tolling noon. Nottingham slipped into his old coat, threadbare at the cuffs, and pulled the stock a little tighter at the neck. At the White Swan next door the ale would slake his thirst and the stew would fill his belly.

Sedgwick was already seated at a bench, a mug half-empty on the table, the remains of a bowl of pottage next to it.

'Quiet morning?' the Constable asked.

The deputy sighed.

'Anyone would think they wanted us out of a job. Someone had his pocket picked up by the Market Cross and that's been it.'

'Did you catch the thief?'

'Long gone, of course. Didn't even have a description.'

'Take a look around on the other side of the river this afternoon. See what's going on over there.'

'Yes, boss.'

'Meanwhile I'll go and find this new pimp of yours and make sure he understands how things work here.'

The food arrived and he ate in silence, surprised to find himself so hungry. He wiped the plate clean with his bread and downed the last of the ale.

'We'd better do some work,' he said finally, and they rose together to walk back out into the bright daylight. Sedgwick stopped and sniffed the air.

'Something's on fire.'

'Where?' Nottingham asked urgently. 'Can you tell?' They stood still, listening, then began to pick out a clamour of voices down towards the river. Together they began to run.

Two

The noise became louder, people shouting in panic then the frantic, outraged roar of a blaze. As they neared, the Constable could see dark smoke pluming low above the Calls before tailing into the sky. Christ, he thought, running faster. So many of the houses there were built from timber, old, dry and run down, crammed with the poor and hemmed tight between tanneries, dye works and cloth finishers. If the fire took full hold the whole block could catch in a moment.

Close to, he could feel the fierce heat and glow as the ancient wood caught and burned. So far it was just one house. Small tongues of fire flicked out through gaps in the woodwork, like a hunger that demanded to be fed. The sound around him filled his ears and the thick air made his eyes water, tiny crumbs of hot ash floating to leave him coughing and spluttering.

People had gathered at a distance, pushed away by the heat, already speculating on the dead left inside and taking wagers on the damage. Angrily he pushed his way through them and into a ginnel barely wider than his shoulders, darting along it to the thin, dusty ground of Call Brows and the river.

Men had already set up a bucket line and more rushed to join them, hauling water from the Aire to try to douse the blaze. They worked with quiet, desperate intent; it wasn't just a house up there, it was their own homes and businesses they wanted to save. Without a word Nottingham shouldered his way in, squeezing between Hammond the tailor, face full of fear, eyes wild, needles still sticking from his shirt collar, and a muscled man he didn't know who'd thrown off his coat and rolled up his sleeves, his mouth set grimly. For a full hour the Constable bent his back, moving buckets to and fro, pausing only for quick glances towards the building. There was a sharp, shattering explosion of glass as the heat blew out a window, followed by the slow, menacing rumble of a floor giving way. Anyone trapped inside had to be dead, he thought, and prayed God they'd all managed to escape.

The men battled together, throats too rough and dry from the smoke to speak. His muscles ached and there was pain in his arms and fingers with each movement. Sweat stung his eyes. But he carried on, just like all the others around him. They had no choice. He was sure he could take no more when a yell rose from the house. The Constable jerked his head up, fearing that the fire had started to spread.

Instead there were hoarse cheers and shouts, ragged at first, then growing. They'd won, they'd beaten the blaze, taken the life from it to leave it hissing and steaming. He let the bucket drop to the ground and scooped up handfuls of water to drink and splash over his face, the river coolness like balm on his skin. He straightened up slowly, pushing at his spine with his knuckles as he stretched. Like his neighbours he was grinning wide, pulled and buoyed by victory.

But he didn't have their time for celebration. He made his way back through to the Calls, legs cramping and protesting at each step, hands rubbing at the ache in his shoulders. The crowd was still outside the house, more of them than before, still lively and laughing now the danger had passed. He spotted the deputy, a head taller than the others, and waved him over.

'Get a couple of the men here to watch the place and make sure it doesn't start up again,' he ordered, his voice low and scratchy. He nodded towards the people milling around. 'They'll keep this lot out of the place, too. Make sure Rob knows to have someone guarding it all night, too. It won't be cool enough for us to look inside before the morning.'

'Yes, boss.'

Someone was passing a jug of ale. Nottingham quickly reached for it and took a long, welcome drink before handing it on. 'That was warm work,' he said wearily. 'At least we managed to save it. Did you find out who was living there?'

'No one,' Sedgwick answered. 'It was empty. There'd been a family but they left last week.'

'Lucky for them,' the Constable said. He looked at the wisps of smoke still curling up from the blackened wood and the dark patches of soot bright against old, stained limewash walls. The air was acrid, rasping like a file against the back of his throat.

He turned away, staring at the damage, the heat still strong enough to keep people back, and wondered how the blaze had started. It could have been anything, any spark would have ignited a place like this.

The Constable walked down the street towards the Parish Church, where the air smelt cleaner. He rested against the wall of the graveyard where fresh spring moss covered the coping stones, hawked up phlegm, breathed deeply to clear his chest and wondered. Perhaps they'd understand more tomorrow. The odds were that it had been an accident.

By the time he reached his home on Marsh Lane he could feel all his years in his muscles. The sweat had dried prickly and salty on his flesh. The back door was open, sun coming in to warm the kitchen. Over in the fields white linen like ghosts was spread over green bushes, still drying from yesterday's wash. He poured a full cup of ale and downed it rapidly, scarcely noticing the taste, then followed it with another. The coat and breeches felt heavy against his tired body. He watched Mary working in the garden, planting the seedlings she'd carefully coaxed through the late winter.

She was bent in concentration, her fingers moving in the dirt with quick certainty. Nottingham couldn't see her face but he knew her eyes would be bright in the sunlight and her mouth curved in a tiny smile of pleasure at her work. The older he grew, the more he understood that death came closer each day, the greater the tenderness and love he felt for her.

She turned as he came outside and stood, her eyes widening with worry.

'My God, Richard, what happened to you? You're all covered in dirt and soot. You smell like—'

'—fire,' he told her. 'It's all right, it's out now.' She opened her mouth to speak. 'I was just part of the bucket chain,' he said. 'Nothing dangerous.' He held out his hands, palms upwards to show the redness and blisters from the handles.

'Was anyone hurt?' she asked.

'Evidently the place was empty. We managed to put it out before it could spread.'

'Thank God for that.' She licked her thumb and rubbed a smudge from his cheek. He grinned at the gentle roughness of her fingertip against his face. Her hair was greyer each year and the pain of Rose's loss still lingered in her eyes, but he held her closer to his heart with each season, even after more than twenty years together.

'You'd better go and wash and put on some clothes that don't stink,' she told him. 'Are you hungry?'

'I'm fine for now. How's the garden coming?'

Mary smiled.

'I've put the herbs over there.' She pointed to a cleared corner where the earth looked dark and rich. 'And I'm just planting the onions.'

Clean and in a fresh shirt and breeches, he sat and read his way through the new edition of the *Mercury*. As usual it was filled with news taken from the London papers, things that didn't concern or interest him. The great men would do their damnedest in the capital, but all that mattered in his world was here in this city. He skipped past the advertisements offering outrageous claims for efficacious pills and potions to thumb through the Leeds announcements and their snippets of scandal and innuendo. There was nothing he didn't already know or hadn't proved for a lie.

By the time he'd finished, Emily was lifting the latch with Lister just behind. He smiled to watch the lad trailing her like an eager pup.

'Hello, love,' he said. 'How was your teaching?'

She untied the bonnet and shook out her hair.

'I wish Mrs Rains would let me try some new things,' she replied with a small pout. 'I think we could have the girls reading and counting much better if we did.'

'If anyone can persuade her I'm sure you can,' he offered, hoping the girl hadn't been too insistent.

'We were talking about it on the way home.' Emily reached out and took Lister's hand, squeezing it tightly. 'Did you see there'd been a fire on the Calls, Papa?'

'I was there,' he told her and turned to the lad. 'Rob, talk to Mr Sedgwick when you go in tonight. Make sure you keep a couple of men standing guard on the house that burned. We don't want it flaring up again or anyone going in. You'll have to move the others around so everything's covered.'

'Yes, boss,' he answered, and Nottingham saw the quick flash of relief at the change of subject. 'I'd better go. I need to eat and be ready.'

'Better not be late for work.' They grinned at each other in brief shared understanding before Lister left. They were a good couple, he thought. He was a solid, steadying influence on Emily, tempering her away from wilder moments. And she brought something out in him. He'd come to care about people. Between the job and courting, he'd become a very likeable young man. She could do a great deal worse than end up with him.

The Constable didn't want to enter the house until full light. It was simply too dangerous to risk blundering around among shadows and debris. Rob had stayed on to help and two of the men were hauling ladders. Yesterday's sunshine had given way to high pearly cloud, but the soft spring warmth remained in the air.

'I heard something odd after you'd gone yesterday, boss,' Sedgwick said.

'What's that?'

'A woman thought she saw someone coming out of here before the fire.'

Nottingham turned sharply. 'What? Someone set this?'

The deputy shrugged.

'We'd best see what we can find, then,' the Constable said grimly.

The walls still stood, damaged and scarred, but solid. Inside, though, there was little left. Holes in the roof let light pour in like water. The floors had given way in places, fallen all the way through to the cellar where beams lay broken and burned.

'See if there's anything upstairs,' Nottingham told the deputy. 'Watch those steps, though. Lizzie'll kill me if you end up hurt. Rob, you come with me.'

They lowered one of the ladders and the Constable climbed down to the cellar warily, turning slowly and picking his way across patches of the beaten earth floor, stirring up a fog of fine ashes with every step. The cloying smell of smoke filled the place, rubbing his throat raw as he breathed. The fire had done its work well. Apart from the wreckage there was little to see, just a few small pieces of rubbish pressed down into the dirt, the detritus of lives that had been lived there. He wondered again how the blaze had begun. Had the woman really seen someone leaving here? Why would anyone want to burn *this* place?

He moved on cautiously, hands exploring under timbers that were still warm to the touch. He'd almost finished when his fingertips pressed against something. He felt slowly along the shape, pursing his lips, his face grim.

'Some light over here,' he ordered briskly. 'Get Mr Sedgwick down here and let's get this shifted. I want to see what's underneath.'

The wood had collapsed to make a roof over her. Without that she'd have burned like everything else, the house her funeral pyre. Lister and Sedgwick worked slowly and methodically to pry away each piece, gradually uncovering her as the Constable watched.

Even with the shelter there wasn't much left, little more than a husk of who she'd once been. What remained of her flesh was cooked crisp, all blistered and cracked with the smell of roasted meat. Her hair had been scorched to the scalp, the bone showing through in awful, vivid white. The features of her face were almost all gone; the only things left were her nose and mouth; there was a split in her upper lip, and a jut of bone that could have been a break or a cleft palate. Only her shape gave away her sex, with a mound on her belly. Had she been pregnant?

'Let me take a look.'

Nottingham crouched and moved closer to see her. Her hands were crossed over her breasts, the skin of her arms fused to her sides by the heat. It all seemed wrong, he didn't understand it. He reached out to what remained of her fingers, feeling the brittleness of her flesh crumble under his touch to leave hard, opaque bone. Someone battling to live, to escape, wouldn't have ended up like this, in this position of grace, he thought.

Slowly, gently, he blew the ash off her stomach, brushing away small fragments as he tried to make out what was there. Then he understood. The colour left his face. He stood abruptly and walked across the cellar, pushing his hands against his head, taking short, painful breaths, as if all the air in the place had withered. He squeezed his eyes closed to try and force the vision away. He believed he'd seen all the images of evil in his time, counted and stared deep into them to know them. But he'd seen nothing like this. This was beyond nightmare. A baby, and too small for a newborn. Whoever did this must have ripped it out of her body.

'What is it, boss?' the deputy asked.

'See for yourself.' The words came out as a croak and he hawked to clear the bile out of his throat. 'Look at her, John.'

He watched as the deputy bent then backed away suddenly as he realized what he was seeing. He stood, shaking his head help-lessly. It was beyond all comprehension.

'Fuck.'

'Rob, go and fetch the coroner.' He paused to glance at Sedgwick. 'Send the rest of the men away.'

Lister dashed off, just leaving the two of them to wait with the body.

'How?' the deputy asked, unable to take his eyes off her.

'I don't know.' The Constable's face was dark, his gaze returning to the body. 'I thought I'd seen it all, but this . . .' He didn't own the words to describe what he felt. 'If the wood hadn't fallen that way we'd never have known. There'd have been nothing left.'

They stood with the perfume of the destruction filling their nostrils.

'Seems like that woman who thought she saw someone leaving the house before the fire might have been right,' Nottingham said.

'I know.' Sedgwick's voice was empty.

Nottingham knew he couldn't pause to think too deeply yet about what was in front of him. He needed to keep his mind working.

'You'd better talk to her again. See if you can get anything more from her.'

'Yes, boss.'

'We'll take the body back to the jail ourselves. For right now I just want us and Rob knowing about this.'

The light filtered down on them, so pale it seemed unnatural, something from a tale of ghosts and devils. Finally Brogden the coroner arrived, Lister at his side. He climbed down to the cellar awkwardly, testing each rung of the ladder before trusting his ample weight on it. At the bottom he stopped to inspect his costly clothes, brushing away a few flecks of dirt.

He could afford to dress well. In addition to being Coroner of Leeds, Brogden was also the city's Sergeant-at-Mace and Clerk of the Market, all titles that lined his purse deeply for little work, bringing him more than most people would earn in five years.

He picked his way fastidiously through the rubble and wreckage, careful not to scuff his freshly-shined shoes with their glistening buckles.

'Where's the body?' he asked, and the Constable indicated with his head. Brogden didn't move any closer. 'Was she burned to death?'

'We don't know yet.'

'No matter.' He waved his hand idly. 'She's dead, anyway.' He turned to leave and stopped. 'Was there something else?'

'Take another look, Mr Brogden,' Nottingham told him. 'See what's on her belly.'

The coroner peered for a moment, then pulled back, horrified, looking mutely at the others before leaving. That would live on in his dreams for many nights to come, the Constable thought.

'Right, let's get her back. Rob, you go and get a sheet so we can cover her. We'll find something to put her on.'

They were careful moving her, the body fragile as ash, so light she might have been made of smoke. But lifting her from the cellar was difficult, slow work that brought the taste of vomit hard into their mouths.

Finally they had her on a door that hadn't been damaged too badly, just scorched on its edges, and carried her up Kirkgate to the jail where they put her in the cell they used as a mortuary. The Constable lit two lamps; even on the brightest day the light in the room was dim.

He set up a mug of ale, a bowl of clean water and a cloth, tied a kerchief around his face and took a deep breath. Slowly, gently he eased the cover from the corpse. Then he soaked the cloth and tenderly began to wash away the ash and grime from her belly.

He worked silently, stopping only to spit and rinse the taste from his mouth with small sips of beer. Finally, with the water in the bowl death-dark and thick, he stood back.

The foetus rested on the girl's stomach. It was tiny, hardly any longer than his hand, but there was no mistaking the babe. Its head was large, almost too big for the fragile body; he could discern the features, the eyes and mouth, the fingers and toes, the chest now empty of all life, legs bent and stopped as if the boy had been trying to push his way up to her breast.

He saw the black line where the girl's belly had been slashed open and the child torn out. The cord had been raggedly cut and they'd both been left to vanish in the blaze, to become no more than cinders. He gazed at them again with a deep, overwhelming sorrow.

Finally he covered the bodies again and walked silently back out to the office where Sedgwick and Lister waited.

'Well?' the deputy asked.

The Constable hesitated a long time before answering, running a hand through his hair, not sure he could even speak.

'That's definitely a baby on her belly,' he said finally. 'Not even born yet. The killer sliced her open and took it out of her.'

'Christ.' Sedgwick turned away quickly.

Nottingham looked over at Lister. The lad was too young to understand the full horror on the slab. He'd never been a parent, never lost a child. He couldn't know the pain, couldn't feel it in his gut, aching and gnawing.

'Whoever did it set the fire to burn them up,' he continued bleakly. 'We were just lucky the bodies survived or we'd never have known anything. I want you two out talking to people along the Calls. Don't mention the corpses but find out everything you can. See if you can discover who owns the place, who used to live there, who'd have known it was empty. You talk to that woman again, John, and then see if anyone else saw anything odd. We need to find out who the dead girl was. Someone's got to know her and miss her.' He paused and his voice turned hard. 'I want the bastard who did this.'

The men left. Alone, the Constable sat to write his daily report for the mayor, uncertain how he could begin to describe what he'd seen. He eventually settled for the barest sketch. He was sanding the paper dry when the door of the jail opened and a man walked in.

'I'm Hezekiah Walton,' he said. 'I'm looking for the Constable.'

Three

Nottingham glanced up at the man and smiled genially.

'I'm Richard Nottingham, I'm the Constable of Leeds,' he replied. 'How can I help you, Mr Walton?'

The man bowed slightly

'Do you know a family named Cooper?' he asked.

'There are plenty of people named Cooper in Leeds.' He gestured the man to a seat.

'These won't have been here too long, a month or two at most,' Walton said. 'Up from London, parents and two boys about ten and twelve.'

The Constable stared at the man.

'And what's your interest in them?'

'I'm a thief taker,' he explained. 'The father stole twelve guineas, some plate and lace from the people who've employed me to find them.'

Nottingham leaned forward with interest, steepled his arms under his chin and studied Walton carefully. He looked to be in his late thirties, with thick streaks of grey in his long hair. He was unshaven, the bristles dark against his skin, his clothes coloured with dust from the roads. His coat and breeches were charcoal grey, well cut but old and worn, the long waistcoat once good ivory silk. A sword and scabbard hung from the waist, the leather of the blade handle shiny with use.

'They could live handsomely on that for a few months,' the Constable said. 'What makes you think they've come up here?'

'Someone told my employer they'd left for Leeds. So I'm here to find them.' Walton smiled, showing gaps in his teeth.

'I suppose they could have come,' the Constable conceded slowly. 'People arrive every day, Mr Walton. But I haven't heard of any family like that named Cooper.'

'I'll need to search for them.'

'Of course,' he agreed. He'd expected that; he knew how thief takers worked, though there had been none in Leeds; they were mostly a London breed. They existed on the edge of the law, hired by victims to find those who'd robbed them, or for a fee to act as go-betweens for the return of property. Some even stole the goods themselves, he'd heard, and sold them back for a reward. But it surprised him to find one so far from home. 'What will you do if you find them?'

'Take them back with me,' Walton answered with a grin. 'Let them face justice. And I'll collect my money.'

'They must be paying you well for you to come up here.'

'The money's good if I find them,' the thief taker answered impassively.

Nottingham sat, rubbing his chin slowly.

'You're quite welcome to look for these people in Leeds,' he said finally. 'But I'll expect the same of you as anyone else. You obey the laws while you're here. You understand that?'

'I do,' the man replied with a nod.

The Constable cocked his head.

'Then you're free to do your work, Mr Walton. I hope you find the people you're looking for.'

The man bowed again and left. Nottingham let out a long, soft sigh and shook his head. The last thing he needed was a thief taker. From all he'd heard, most of them were ungodly rogues, willing to go one way or another for some ready silver. But this one . . . his manner seemed too certain, and something in his tale about the Coopers rang false. Two hundred miles was a long way to give pursuit. Either he really was being very well paid or there was a truth he wasn't telling. Probably he imagined everyone outside London to be a bumpkin. It would be worth keeping an eye on Mr Walton.

For now, though, a different business needed his attention. He walked down Briggate, gazing around at the houses, some put up just the previous year, others dating back to Queen Bess, their fronts low, bowed and sagging, wood blackened with age. He stopped where the entrance to a court of tenements snaked back from the street between two buildings. The passageway was barely wider than a man, and disappeared quickly into deep shadow. He leaned against the stone wall and waited, the image of the burnt girl and her baby all too sharp in his mind.

Just a few minutes later a man scurried out and past him, his wig and hat pulled low, but Nottingham paid him no mind. In a few more moments she was there, stepping out into the light and blinking, her hand still adjusting her dress, tugging up the bodice and smoothing the hem.

'Hello, Jane, love.'

'Mr Nottingham.' She was small, barely reaching to his shoulders, her dark hair falling out of its pins and all a-tumble on her neck. From a distance she looked young, with soft eyes like velvet; seen close, the lines around her mouth gave the lie to that tale.

'Business good?' he asked.

She shrugged. 'I'm not starving yet.' She looked up at him, holding a battered fan to cover the hint of a smile on her face. 'It's not often I see you these days. You must want something.'

He laughed, knowing it was true.

'Have you heard of Joshua Davidson?'

'No,' she said with tired certainty. 'Who's he, anyway?'

'He's new here. I've heard he's doing some pimping.'

She shrugged again.

'I want a word with him' he went on. 'There's a few coins in it if I can get his address.' He reached into the pocket of his breeches and jangled the silver. Jane sighed.

'How soon?'

'A quarter of an hour? I'll be at the Old King's Head.'

'Go on, then, seeing it's you,' she agreed. 'I'll ask around. But I'll still want paying even if I can't find owt.'

He nodded his agreement and strolled away. The inn stood at the corner of Currie Entry, an old building of dark panelled corridors and tiny private parlours, the window mullions stained by years of smoke, the wood of the tables so scored and rough a careless man could cut a hand on it. He bought a mug of ale and sat by himself in the corner. A few of the customers cast awkward glances at him but he just stared back, slowly enjoying the drink and letting the time dissolve.

He thought once more about the girl lying in the cold cell with her dead babe and the taste of ashes filled his throat like dirt. Whoever could kill them that way and set that blaze was someone who'd given up his soul. Once they had him, the Constable would relish seeing him gasp and choke at the end of a noose on Chapeltown Moor.

First, though, they had to find him. With any luck, Sedgwick and Rob would learn something useful. But somehow he feared this would be no easy trail. Nottingham drained the rest of cup in a long swallow and pushed it away. He was just about to stand when Jane entered, eyes glancing around until she spotted him.

'I hope you're grateful,' she scolded breathlessly. 'I've been all over the bloody place, I had to ask four different girls. Whoever this Joshua Davidson might be, most people have never heard of him and they don't care. But he's over on Mill Hill, right across from Shaw's Well.'

'Thank you,' he told her, putting two coins down on the bench. Her hand darted out from under the fan to retrieve them, so quick that if he hadn't known he'd never have noticed she only had four fingers. Two years before, her pimp had imagined she'd been cheating him and had exacted his price. A fortnight later he'd been pulled from the Aire, a knife forced to the hilt in his chest before he'd been tumbled in the water.

The Constable walked down towards the Bridge then turned on to Swinegate, as he had so often before, threading through the press of people in front of the shops. Hammering echoed from the smithy, the reek of horse dung hung about the ostler's yard. There were puddles of piss in the road where night soil had been thoughtlessly tossed. Up in one of the houses a child was crying loudly, even as its mother tried to calm it. Amos Worthy had lived along here, six months dead now and already forgotten by most. Even his money and power couldn't halt the cancer that whittled away at his large body until all that remained was withered and useless. Now the door to his house was closed tight and Nottingham wondered if someone else was living there, or if the place held only memories in the cobwebs and the dust on the floor. In a curious way he missed the man, the devil he'd come to know all too well.

The was no real slope to Mill Hill, just a name and tumble of houses across from Shaw's Well, ramshackle old buildings whose timbers were strained and cracking, barely standing and held together by habit and the sheer grace of God. He pushed the fringe off his forehead, knocked on the door, heard the sound echo inside, and waited.

Finally a man answered, his fair hair tousled. From the way he wore his clothes he'd just dressed, an old, mended shirt hanging down outside a pair of faded breeches and the waistcoat inside out. He was perhaps twenty-five, pasty-faced and thin.

'Are you Joshua Davidson?' Nottingham asked. The man straightened his back and waited a moment before answering, as if wondering whether to admit the fact.

'Aye,' he said, 'that's me. What can I do for tha?'

'I'm Richard Nottingham. I'm the Constable of the city. I'd like to have a talk with you.'

Davidson looked at him, eyes wary and curious. 'I've done nowt wrong.'

'I didn't say you had, Mr Davidson. But we'd do better not standing on your doorstep.'

'I suppose tha'd best come in, then.'

The man turned and limped down the hallway, heavily favouring his right leg, moving with awkward, unequal grace. In a parlour furnished with only an old, chipped settle he leaned against the wall and waited.

'I hear you have some girls, Mr Davidson.'

The man weighed the statement and then bobbed his head quickly.

'Aye,' he admitted. 'There's just the pair of them. Me sisters. I look after them.'

'Where did you come from?'

'Wakefield. Not that there was ever owt there for us, mind,' he said sadly. ''Appen we can make a bit of brass up here.'

'And have you?'

The man shrugged noncommittally. 'Early days yet. We've barely been here a month.' Davidson sounded cautious. 'I'd not have thought the Constable would have bothered with us, mind.'

Nottingham smiled. 'I'll just tell you what I say to all the other whoremasters. I know men are going to pay to have girls. They always have, I'm not a fool. You stick with that and you'll have no trouble from me. Get into anything else or cause any trouble and you'll be out of here in a day. Understood?'

'Aye.' Davidson agreed readily. 'I'd find some work myself if I could, and we'd have none of this. It's not summat I like but we need to eat.'

'Your leg?' the Constable asked.

'Run over by a cart about ten year back,' he explained. 'It never did set reet. I were a messenger lad before that. Can't run so fast now.' He gave a small, wry grin. 'Don't worry, sir, you'll not have a problem with us.'

'Good. Then I wish you well in Leeds, Mr Davidson.'

John Sedgwick sat on the bench in the dram shop, Lister at his side. It was the main room of a shabby cottage made over to sell gin, the trappings cheap and gaudy, their poor shine long since worn away.

The woman across the table from him had been worn to the nub by time. The hair under her cap was sparse and metal-grey, only a few discoloured teeth remained in her mouth and her clothes were fifth-hand rags from market trestles, but there was still a small, glittering spark of intelligence in her eyes. Her hand clutched the glass tightly. The deputy signalled for another taste and waited until it arrived.

'Let's go over it again, love,' he said, filling her cup as she watched greedily. 'What time did you think you saw someone coming out of the empty house?'

She took a drink and let it swirl in her mouth before answering.

'I told you, I don't know, do I?' She paused, then said, 'I think the Church might have rung seven.' Her voice was rough and metallic. 'It were coming nigh on light, I know that. Had to be to make him out.'

The deputy nodded. It was the third time through the tale and he was ready to press her for details.

'What were you doing?'

'Emptying t' pots. All the piss has to go somewhere, doesn't it?'

'Did you see where he came from?'

She shook her head quickly and took another small nip of the gin, looking fondly at the remaining liquid. 'He were just there, so it must have been somewhere close, I know that.'

'Could he have come through the ginnel?'

'Mebbe,' she said eventually, with a grudging shrug. 'I looked up and he were crossing the street.'

'Did you see his face?'

'Just his back.'

'Can you remember what his was wearing?' Lister asked and she slowly shifted her gaze to him. Sedgwick pulled three small coins from his waistcoat pocket and let them fall on the wood.

'Just ordinary,' she said.

'What's ordinary?'

She drained the glass, making sure she took every last drop.

'I don't know. Dark coat, dark breeches, hose, shoes.'

'What about his hair?' the deputy wondered. 'What colour was that?'

He watched her thinking, trying to remember. Finally she just shrugged again.

'I don't know.'

'That's all right,' he told her, pushing the money across the table and standing up.

Outside, the deputy kicked at a stone, and sighed as it skittered across the dirt.

'She'll be in there until it's all gone.'

'She wasn't much help,' Lister said.

'I still think she saw summat. She wouldn't have stuck to it like that if she hadn't. We'd better go around and talk to people along here, see if anyone else noticed anything. You take the houses on that side, I'll take these.'

'I'd rather be on my way home to bed.'

Sedgwick grinned.

'You can do that once you've talked to them. What do you think we pay you for?' He ruffled Rob's hair and gave him a friendly push. 'Come on, there's a dead lass and her baby to think about.'

The deputy found few people at home. Most were off at their work, wives and husbands both. Children of all ages ran wild between the houses and on the road, scattering and reforming like flocks of birds. They ran to him eagerly when he brought a coin from his pocket and let the light play on it. He squatted, looking from one face to the other, some still clean, others with the grime of a week or more on their skin.

'Listen,' he said, raising his voice to quiet them. 'You, hush. I'm trying to find out about the fire over the road. Who saw it?' They all nodded and started to speak but he was louder. 'How many of you were out before it started?'

Three of them raised their hands.

'Right. You lot come over here.' He waited until they gathered close, the others wandering off, already bored. 'This is important,' he told them. 'What did you see before the fire? Was there anyone around the house?'

Two of the boys shook their heads but one girl looked thoughtful.

'You mean a man?' she asked.

'Anyone or anything,' Sedgwick said gently.

She rubbed a runny rose with the back of her hand and closed her eyes to fix the picture in her mind.

'Them as lived there had gone last week,' she began. 'I heard them move out in the night when it were quiet.'

'What's your name, love?'

'Meg. Meg Smith.'

'Right, go on, Meg,' he encouraged her.

'Yesterday my mam woke me up early to go and buy a jug of ale for my da so he could go to work,' she said.

'What time was it? Do you know?'

'Don't know,' she answered, 'but it wasn't light yet. Just a bit lighter over there.' She pointed at the horizon and looked at him questioningly. He nodded his understanding. 'The door was open.'

'Of the house, you mean?'

'Yes.'

'Did you see anyone?'

She shook her head. 'Not until I was on my way back. There was a man coming out. He closed the door behind him and then he went down towards the church. I don't think he saw me.'

The deputy smiled at the girl. 'What did he look like? Did you see him properly?'

'Not really,' she replied slowly, concentrating. 'He was big.'

'As big as me?'

'I don't know,' she said doubtfully.

'What was he wearing?'

She thought and finally shook her head. 'Just clothes.'

He smiled at her. 'Anything else you can remember?'

'No,' she answered with quick honesty.

He took her small hand and folded it around the coin.

'You take that and keep it for yourself, Meg. Don't let your mam or your da know you have it, all right?'

'Yes.' She ran off to join the others, her fist tightly clenched.

It wasn't much, but at least it was a start and it made the woman's story less of a drunkard's dream. Now he had to hope others had been out and about, their eyes sharp and able to give a better description. Down here, though, there wasn't much hope of that. They'd learned to look at the law with distrust and knew it was better to say nothing than a word too much.

He waited until Lister had finished his few brief questions of a man, and walked over to him.

'Anything?'

'Nothing,' Rob answered wearily.

Sedgwick looked at the lad, his face drawn, the skin dark under his eyes. He'd need to be rested to work tonight.

'You get on home. I'll cover this.'

'I will. It's always harder to sleep during the day, isn't it?'

'You get used to it,' the deputy told him with a laugh. 'Like everything else in this job.'

Once Lister had gone he set to work again. He knew there was a chance he'd discover more if he worked alone. Rob was good at plenty of things, and he'd learned well since starting the previous summer, but he didn't yet have the skill of talking to the poor. He'd never been one of them, he couldn't read their faces yet or understand what might be in the things they didn't say. He'd learn, in time, but right now things would go faster without him.

He spent the rest of the afternoon moving from house to house along the Calls, going all the way down to the Crown Inn by the graveyard of the Parish Church. The bells rang the hour a few times as he tried to cajole and charm the folk he found, but for all his hope and persistence there was little of help. Only two thought they might have seen someone and neither had paid attention to a figure on the street in the early morning.

Finally he'd had enough. His throat was dry from asking questions, his feet ached from standing, and he wanted to be at home with Lizzie and the baby. He stretched out his back and set off for the house on Lands Lane.

He felt the pride swell in him each time he unlocked the door. It only had a single hearth and a bedroom atop a large kitchen. But it was a house. All his life he'd lived in rooms, sometimes shared with other families, some dark and dank spaces. This felt like riches and grandeur. James had explored the place like another country and Lizzie had walked around slowly, touching everything in disbelief and wonder. The boss had upped his pay back in September, just after the new mayor took office, and they'd been able to afford this.

Lizzie looked up from her chair, a weary smile on her face. Isabell was in her arms, taking the nipple, only her head showing from the swaddling.

'How is she?' he asked.

'Slept well, for once, but she cried all morning.' She sighed and switched the baby to the other breast. He took her free hand, rubbing the palm lightly.

'You look tired.'

She snorted. 'You show me a mother who isn't. We get by, like we always do.' She stood as the baby finished and passed her to him. 'You can look after her now. There's the last of yesterday's pie if you're hungry.'

He held Isabell, her head over his shoulder, patting her back to wind her. He loved moments like these, revelling in the tiny girl with her warm, milky smell, the tenderness of her skin and the softness of her hair.

'Aye, I could eat. Where's James?'

'He's still out playing.'

A dark look crossed his face.

'Leave it, John. Don't worry, it's still light.'

But he knew he'd fret anyway. The boy was five but he already had the wild spirit his father recognized all too well. For a while James had seemed happy; Sedgwick's wife had gone off with a soldier and Lizzie had moved in, everything to James that his mother had never been. Then they'd moved to the house and Isabell had been born. Now so much of Lizzie's time was taken with the baby, leaving James on his own, and he'd learned to leave quietly and stay away for hours.

The deputy had tried reasoning with him and punishing him, mildly and harshly, but none of it had helped. After Easter the boy would start at the charity school; until then Sedgwick was determined to keep him in line.

Lizzie put the pie and a mug of ale in front of him and took the baby.

'Did you tell him not to go out?' he asked.

'Yes,' Lizzie admitted, rocking Isabell gently in her arms.

'If he's not back by the time I've finished this I'll go and find him.'

'John . . .' she began, then stopped. He ate silently and purposefully, cutting and chewing, washing the food down. Then he pushed the chair back and stood, eyes like thunder.

'I'll be back soon enough. If he comes in—'

'I know,' she said.

The boy was exactly where he'd expected, playing in the old, tangled orchard that had once been part of the manor house. There were other lads there, all of them older, and Sedgwick stayed quiet, watching them from a distance. Five of them moved together; James and another outside the group ran behind.

He sighed. It reminded him all too much of himself, and he knew he couldn't let his son make the same mistakes. Quickly he strode out and grabbed James by the wrist, the others shouting and scattering quickly.

'Right, you're coming home with me.' He began to walk, the boy squirming and wriggling in his grip, on the edge of tears. The deputy dragged harder, then stopped after a few yards and knelt so that their faces were close. 'I'm only going to say this once,' he told James, his fingers tight on the boy's thin arm. 'You're going with me. When we get home you're going to say sorry to your mam for disobeying her, and then you're going to bed.'

'But I haven't had my supper,' James complained, starting to cry and snuffle.

'And you'll not be getting any, either.' His voice was harsh and serious and he looked into the boy's eyes. 'I've had enough of this. You need to start doing as you're told. Do you understand me?'

The boy kept his head down. Sedgwick put a hand under his chin, forcing it up, seeing the tear tracks like icicles on his cheeks and the misery in his eyes.

'I said, do you understand me?'

James nodded slowly. The deputy breathed deeply, wondering just what he was going to do with his son. Then he stood up and held out a hand. The boy stared at it for a moment, no expression on his face, and reached out to take it.

Four

'So there was a man in the house before the fire but we don't know anything about him?' the Constable asked.

'Seems that way. The ones who saw him weren't paying attention,' Sedgwick explained. 'Why would they?'

It was still early, the weather cooler with the promise of rain drifting on the wind. Lister had put more Middleton coal on the fire before the others arrived and the room was warm.

'How about you, Rob, did you find anything?'

'No, boss.'

Nottingham sat back.

'We'll get her buried today,' he said thoughtfully. 'Nobody's come forward to say someone's missing. That means she probably doesn't have any family around here.' He looked at the others. 'Any ideas?'

'A whore?' Lister wondered.

'Whores have friends and families,' the Constable reminded him gently. 'Still, it's worth asking round. See if any have gone missing, ones who were pregnant.'

'What about servants?' Sedgwick suggested.

'That could be,' Nottingham agreed slowly. 'Maybe dismissed because of her state. Why don't you talk to some of them? You know how they gossip with each other, someone might have heard something.'

'I'll try,' he said doubtfully. With so many servants in the city they'd need God's own luck to name the girl.

'I know. But we'll need to know who she was if we're going to find who killed her. We can't let anyone walk free after that.' He paused, then added, 'By the way, there's a thief taker from London going about. He's looking for a family called Cooper, husband, wife, two lads. That mean anything?'

They shook their heads.

'I had a word with Davidson, too, John. I don't think he'll be a problem. Seemed meek as a lamb to me.'

'Let's hope he doesn't get any ideas, then, boss.'

The men left and Nottingham walked back into the cold cell. The girl was still covered by the sheet, the stink of her cooked flesh slowly turning rancid. He pulled down the cloth to show what remained of her face and stared at its emptiness, trying to picture how she must have looked.

He was still there, lost in thought, when the undertakers arrived, and watched as they bundled her carelessly away. They'd take her and the baby to the pauper's cemetery on the other side of Sheepscar Beck. A curate would sketch a few words over the two of them, then a covering of quicklime and a few inches of earth would see them into eternity. There'd be no record of where they lay.

After a little more than a week he gave up. There was only faint talk and wispy rumour of whores or servants gone missing. The Constable had Lister investigate but everything came to nought. They knew no more than they had in the beginning, and there were other, pressing matters, petty things that took time and attention.

Still, it gnawed at him, the way every killing he hadn't been able to solve stuck inside. Her murderer was still in Leeds. Maybe he thought he was free, maybe guilt woke him in the middle of every night and left him glancing over his shoulder everywhere he walked. He wanted the chance to find him and look for the secrets in his eyes.

The Constable had been on the other side of the river. Thieves had struck the grand house of a merchant on Meadow Lane, taking silver plate and coins, a pretty return for a few minutes' work.

They'd come in the night, worked quickly and silently not to wake the household. In all likelihood someone inside had helped them; he'd send the deputy over later to talk to the servants. A word, a hesitation, a look: that would be all it took.

The day had a pleasant spring warmth, the early April sun comfortable rather than overpowering. As he passed a bush a small flock of sparrows wheeled away in a brief rustling of leaves and beating of wings. He dawdled across the bridge back into Leeds, leaning on the parapet for a while, gazing down at the light shimmering on water and letting his thoughts drift away. The voice roused him.

'Mr Nottingham.'

He turned to look at the thief taker. He'd heard nothing of the man since he'd come and introduced himself, and was surprised to find him still here.

'Mr Walton,' he acknowledged. 'Did you ever find the people you needed?'

'No.' Walton frowned. 'If they were ever here at all they'd long gone by the time I arrived. I couldn't find a sniff of them.'

'I'd have expected you to be back in London, then.'

'I've been thinking I might stay here a while.'

'Oh?' The Constable was astonished. 'You like Leeds?'

The man shrugged. 'I've lived in worse places. And there's no thief taker here,' he added.

'Maybe we haven't had need of one,' Nottingham suggested wryly. 'We catch the people who break the law and deal with them.'

'Maybe,' Walton agreed with a small dip of his head. 'But there's money to be had reuniting people with property taken from them.'

'As long as it's all legally done,' the Constable said, leaving his meaning clear.

The thief taker gave a short, cold smile. 'Ask after me in London. I'm an honest man. "A good name is better than precious ointment." That's what it says in the Bible, and that's how I live, Constable.'

'I don't doubt your honesty,' Nottingham told him. The man's gaze was dark and intense. 'Just don't hinder us in our work.'

'Of course.'

'You think you can make a living?'

'I do,' Walton replied with conviction. 'I've been listening to people talk. Seems there's plenty of need for my services here. Things vanish, things are stolen, things that might not be reported that people will pay to have returned.'

'That sounds very close to the edge of the law, Mr Walton,' the Constable said slowly.

The thief taker shook his head and glanced down at the water. 'Quite legal, Constable. It's a good trade in London.'

'We're not London.'

'You're like any other provincial city,' he said with contempt. 'You look to London and wish.'

Nottingham turned and looked at him. 'Do we?'

Walton smiled, showing the dark gaps in his teeth. 'You do. And people here have their secrets, too.'

'I'd be very careful if I were you, Mr Walton. You don't know us here.'

'Not yet, perhaps,' he conceded. 'But I've been watching and learning. I have an advertisement in next week's newspaper. We'll see if there's a demand for what I do.'

'And if there's not?'

The thief taker gave a confident grin. 'There will be. People are people, it doesn't matter where you go.'

'I'll be watching you,' the Constable told him.

'Of course.' Walton raised his hands. 'What do I have to hide, Mr Nottingham? I've told you my plans.'

'I'll wait and see what happens.'

The man ducked his head. 'I'll bid you good day, Constable.'

He watched the man walk away with his sure stride, looking around as he went. Nottingham didn't trust him. Beneath the words he could make out the stink of evil, strong and sulphurous. He'd paid Walton little mind before; now that would have to change. Rob's father published the *Mercury*; they'd be able to see the advertisement before it appeared. Then he could keep an eye on the man.

He made his way back up Briggate, past the shit and piss that clogged the runnels in the street, hearing the Saturday market in full cry beyond the Moot Hall, the vendors yelling, 'What do you need? What do you lack?' and the sounds of voices shouting and haggling furiously.

He turned the corner on to Kirkgate and saw the woman waiting by the door of the jail. Her hands were clasped in front of her and she glanced patiently at all the faces that passed, her face expressionless.

'Mistress?' he asked. 'Can I help you?'

'I'm waiting for t' Constable,' she said.

'I'm Richard Nottingham,' he told her. 'I'm the Constable.'

He waited until she was seated. Her features had the sharpness of someone who'd never eaten her fill, the skin drawn and wrinkled. She was no older than him, he judged, but time weighed her down. Work had gnarled the knuckles of her hands into awkward shapes, the skin raw and red. Her dress was dowdy and ill-fitting on her thin body, the material worn thin.

'How can I help you?'

She held his gaze with her clear blue eyes.

'I'm Alice Wendell. It's about my lass,' she said. 'Mebbe it's summat and nowt, but I don't know where she is.'

'What's her name?'

'Lucy. Lucy Wendell. She turned sixteen last month.'

He said nothing. At sixteen the girl could have gone off anywhere, with anyone.

'How long's she been missing?' he asked.

'I don't know,' she answered and he looked up sharply. 'She were working as a servant but she never came home on her day off. And when I went to ask about her all they'd say was that she'd been dismissed. Wouldn't even tell me when she'd gone.'

'What do you want me to do, Mrs Wendell?' Nottingham wondered.

'Go and ask,' she said bluntly. 'They'll tell you when they let her go. You're the Constable.'

'I'll do that if you want,' he offered, 'but it might not help you find her.'

'Aye,' she agreed. 'I know that. It's somewhere to start, though. She were never the brightest lass, you see. It was always better when there was someone to look after her.' Her face softened as she talked about the girl. 'Me, her brother, the people where she worked.' When she lifted her face he could see her anguish. 'I don't know what she'd do on her own.'

'Who was she working for?' Nottingham asked.

'Cates. You know him, the merchant? She was a maid up with him and his family.'

He knew them. They owned one of the new houses up at Town End, out where Leeds was pushing out into the countryside and the air was cleaner. Ben Cates had done very well from the wool trade over the years. He'd served on the Corporation, an alderman who'd used his connection to gather even more riches to himself.

These days, though, he left most of the work to his sons, Robert and William. But from the fragments of gossip the Constable had heard, he wasn't ready to give them their heads completely yet; he still kept a wary eye on the business.

'I'll go and have a word with them and find out what I can for you,' he said. 'And how will I find you, Mrs Wendell?'

'Down on the Calls. They know me there.'

'Where they had the fire.' He thought of the body they'd found. Could she have been the girl?

'Aye,' she agreed sadly, 'it were a bad business, that. Only t' other end of the street from me an' all. Just as well those Grants had done a flit the week before, they had three little ones.'

'I'll go and talk to Mr Cates this afternoon,' the Constable promised.

'Thank you.' She stood, back carefully straight, head high.

'I have a daughter myself. I understand.'

She gave him a short nod and left. He sat back and sighed. He'd heard the pain behind her request and understood just how much it had cost her to come and ask this favour from him. She was like so many women he knew in Leeds, strong because she had to be, relying on no one to get through life, trying desperately to keep the edges of her family from fraying apart. But there were few happy endings for the poor in this world.

He'd go and ask his questions and find the answers. They wouldn't give her any comfort, and she knew that as well as anyone, but she needed them anyway. Cates had seemed reasonable enough whenever they'd met. By all accounts he was a hard man but at least he wasn't a bad one.

The merchant was at home, working at the polished desk in his library. An expensive, full-bottomed wig had been casually thrown aside on a table, a thin dusting of powder on the wood around it. The windows were open on the garden, drawing a light breeze into the room. Nottingham saw the books packed tight on shelves along one wall, and thought how much Emily would love something like this one day.

'Constable.' Cates rose and extended his hand. The man had grown portly in the last few years, Nottingham thought, chins fleshy and sagging into his collar and over his stock. His coat was good wool, flatteringly cut, the breeches tight around a pair of heavy thighs, his long waistcoat gaudy yellow and blue silk. 'Sit down. What brings you here? Nothing wrong, is there?'

'No,' the Constable answered, settling carefully on a delicate chair of fine wood, its legs thin as spindles. 'Just a question about someone who used to be a servant here.'

Cates snorted. 'Lucy Wendell?'

Nottingham nodded.

'Her mother was round here yesterday, wanting to know about the girl,' he said brusquely. 'I told her I'd had to dismiss her.'

'She was hoping for more. The girl seems to have vanished.'

'No surprise,' the merchant said dismissively. 'I've had dogs with more brains than her. Someone had to watch her the whole time or she'd be off in a daydream.'

'I see.'

'That wasn't the reason I got rid of her. I could have lived with idleness, you can whip it out of them. But she was pregnant. I hadn't noticed, what with her apron, but my wife saw it. I had her in and asked her.' He shook his head. 'I'm not sure she even understood what I meant. But I had to turn her out. Didn't want the girl whelping here.'

'What did she say?'

Cates waved his hand. 'Cried, the way they do. But she was out that afternoon.'

'How long ago was this?' the Constable wondered.

'A month?' The man thought. 'Aye, it was four weeks ago, I remember. We'd just made a big sale to Spain the day before.'

'How long did you employ her?'

Cates calculated for a moment.

'Six months, as near as dammit. Too long, really, for what little she could do.'

'Thank you.' Nottingham stood. He'd learned what he needed.

'You're wondering why I didn't tell her mother, aren't you?' He sighed. 'How do you tell someone her daughter's not only stupid but a slattern as well?'

'I understand,' the Constable told him.

'I didn't think she'd come to you.'

Nottingham looked at him calmly. 'I don't think she had anywhere else to turn, Mr Cates.'

He walked back down Briggate. The market had ended and the men were packing away their wares, laughing and boasting and comparing profits. Somewhere in the distance he could hear the rough, raw scrape of a fiddle. Ragged, hopeful children darted out of the shadows to grab at fruit that had fallen, holding it close, a meal for the night, survival until tomorrow. He'd been one of them himself, long ago in a lifetime he'd put away. After his father, one of the merchants, had thrown out his wife and son, they'd had to scrabble on the streets. His mother had become a whore and Nottingham had lived by theft, work, anything to keep body and soul together.

A pair of women wandered like ghosts through the detritus, eyes sharp for anything they might be able to use, scraps of food, pieces of tin, a dress too ripped or threadbare to sell. They moved silently, hopelessly, so pale and thin they looked like wraiths caught between life and death. One he'd seen for at least five years, her back bent and her grey hair lank, no expression on her face. He took a coin from his breeches and slid it into her cold hand. She didn't even look up at him. Sometimes he believed that the line between the poor and the dead could barely be seen.

Once he reached the Calls he only had to ask once to find the address he needed. It was a single room in a cellar, the only light a window high in the wall that would never catch the sun.

She owned little, but she kept it clean, the place spotless and scrubbed, a coat and dress hanging from a nail on the wall, a sheet folded carefully over the straw of the mattress in the corner.

'You've seen him, then?' Alice Wendell asked, her back straight, her gaze direct.

'Yes.'

She waited quietly for his response, her face composed, eyes intent on him.

'Cates dismissed her four weeks ago,' he began. 'He wasn't happy with her work, but mostly it was because she was with child.' He paused. 'That's why he didn't want to tell you.' The woman remained still. 'He said she didn't even seem to know she was going to have a baby.'

'Aye, that'd be Lucy,' she said in a soft, tired voice. 'She's a lovely lass but she's not always in this world. Someone will have had his way with her and she'll not even remember who it was.'

'I'm sorry,' the Constable told her. She put a hand on his arm.

'Nay, it's not your fault, lad. There's plenty happy to take advantage of a girl like that. Now I have to find her before anything else happens.' The woman sighed. 'She'll be too ashamed to come back here where I can look after her.'

'I can have my men keep their eyes open for her.'

'Thank you.' For the first time, she gave a brief smile. Four weeks was a long time; he knew she understood that. The chances of finding the girl were small. But it cost nothing to have the men keep watch.

'What does Lucy look like?'

'She's easy enough to spot, is our Lucy. Lovely long, pale hair and blue eyes. But you can't miss her. She has a harelip.'

'A harelip?' His head jerked up and he thought again of the girl from the fire.

'Aye,' the woman said with slow resignation, as if she'd had to explain it too many times before. 'You know what they say, don't you? If a woman sees a hare when she's carrying the child, it'll be born with a harelip. Well, I never saw one when I was big with Lucy, I'll tell you that for nowt.' She shook her head angrily. 'All those bloody tales and she's had to pay for it her whole life. They've allus made fun of her.'

'Is there anywhere else she could have gone?'

'Only to her brother. There's just been the three of us since my man died, and they were just bairns then. But our Peter would have brought her back here if she'd turned up, I know he would.'

'Where does he live?' Nottingham asked.

'Queen Charlotte's Court, up off Lady Lane. Him and his girl have a room up there.'

'How tall is Lucy?'

'There's not much to her,' Alice Wendell said tenderly. 'Thin as a branch and smaller than me.'

He looked at her, seeing the love for the girl in her eyes, and knew he had to tell her. 'You'd better sit down, Mrs Wendell.' She looked at him curiously.

'We found a body in the fire last week,' he began. He'd spare her the brutal details. 'A girl who was pregnant. From what I could see, she might have had a cleft lip. It looks as if someone killed her before the blaze.'

For a moment he wasn't certain she'd understood him. Then slowly, by small degrees, her face crumpled and she brought up her worn hands to cover it.

'I'm sorry,' he told her.

'Why?' she asked eventually, her words muffled. 'What was she doing there? Who'd do that to my Lucy?'

'I don't know. But I'll find out.'

He stood, knowing there was no solace he could give now, then he closed the door quietly behind him, leaving the woman to a lifetime of mourning.

Back at the jail he sat and stared. The girl had been gone four weeks, and a little more than seven days had passed since they'd found the bodies after the fire. Now he had a name for her: Lucy Wendell. Pregnant and with a harelip, who else could it have been? He had somewhere to begin.

But that meant she'd been somewhere for three full weeks before she was murdered. Twenty-one days was a long time.

Five

Lister was yawning, barely awake after the long Saturday night. There'd been something in the air; he'd lost count of the fights they'd broken up, men filled with ale and looking for violence. They'd cracked heads, put some in the cells to face the Petty Sessions, and taken blows. His cheek ached where someone had hit him and he had a kerchief wound round his hand to staunch the blood from a cut to his palm. At least no one had died, although one seemed unlikely to survive, cut deep in the chest with a long tanner's knife.

A light, misting ran had drifted in with the dawn, softening the outlines of the buildings through the window of the jail. Soon the bells of the churches would begin to ring for Sunday services, the carillons echoing around to remind the faithful, and the people would parade around in their best clothes. He'd be home and in his bed, trying to rest before calling on Emily in the afternoon.

He stretched out his legs on the flagstone floor and looked at the Constable.

'Sounds like it could have been worse,' Nottingham said.

'Maybe,' Rob agreed cautiously.

'You wait until they're a real mob,' Sedgwick told him. 'It's been a while since we had that.'

'I have a name for the girl who died in that fire down on the Calls,' the Constable said. 'Lucy Wendell.'

This was the reason he'd come in early this Sabbath morning, Lister realized. He and the deputy both shook their heads. The name meant nothing.

'It looks like she was missing for three weeks before the blaze. She'd been working as a servant for the Cates family. They dismissed her because she was pregnant. I've talked to her mother. The lass didn't go home after that. There's a brother lives in Queen Charlotte's Court. John, you go up there and talk to him. Rob, do you know either of the Cates boys?'

'I know William best.'

'I talked to Ben Cates. It seemed straightforward enough, but when you have a chance, talk to William. See what you can find out about the girl.'

'Yes, boss.'

'How do you know it's the same girl?' the deputy asked. 'There was precious little left of her.'

'Lucy Wendell was pregnant and she had a harelip.' He shrugged. 'I doubt we'd find two round here like that who've gone missing. Don't let on to anyone that she's dead yet, though. I want to find out what happened to her.' The Constable stood, ready to leave. 'Anything else?'

He made his way down Marsh Lane, Mary on one arm, Emily on the other. This was always the proudest moment of his week, walking to church with the pair of them. He'd put on his good suit, and the women wore dresses sponged clean and bright. They hunched into their coats to keep off the dampness but he kept his face to the drizzle, feeling it fresh on his skin and combing it into his hair with his fingers.

On Kirkgate rich and poor lived cheek by jowl, in houses that had been grand back when James was king or in sad wrecks of dwellings that let in the weather. St Peter's stood set back from the press of them; the old, dark stone church towered over them all. Nottingham smiled wryly at the way people lowered their voices to a respectful whisper as soon as they entered the lych gate. He just hoped he'd stay awake during Reverend Cookson's sermon. For a man supposedly filled with the spirit of God he droned worse than an insect.

He'd never been one for believing, and since Rose's death the year before the prayers seemed like nothing more than empty words that hung on the wind before blowing away. He came because he had to, because his position demanded that he be seen here. He exchanged greetings with aldermen and merchants, bowed to the mayor and received a wink as they made their way to the pew. Mary sat quietly, years of faith behind her, but Emily shifted restlessly on the seat, willing the time to tick away to afternoon when she'd see her young man. Young love, always eager, he thought, and reached out to take his wife's hand. He relished her joy and solemnity, every shade of her moods.

'You stayed awake for most of the sermon,' she said approvingly as they filed back out into the daylight. The morning had cleared, bringing patches of blue sky to the west.

'Not by choice,' Nottingham complained. 'How long did he talk?'

'He turned the glass twice, so a little over an hour,' Mary told him.

He sighed. 'And it's nothing he couldn't have said in ten minutes.'

'Richard!' she hissed, nudging him with her elbow as he raised his hat politely to Mrs Atkinson, the alderman's wife. Emily was deep in conversation with her friends, talk punctuated by the sweetness of girlish giggles.

'Let's go home,' he said. 'She'll follow when she's ready. She still has to get herself ready for Rob.'

'She loves him, you know,' Mary told him as they walked down the street, skirting around the stinking puddles and pools.

'Are you sure?' he asked, surprised.

She looked at him in astonishment.

'I'm her mother, of course I'm sure. She'd marry him tomorrow if he asked.'

'Let's hope he doesn't, then,' he said. 'They've only known each other a few months.'

'Sometimes you can tell in a few days, you know. You seemed certain enough as soon as you knew me.'

He grunted, reaching to his neck and loosening his stock. 'That's better. They're not old enough to be wed yet. And they don't have any money.'

'Not having money didn't stop us,' she reminded him.

'We were older than them,' he countered. 'I was twenty, Rob's just eighteen. Emily's only sixteen. You were eighteen.' But as he looked at her he knew words couldn't win this. There was something deeper. 'What about Rob? Do you think he loves her?'

Mary's eyes shone, her face as open as sky. 'Haven't you noticed how he looks at her whenever she's in the room? He's as besotted as she is.' He saw the pure delight in her smile. After losing one daughter, she wanted the other to be happy.

'Give them time,' he told her. 'Last year you were glad to have her home with us.' He recalled Emily on the doorstep in tears, trying to explain how she'd left her position as a governess after her employer attempted to force her to lie with him.

He put her arm in his as they walked slowly back up Marsh Lane. By the beck the trees and bushes were green, the bluebells giving thick, glorious spots of colour on the ground.

'If it's what they want, they'll do it in time,' he said.

'What about Rob's father? What does he think?' Mary wondered.

'I've no idea,' the Constable answered. 'When I've seen him we've never talked about it.' He unlocked the door to their house and stepped aside for her to enter, the way he'd always done, the way his mother had taught him. Mary bustled into the kitchen. A few minutes later Emily dashed in, as always on the edge of lateness, gathering her skirt and rushing up the stairs to her bedroom. He sighed.

The deputy knew Queen Charlotte's Court well. He'd been here many times before. There'd been fights, stolen items, even bodies in the rubbish that crowded around the decrepit buildings. It was a place where people survived rather than lived. Precious little light came in, and rancid smells collected in the deep mud. There was no joy in life here.

It only took a brief word to discover where Peter Wendell lived. It was a rooming house with the front door missing and wood on the stairs going rotten, never built to last but still here, making money for a landlord who only cared that his tenants paid on time.

Wendell answered his knock promptly. He looked close to twenty, his face not yet fully settled into shape, thickset, with dark hair cut close to the skull and shirt sleeves rolled up to show bulging muscles. His eyes were blurry and bloodshot, and the smell of last night's drink was strong on his body.

'Aye?' he asked.

'I'm John Sedgwick, the deputy constable.'

'Oh aye?' He pushed his chin forward in a challenge. 'You got business here?'

'I want to talk to you about your sister.'

The man cocked his head. 'Better come in, then. Don't want the world knowing my life.'

There was a pallet in the corner with a grimy, stained sheet thrown hastily over it, a scarred table close to a dirty, cracked window, and two stools. A girl, haggard and thin, stood in the corner, pulling a threadbare shawl around her shoulders.

'So what about my sister, then?' Wendell asked.

'Have you seen her lately?'

The man shook his head slowly and turned to the girl.

'How long is it?' he asked her. 'Two months?' She just looked back at him blankly. The deputy could see the garden of bruises on her arms and wondered how many more there'd be on her body. 'Aye, two months, summat like that. Why?'

'She's missing. Your mam's worried about her.'

'Well, we've not seen her,' he said, brushing the problem aside as if it had no importance. 'She's working for that man up at Town End.'

'They dismissed her.'

'Oh aye?' For the moment there was a flicker of interest in his eyes.

'Where do you work?' Sedgwick asked.

Wendell looked at him. 'What's that matter to you?' The man's voice was surly.

'I'm just curious.' The deputy smiled. 'It's my job.'

'The blacksmith on Swinegate. I'm a farrier.'

'Good work, is it? Steady?'

'It's fair.' The man kept his bulk close to Sedgwick, arms crossed over his chest.

'I'd have thought you'd earn enough to afford somewhere better than this.'

'You think what you like,' Wendell said sullenly.

'You know anywhere your sister could have gone?'

'She'd have come here or gone to see me mam,' he answered without hesitation. 'We're all the family she has.'

'No one else?'

'No.' He paused. 'You don't know about our Lucy, do you?'

'What do you mean?' Sedgwick asked.

'She's a sweet lass, right enough, but she's not all there in the head.'

'She's bloody simple,' the girl muttered, but Wendell silenced her with a quick, vicious look.

Sedgwick waited for more.

'I'd have looked after her if she'd come to me.'

'She was pregnant,' the deputy told him. 'That's why she was dismissed.'

'I'll look for her,' Wendell said with a sharp nod.

'That's our job . . .' Sedgwick let the words trail away.

'I said I'll do it. You're not family,' the man said firmly, his jaw set, his gaze hard. 'It's different.'

There should have been no business done on a Sunday, no food or drink for sale on the Sabbath. But behind closed doors the alehouses and dram shops turned a pretty penny every night of the week. Where there was money to be made, God could easily be forgotten.

Lister had to try three places before he found William Cates. He knew the man would be out rather than face the deathly stillness of an evening at home with his parents and his pious brother, the pair of them as different as stone and water. Robert lived for business and the church, treating both as holy and cherishing profit as a sacrament. Will preferred the noise and liveliness of a crowd, the distraction and pleasure it brought. But he was the one with the natural gift for the wool trade. He could spot a good cloth at ten paces, knew who'd buy it from him and for how much. Robert did the work but Will filled the coffers.

Lister bought a mug of the alewife's special brew and stood close to the fire. It was still chilly enough after dark to need heat even as each day grew a little warmer.

'Rob, over here.'

He looked up and saw Cates wave. The men around him moved on their benches to make room.

'We don't often see you out on a Sunday,' Cates laughed as he settled. 'I thought you'd maybe taken religion.'

Lister smiled. 'I don't have the time any more. I'm working and I'm courting these days,' he explained sheepishly.

The men all laughed knowingly.

'You should never let that stop you having a good time,' Cates advised him, signalling to the pot boy for another jug. 'Still, I suppose when you're a Constable's man, eh? You enjoying it?'

'Best job I've ever had,' Rob answered honestly.

'And you've had a few in your short time.'

Lister grinned and took a long drink. He glanced at the others, chattering and joking, and leaned forward. 'I wanted to see you, Will. Can you make a few minutes tomorrow?'

'Me?' Cates looked puzzled. 'I suppose I can. Is it important?'

'It's probably nothing, but . . .'

'Work?'

'My work,' Rob said.

'All right,' Cates agreed after a moment, giving him a curious look. 'The Rose and Crown at noon. We'll get a parlour.' He paused. 'Are you sure it's nothing bad?'

'Don't worry,' Lister said. 'I just thought it would be better away from the warehouse or home.'

Cates sat back and gave a hearty laugh. 'The good things in life usually are.'

Rob finished his ale and stood up.

'Gentlemen,' he said, and left.

The city was quiet, and a low, heavy moon hung over the horizon. As he walked home, hands pushed into the pockets of his breeches, Lister thought back to the afternoon with a smile. He and Emily had strolled out along the river, seeing the wildflowers start to bloom and hearing the rich birdsong in the hedgerows. He'd led her into a copse and pulled her close, kissing her hard and feeling her body pushing against his.

They'd stopped, the way they always stopped, the pair of them flushed and guilty. He'd looked at her, seeing her eyes wide and expectant, her mouth so red. He'd stroked her hair and rested her head against his shoulder. Finally, once his heartbeat had slowed again, he'd led her back out into the sunshine to continue their ramble. They said nothing, the pressure of her hand tight on his, her small, thin fingers grasping him.

Later, at her door, he held her again, their passions cooler as the evening scents rose from the ground.

'I love you,' she said. He smiled and rubbed his fingertips against her cheek.

'I love you,' he told her and gave a small, dry laugh. 'So now we've said it.'

'I mean it, Rob.' Her voice was earnest.

'So do I. I've never told it to anyone before,' he insisted. The men he knew didn't love. Instead they valued girls for their fortune or position, for their beauty or the slimness of their waists. This was different, a strange land where he had no language. 'But what do we do about it?' he asked.

'We just love each other, that's all,' she answered confidently. 'And we don't stop.' She stood on tiptoe, put her lips against his, smiling, then opened the door and vanished inside.

He'd wandered back into Leeds feeling light and content, the gentle happiness still filling him as he unlocked the door on Lower Briggate. The smell of ink filled the place, seeping out of the room where his father wrote and printed the *Leeds Mercury*.

James Lister had purchased the newspaper the year before from the widow of its founder. He'd already been writing for it, penning idle pieces of gossip that saw print each week, but his income was solid enough not to need the money. Taking on the whole business had been a gamble, but one that seemed to be paying off. The *Mercury* had increased its profit in the last twelve months, and Lister was slowly altering the balance of news to make it a respectable local press. Rob had worked for his father briefly, trying to learn the trade. But he had no way with words, the backwards letters of the press confused him and he had no desire to end up as a printer's devil, hands black with ink.

He made his way softly up the stairs. His mother would already be in her bed, ready to rise early and supervise the servants on the Monday wash. A light was still burning in the parlour and he saw his father, sitting and waiting, waistcoat unbuttoned to let his ample belly spread, a book open on his lap. It would be Defoe, he was willing to put his wages on it. It was always Defoe.

'I didn't think you'd be so early,' James Lister said with a smile. 'Come and sit for a little while.'

'I'm tired. I've been working.'

'And you were courting earlier.' Lister's voice was gentle, almost laughing. 'You had the afternoon with Emily Nottingham, didn't you?'

'Yes.' He leaned against the door jamb, half in the shadows.

'I like her, she has a spark.'

'She does,' Rob agreed with a broad smile.

'How long has it been now?'

'Eight months, father,' he replied. 'As I'm sure you know full well.'

Lister nodded slowly. 'I just wanted to be certain.' He raised his head. 'It's long enough to be serious.'

'Yes, it is.'

'What about the girl?'

'How do you mean?' Rob asked.

James Lister spread his hands in exasperation. 'Are you just a way to fill her time or is she in love with you?'

'She's told me she loves me.'

Lister raised his eyebrows. 'And I suppose you've said the same to her?'

'I have,' Rob admitted, feeling himself redden.

'They're not idle words, I take it?'

'No,' Rob replied fiercely. 'Of course not.'

Lister stroked his chin thoughtfully. 'You know there were rumours about her a year and a half or so back? People said she was running wild.'

'She told me all about it,' Rob said, an edge in his voice. 'But there was never anything improper.'

Lister removed his spectacles and polished them with his kerchief. 'Has there been with you?' he asked.

'No, there hasn't.' Rob paused. 'Why are you asking me all this, anyway, father?'

'Because I don't want you coming home one day and announcing you're betrothed to the girl, that's all,' he said, his voice firm as iron.

Rob bristled. 'Why not? I love her, so does Mother – you just said that you like her yourself.'

Lister shook his head as if his son was stupid.

'Liking's fine, loving's fine, I suppose,' he said, 'but she's not a girl for you to marry.'

'I thought you respected Mr Nottingham. You recommended me to him for a job.'

'He's a good enough Constable,' Lister acknowledged. 'And he can be fine company at times. But he's not the right class socially.' All the pleasantry had gone from his voice. 'Tell me, what do you know about your Constable? About his past, I mean.'

'Nothing, really,' Rob admitted. 'I've never felt the need. I know there was money when he was young, but it went and he lived as best he could.'

'His father was a wool merchant – quite middling, the wife brought all the money to the marriage,' his father explained. 'He discovered she was having an affair and threw her and their son out. She had to make her living as a whore while the lad begged and stole.'

Rob stayed silent, staring at his father. He'd heard hints of the story, nothing more. But the Richard Nottingham he knew was the Constable, an excellent one, too, a man he admired, that he'd learned from.

'I don't see how that affects Emily,' he said, concentrating on keeping his voice under control.

Lister snorted. 'I'd hoped you'd managed to acquire a bit of common sense by now, Robert. We're a respectable family. We have a long line, we have some money, we're not scrabbling in the dirt for our pennies. We have a reputation. I won't have my son marrying the granddaughter of a whore.'

'So the Constable's daughter isn't good enough for your son?'

'No, she's not,' Lister answered sharply. 'You see how her father dresses; the man might as well be wearing rags. And the girl? She works, she teaches.'

'What are you saying I should do?' Rob asked. Anger was growing inside him, but he kept it carefully tamped down, his fists clenched tight at his sides, nails digging into his palms.

'Drop her. Or keep on walking out with her if you want. Bed the bitch if you can, if she's slut enough. I don't really care.' He turned his gaze on his son. 'But I won't have you marrying her. Your mother and I will find you a suitable wife.'

Rob pushed himself away from the door frame. 'Is that advice or a demand?'

'It's whatever you want to make of it,' Lister told him. 'But you'd do well to remember that there are consequences for every action. I want a good match for you. Take a little time and think about that.'

'Goodnight, father,' he said coldly and ran up the next flight of stairs to his bedroom.

Six

An early mist had come down as the Constable walked into Leeds, giving a cobweb light to the land. Somewhere off in the trees crows were cawing and he could hear the soft smack of hooves on the earth, but he couldn't see them. Once the sun rose it would all burn away and bring another bright spring day, but for now he might have been alone in the world with its soft, beautiful chill.

Three weeks, he thought. Someone must have seen Lucy Wendell in that time. She'd need to eat and drink, she'd want somewhere to sleep. If she'd had any money at all it would have been precious little, not enough to keep her for all that time.

He was still brooding when the deputy arrived at the jail, rubbing the sleep from his face. He sat on the bench, stretching out his long legs.

'Bad night?'

'Isabell kept waking and I don't know what I'm going to do about James.' He chuckled drily and shook his head. 'Aye, other than that it was fine.'

'Have you seen Lucy's brother yet?'

'Yesterday. He claims he hadn't seen her.'

Nottingham waited.

'But?' he asked.

The deputy shrugged. 'There's something about him I don't like. He said he'd go searching for her, keep it in the family. From the look of him, he spends most of his money on drink and beats his girl.'

'Plenty of men do that,' the Constable countered.

'I know.' Sedgwick yawned and rubbed the back of his neck. 'I just had the feeling he wasn't telling me the full truth.'

'You didn't tell him she was dead?'

'No.' Sedgwick poured himself a mug of small beer. 'Are you even sure it's her, boss? There was so little left, how can you tell?'

'It's her, John,' he said. 'I'm certain. That had to be a harelip.' He pushed the fringe off his forehead. 'All it means is we still don't know anything. I'm going to ask at the inns. She might have gone looking for work after Cates dismissed her. Someone took a lot of trouble to try and make her disappear. If it hadn't been for pure luck we'd never even have known she'd lived, let alone that she was dead. She'd just have been ashes. We need to find whoever could do that.'

'Have you thought more about asking around the whores?'

'It's a good idea,' Nottingham said with a nod. 'Why don't you do that?'

'Yes, boss.'

'Was there anything else yesterday?'

'A body from the river. Scudamore Mitchell, you remember him?'

'Is he the carpenter whose work kept falling apart?'

'That's the one. His friends said he'd been drinking Saturday night, probably fell in. And there was another who was cleaning his fowling piece and blew off his foot.'

'Nothing suspicious?'

The deputy shook his head, no longer surprised by the things people did. 'No, just stupid. He might live, if he's lucky.'

The Constable stood. 'Write them up,' he said. 'I'm going to start talking to the innkeepers. Lucy didn't just vanish for three weeks.'

He began at the top of Briggate, at the Rose and Crown. People were already hunched over the benches, breaking their fast with bread and cheese and ale. Martin, the owner, wiped his hands on his leather apron and tucked money away in the pocket of his long waistcoat. His wife would be in one of the outbuildings starting a new draught to brew while their daughters worked in the kitchen, preparing the vegetable stew for dinner.

'You'll have something to drink?' He began to reach for a mug. 'How can I help you, Constable?'

'Nothing for me today,' Nottingham said pleasantly. 'Just a few questions. Do you have many seeking work here?'

'A few,' Martin replied with a laugh. 'Got to be careful who you take on in a place like this or they'll be tipping the profits down their gullets.'

'I'm looking for a girl who might have asked about becoming a servant.'

'Oh aye?' He folded his arms. 'Never a shortage of those. There's always too many lasses looking for work.' He winked. 'And some reckon they can make some brass on the side from the men.'

'You'd remember this girl. She had a harelip.'

The man grimaced and the Constable noticed the small hand movement he made to ward off evil. Harelips were bad luck, cursed by God, their words twisted, their looks ugly. People shunned them lest their own babes became the same way.

'Not had one like that here,' he replied. 'I wouldn't have hired her, anyway. She'd drive business away.'

The Constable made his way down the street, stopping at all the inns to ask and receiving the same answer everywhere. She'd never sought employment at them and none would have taken her on. By the time he reached the Talbot he was downcast; the search seemed fruitless, but he'd go in and ask anyway.

With its cockfighting pit and gambling, the Talbot was a place he hated. The men were called there two or three times a week to quell fights or arrest a pickpocket. He'd have closed the inn if he'd had the power. As he entered he felt the conversation hush. The landlord spat on the stone floor and turned away to examine the spigot on a cask. Nottingham walked up to the serving trestle and waited.

'Mr Bell,' he said finally, and the man looked at him.

'I'd not seen thee there,' the man said flatly. 'You'll have a drink with me, Constable?'

Bell was a large man, strong and with the edge of danger in his temper. He'd fought bare knuckle when he was young and had the makings of a champion until he'd shattered the bones between his knuckles and wrist. Now there was a thick layer of fat over the old muscles, and the scars on his face and hands stood as the only reminders of his past.

'Not today,' the Constable answered with a smile. 'All I'm looking for is some information.'

Bell eyed him warily.

'Have you had a girl with a harelip asking for work here? It would have been a few weeks ago.'

The man chuckled.

'What? Alice Wendell's lass, you mean?'

'Yes,' Nottingham said with surprise.

'No,' he answered firmly, 'she's not been in here. She knows I'd never take her on. They wouldn't be happy.' He tilted his head toward the customers. 'I've known her since she was a nipper. Lovely girl, do anything for anybody, mind, but not a clever lass. Why are you looking for her, then? She done something?'

'She's missing. I told her mother I'd ask after her.'

Bell frowned. 'That's bad news. I always had a soft spot for young Lucy. I'll keep a lookout for her.'

So, nothing, he thought as he walked back to the jail. He could go through all the alehouses and dram shops, but that could easily take half a week. He sat at the desk, lost in thought. Lucy Wendell had been somewhere, and he was certain it had been in Leeds. It was probably the only place she knew, the only one where she'd feel that she might be safe. And in the end even that hadn't helped to save her. He loved the city but sometimes it seemed cursed and dangerous.

Someone had bedded her and put a child in her. Whoever had done that had almost certainly been the one to kill her, too. That would take the start of this tale back several months, to when she was working for Cates, and that was food for thought. Men took advantage of girls working for them often enough, then dismissed them if their bodies quickened. He'd never heard

of anyone killing a lass because of it, but men had certainly killed
for much less.

By noon there was a high, gentle haze, as if someone had carelessly smudged sky and cloud together. The whores were out on
Briggate, touting for business. Some held their fans coyly over
mouths of broken teeth, eyes dancing, while others were more
brazen, giving loud invitations to the men passing.

The street was busy as ever, servants and mistresses ducking in
and out of the shops, argumentative carters guiding their teams
on the roads with raucous shouts, the traffic stuck on either side
of the Moot Hall, angry and yelling, fights brewing in frustration.
The air was filled with sound, the city loud and vital.

Sedgwick knew some of the girls, but they were always
changing. Lizzie had been one of them when they first met, a
life she'd been happy enough to leave behind. Many of these
would go elsewhere in a few weeks or months. A few would
stay for years, growing old and weary far too soon in the
profession.

He saw Caroline, a girl who'd been fresh on the street back
when he'd started out as a Constable's man. Now lines ran deep
on her face, and she tried to hide them with white lead and
beauty spots and pulled her bodice lower to try and attract the
attention that had come easily when she was young. She'd seen
them all and was sometimes a mother to the lasses of eleven or
twelve who arrived lost and fearful.

'Lovely day for it,' he said with a wink.

She raised her eyebrows and pursed her lips. 'If you say so,
Mr Sedgwick.'

'Sun shining, spring and the sap rising, should be good for
trade,' he told her playfully.

'You'd better not be looking to buy,' she warned him. 'Your
Lizzie wouldn't be happy. And don't you doubt I'd tell her.'

He laughed. 'I don't think I'd dare, love. She'd have my balls
off. I'm just asking a few questions, that's all.'

She cocked her head. 'Go on, then.'

'Did you see a girl with a harelip working a few weeks ago?'

'Her? You're asking about her?' she said and he felt his pulse
quicken.

'You saw her, then?'

Caroline nodded her head sadly. 'She never had a chance out here, poor little thing. Who's going to pay for a lass like that? Especially one who's carrying a child. Although I know some of you men have strange tastes,' she added darkly.

'Did you talk to her at all?'

She shook her head. 'Never had the chance, Mr Sedgwick. She were only out here two nights. The first she was too scared to do owt and the next she came all bruised. Then she didn't come back at all.'

He could feel the dryness in his voice. 'How long ago was this?'

He waited as she concentrated.

'I don't know,' she admitted finally. 'I can't think.'

'Was it before that big fire down on the Calls?' he asked, using it as a marker. Caroline's face brightened. 'Oh, before that, I'm sure of it.'

'Who was running her, do you know?'

She frowned. 'Never heard, and whoever it was, he didn't show his face round here. She was down by the old chantry chapel by the bridge. They often put the new ones down there. A fresh face to catch trade as it comes into town.'

'I need a favour,' he began, then stopped as something caught his eye. 'Can you ask around and see who was running her?' He dashed the words off even as he began to move. 'I'll look for you later.'

He ran quickly and quietly through the crowd, tall enough to keep watching his quarry. In just a few seconds he was able to reach out and hold the boy by his collar. The lad shouted out but no one stopped to help him.

'You know you're not allowed down here.' James was wriggling hard, like a fish fighting the hook. Sedgwick jerked and the boy stopped. 'Don't you?'

James didn't answer.

'Well, don't you?' He kept his grip tight, moving to look his son in the face.

'Yes, Papa.' He could hear the defeat and sullenness in the answer.

'Do you want me to thrash you out here in front of everyone?'

Sedgwick's voice was low, barely more than a hiss, but threatening and dangerous.

'No, Papa.'

'I'm going to take you home and see what your mam has to say.'

'She's not—' James began then shut his mouth.

'Not what?' Anger flooded into his words. 'Not what? Not your mam?'

'She's Isabell's mam now,' James started, unable to stop his words. 'That's all she cares about, what Isabell does.'

He took the boy by the arm and began to drag him, forcing the lad to run to keep pace with his long strides. He said nothing, feeling the fury inside himself, scared he might not stop slapping the boy if he began. Finally, in Lands Lane, the small house in sight, he halted.

'I never want to hear what you said before,' he told the boy. 'I don't know what you remember about your real mam, but Lizzie's been more to you than she ever was. She loves you and she looks after you.' He paused and took a breath, trying to frame his thoughts into words. 'You know Isabell's tiny, don't you?'

'Yes, Papa,' James answered reluctantly.

'That means she relies on her mam for everything. You were the same when you were a baby. It doesn't mean Lizzie's stopped loving you, and it certainly doesn't mean she's not your mam any more. You understand that?'

James nodded slowly. Sedgwick took an old, dirty kerchief from the deep, bulging pocket of his coat, wet it with spit and gently wiped the tears away from the boy's dirty face.

'I'm warning you, though,' he continued. 'You misbehave once more and I'll spank you so hard I'll tan your hide. And don't think I wouldn't do it because you're my son.' He took the boy by the hand again and walked into the house. Lizzie was hunched over Isabell; the baby in her basket was crying as if the world might end. She looked up as they entered, her eyes wide, face drawn in fear, her hair wild.

'Where were you?' Lizzie stood, looking first at the baby and then opening her arms. Sedgwick let go of the boy and James ran to her. She shook her head, eyes closed, rocking back and forth as she held the lad. 'Don't,' she said softly. 'Don't ever do that again. I was looking for you and you'd gone.'

'I won't,' James promised, snuffling as he cried. 'I'm sorry.' Sedgwick carefully picked up the baby, so light and fragile in his large hands that it still scared him. He cradled her, rubbing a fingertip gently over her lips, taking in her warmth and marvelling that he could have a love so huge for something so small. She opened her eyes and smiled up at him, the yelling subsiding into a gentle hiccough.

'Where was he?' Lizzie asked. The boy kept hold of her skirts.

'Down on Briggate.' He looked at James. 'He knows what'll happen the next time.'

She breathed deeply and shook her head sadly and put her arms around the lad's shoulders. She sagged with exhaustion; she looked like a woman close to the end of her tether. Her eyes were sunken, with dark patches shading under them, all the prettiness and life leeched from her face in a wearied expression that was beyond age. Between the baby and James there was no peace for her.

Sedgwick reached out and stroked her arm, moving down to rub the back of her hand tenderly. Then he kissed her and left. There was work he needed to do; the problems at home would need to wait until later.

Will Cates was waiting in a small private parlour at the Rose and Crown when Rob arrived. It was up a rickety flight of stairs and curtained to give some privacy. A jug of wine sat on the table. Lister sniffed it, looked questioningly at Cates, then poured himself a mug and sat down. Even dressed in his best coat and breeches he didn't look rich, but he was presentable enough for good company.

'Now,' Will asked, 'what's all this mystery about?'

'I told you, it's nothing important.'

Cates laughed softly. 'But important enough to meet in private?'

'That was your idea.'

'True enough,' he acknowledged, taking a drink. 'So what is it, Rob?'

'Your father dismissed a serving girl a few weeks ago.'

'Who? Lucy?' Will said in aggrieved surprise. 'You dragged me out to ask about Lucy?'

'I did,' Lister admitted without apology. 'She's missing. No one's seen her since she left your house.'

Cates snorted. 'She's probably too stupid to find her way home.' He narrowed his eyes. 'Anyway, what business is it of the Constable? She's hardly a child.'

Rob gave a heavy shrug. 'I just do what I'm told.'

Cates drained his mug and reached over to pour more of the wine.

'You know Lucy was pregnant? That's why my father really let her go.'

'Yes.'

'I don't know who was more scandalized by it, my mother or my holy brother.'

'Any idea who got her that way?' Rob asked.

Will held up his hands. 'It wasn't me, that's all I can tell you. She might have been too daft to say no, but with that harelip she wasn't someone I'd have wanted in the first place.'

'You've tupped other servants?'

'Of course I have,' Cates admitted without hesitation. 'My first time was with a maid. What's the point of having good-looking servants otherwise? Don't tell me you never have?'

'No.'

Cates raised his eyebrows. 'Dear God,' he said, rolling his eyes. 'Another innocent. I think even my brother's been at the serving girls, and I know for a fact my father has. But Lucy? You've got to draw a line somewhere. I doubt she'd have known what I was doing.'

'I heard she wasn't bright.'

'She was simple,' Cates observed flatly, pouring more wine. 'I don't even know why my father took her on. She couldn't do anything without prodding, and even then it was only half done.'

'So why didn't he dismiss her sooner?'

'No idea,' he answered, 'and far less interest. It's not my business. If he'd give me a halfway decent allowance I wouldn't even be living there.'

Lister sipped deeply and then pushed the mug away.

'More?'

Rob shook his head. He rarely drank wine and didn't want it going to his head.

'What was she like?'

'Lucy?' Cates though for a moment. 'Ugly as Saturday sin with that harelip. But it was always yes sir or no sir and a pretty little curtsey. At least she knew that. If she'd looked better I'd have had her, stupid or not.'

'No one called for her?'

Cates laughed. 'Christ's blood, man, do I look like an authority on what the servants do? I don't know. You'd have to ask them. As long as they do what they're supposed to and keep out of my way I don't give a bugger what they get up to.'

Rob stood. 'Thank you,' he said.

'Is that it? Not going to stay and have something to eat? The landlord said they had a fresh pig this morning.'

'I can't. Work to do.' It was a lie, he had no duty until this evening. But staying meant more drinking and he wanted to be sober to walk Emily home from school.

Cates shrugged. 'It's your choice,' he said.

It was the shank of the afternoon when Richard Nottingham turned the corner from Kirkgate on to Briggate. The sun had finally broken through and the heat of the day clung close to the pavement. It seemed too early in the year to be this warm, he thought.

He opened the door of the house and walked in, his ears suddenly aware of the loud mechanics of the printing press, the rich smell of ink filling his nostrils. James Lister was working, turning the handle, the sleeves of his shirt rolled up, his concentration deep on his task.

'Mr Lister,' Nottingham shouted. Only when the job was done did Lister raise his head.

'Constable,' he said with a smile. 'It's a bad time to call, I'm afraid.' He gestured around the room, at the piles of paper and the finished copies of the new *Leeds Mercury* stacked under the front window.

He was a man who seemed to grow more rotund by the month, his long waistcoat barely containing his belly. Careless ink stains smudged his clothes, and there were black flecks on his white hose and across his florid face. But he had a ready grin and an ear for delicious gossip that served him well.

'What can I do for you?'

'Someone has an advertisement in your new issue,' the Constable explained. 'I'd like to see it.'

Lister looked at him shrewdly and picked up a finished copy, his thick fingers smudging the wet words.

'Anything I should know about?' he asked with interest.

'The thief taker. I'm curious about his services.'

'I remember him. A very curious man, don't you think?' He glanced at the Constable but didn't wait for an answer. 'Told me what he wanted to say and I wrote it down. I don't think he has his letters. There was something not too pleasant about him.' He handed over the newspaper. 'That'll be a penny ha'penny,' he said.

Nottingham laughed and dug into his breeches pocket for the coins.

'It'll be the best money you spend this week,' Lister promised with a smile, eyes twinkling.

'Maybe. I'll leave you to your business.'

'Still a few hours of this. Just think, you're the first in Leeds with all the news.'

He went to the White Swan, next to the jail. The potman brought his ale and the Constable turned the pages of the newspaper, eyes slipping over the print until he found what he wanted.

It was much as Walton had said. For part of the value of the items he'd reunite owners with belongings that had somehow disappeared. For a little more money he'd find the person who'd taken them and bring him to justice. It was an odd, dark trade, but he had to admit it was within the law. What troubled him was that it needed a familiarity with Leeds that the thief taker couldn't possess; the man hadn't been in the city long enough to know people or understand the subtleties of the place. Walton could be contacted in care of the Talbot Inn. Somehow that didn't surprise him. It just meant they'd need to keep a closer eye on the man.

★   ★   ★

Caroline had gone by the time the deputy returned to Briggate. She could have been off with a man, or maybe she'd gone to the dram shop to drink down some strength for the rest of the day. But he couldn't wait for her. There were other girls who might have seen Lucy, who might have the answers he needed.

A couple of them remembered her, the timid, ugly creature who seemed to make no money yet came back the next night with her face bruised button-bright and her eyes full of fear, then didn't return again. But none of them had spoken to her and no one knew who'd been running her. All he could hope was that Caroline had been able to find a name for him; if anyone here was likely to manage it, she'd be the one.

There'd be no point questioning the pimps. These days there were too many of them and the denials would fall too easily from their lips. Instead he went on to other business, the theft of some lace from a shop near the top of Briggate, the report of a pocket picked and two florins stolen. That worried him; it was the third instance inside a week. But without a description of some kind, or the good fortune to catch the thief in the act, they stood little chance: he knew that all too clearly.

Finally he returned to the jail. Nottingham was there, working on another report, sharpening the nib on a quill.

'She was a whore right enough,' the deputy said, folding his long body on to a chair. 'Just not a good one.'

The Constable sat back. 'How do you mean?'

'She only worked two nights. Took nothing the first, according to other girls, came back all bruised the next, and that was it. Never returned after that.'

'Who was pimping her?' Nottingham ran a hand through his hair, pushing back the fringe.

'I don't know yet, boss. Old Caroline's asking round.'

Nottingham thought for a moment. 'How long ago was this?'

Sedgwick shrugged. 'Before the fire on the Calls, that's all she can really remember.'

The Constable gave a long, deep sigh. 'That doesn't help us much.'

'It's a start. I'll keep asking. I suppose the pimp could have killed her.'

'It's possible,' Nottingham agreed. 'If he beat her once he could do it again. That makes him the best we have.'

'What about the baby, though, boss? Why would he want to tear the child out of her like that?'

'I wish I understood that, John. I really do.'

After the deputy had left for the evening the Constable pushed his reports aside. They'd still be there in the morning when he'd be ready to deal with them. He needed to talk to Alice Wendell again.

He locked the door of the jail and walked slowly to the Calls. Leeds was growing quiet, people in their homes, the noises around muted. There was a deep, comforting silence within the sounds of the city, and he reached for the stillness there. Already workmen were busy on the house where they'd found Lucy, he noticed. They'd knocked out much of the bones of the place and put up a new framework, the fresh-cut timber almost golden in the early evening light. The Constable lingered for a minute, amazed as always by the skill of the joiners and builders, then moved on.

He only had to knock once before she answered the door to the cellar room. It didn't surprise him. As soon as she saw him, for just the briefest moment her face fell. Then she gathered herself, mouth firm and back straight.

'Tha'd better come in,' she said.

Inside, the door closed, she kept her gaze direct.

'I'm sorry,' he began but she shook her head.

'Nay,' she told him. 'It's not your fault. I thought you'd be back.'

'I need to ask you some questions.'

'Aye. Go on, then.' Her voice was steady, her gaze firm, but he saw her fingers pressing tightly on the wood of the table. She kept her grief inside, a private thing, not to be shared. The face she showed the world had to be strong.

'How long have you lived here?' he asked.

'Six month, near as spitting. Used to be up in the Leylands. But once it were just me, after our Lucy found her position, I wanted somewhere cheaper.'

'So the folk around here don't know her?'

'Nay.' She paused thoughtfully. 'It were different when we were up there,' she continued, as if it had been another town and not just a quarter of a mile away. 'They all knew us there. Everyone looked out for everyone else. Even more when I had my man.'

'How did he die?' the Constable asked quietly.

'He went mad.' She lifted her eyes. 'Couldn't work, couldn't do owt. Finally it seemed like all he had left was words. He'd never been much for talking, but he began to speak and speak. All day, even into the night when he should have been asleep. Then it was like he'd said everything, used it all up, and he was silent. And then he died.' She gave a small, wan smile. 'It were a long time ago now.'

But no less raw for all the years, he thought.

'What about your son?'

'He were a good lad,' she answered, and he noticed the past tense. 'Looked after things, brought his money home every week. He had a good trade at the smithy. Then he met some wild lads and he fell in with them.'

She shrugged helplessly. He knew the story, he'd heard it more times than he could recall. Drinking, whoring, fighting . . . there was nothing new in the world.

'Our Lucy, she's buried over there with the paupers?' Alice Wendell asked.

'Yes. We didn't know who she was.'

After a short silence she asked, 'Can I bring my lass home? Bury her proper?'

'I don't know,' he admitted. 'I'll find out.'

'Thank you,' she said with a short nod of her head. It was both gratitude and dismissal.

'Is there anything else I can do?'

'I'll be reet.'

He left her, saddened and heartsore. She'd survive because she'd always survived, no matter how much life might have thrown at her. She'd outlived her daughter and that was always a difficult thing to accept.

At the Parish Church he made his way among the graves until he reached Rose's headstone. He bowed his head and let memories of her fill his mind, allowed the joy of remembering her alive overcome the pain he'd felt when she'd died. She'd been gone more than a year now but the scar still felt tender.

Quietly he made his way home, thoughts tumbling in his head. Mary was in the garden, carefully picking weeds from between the plants as the light faded. He lifted her up, held her close, smelling her, kissing her.

'What's that for?' she asked in happy astonishment.

He shrugged and smiled.

Seven

The second of the burglaries came that night, at the home of Alderman Ridgely close to the Red House at the top of the Head Row. The job had been neatly and daringly done, the Constable saw after he'd been called out in the small hours, the lock on the window sash quietly worked open with a knife blade.

The thief had made away with some plate, worth almost ten pounds if the blustering owner was telling the truth. It was a good sum, a fortune to many men. Nottingham sighed and tried to rub the weariness of a broken night from his face. He knew exactly what would happen. The Alderman would have a quiet word with the mayor. Then John Douglas would have to put pressure on him to find the goods and the man who'd stolen them.

Tuesday morning brought rain to blight the early cloth market. He walked down Briggate in his greatcoat and tricorn hat, surrounded by the scent of wet wool, the rich smell of Leeds's prosperity. Wind gusted up from the river, leaving the weavers soaked at the trestles, covering their cloth as best they could. The merchants huddled together, clustering in doorways, the quiet confidence of money in their talk. Once the bell rang they'd forget the weather to look and buy and calculate the profits in their coffers.

Someone had driven cattle into the city to be killed and butchered at the Shambles and the road was thick with muddy cow pats, strong and stinking. He heard the heavy, grievous lowing of the beasts further up the street as they were put to the knife.

Back at the jail he fed the fire and dried off, his coat steaming as the heat took hold. By the time the deputy arrived from his rounds Nottingham was settled with a pie left over from the day before and a mug of small beer.

'Quiet market, boss?'

'The merchants will have made another fortune so they'll be happy. Any word on this burglar?'

'Nothing. No one has any names, no one's been trying to sell the plate. I even went over and asked Joe Buck and he hasn't heard anything.'

The Constable frowned. If Buck, the largest dealer in stolen goods in the city, didn't know, the thief was keeping quiet.

'What about Lucy? Did Caroline come up with the name of her pimp?'

'I haven't seen her yet. She'll be out later.' He glanced out of the window. 'Don't fancy her chances of doing well in this.'

'It's market day. Enough people will be flush that trade will be good. I need that name, John. We've got nothing else.'

From the Moot Hall up to Harrison's market cross at the Head Row, stalls lined Briggate. The patter of rain made a tumbling dance on the ragged sheets the vendors had put over their stalls.

Old clothes, pans and pots, baskets, and more competed for space with withered carrots and potatoes kept through the winter to sell. Chickens squawked in terror as their cages were stacked. The street was a clamour of people inspecting and bargaining. A woman yelled her wares, apples that had been fresh before the flesh had puckered, hoping for a few pennies from the last of autumn. Men and women moved against each other, packed tight. It would be the perfect place for the pick-pocket to strike again, and the Constable needed to try and find him.

Nottingham walked through, fingertips tight on his money, alert for a hand, watching for a glance or a sly movement. Sedgwick was there too, doing the same thing, the pair of them bait in the press of people. They finally gave up as the church bell struck noon. The rain had stopped, but that was the only good thing about the day. They stood by the cross and the Constable rubbed the rough, worn stone.

'He's in there,' he said, looking at the crowd.

'I'll wager we'll have someone in later who's had his money lifted.'

Nottingham shook his head. 'I won't bet against you. Whoever it is, he probably knows our faces.' He paused and glanced at the deputy. 'Caroline should be out and earning by now.'

The Constable walked down the Head Row and along Vicar Lane. After the strident bustle of the market the streets seemed curiously quiet. Carts still passed, servants shuffled on their way back to work, arms laden with purchases, harried looks on their faces, but the noise was that of every day. It should have soothed him but it didn't.

He was on edge and he knew it. He wanted the name of the pimp. They had nothing else, no way into finding out who'd killed Lucy Wendell. Whoremasters killed their girls; he'd seen it too often over the years. One blow too many, in drink or in anger, a harsh touch with a knife. He'd made enough of them swing.

But this murder was different, deliberate and evil. And that was why he had to find the killer.

She was exactly where he expected to find her, a cap covering her hair, wearing the only dress she possessed, a muslin gown with its pattern so faded it was impossible to make out. She'd pulled it down to show off what bosom she still had, the skin wrinkled and aged between her breasts. She held a fan over her mouth, waving it coyly to hide her rotten teeth and the foul smell of her breath. But her eyes twinkled when she saw him.

'You ran off fast enough yesterday,' Caroline said. 'Did your fancy woman see you?'

'I'm safe, she's only around Thursdays and Fridays,' Sedgwick answered with a wink to make her giggle, the years falling from her face for a moment. 'Did you find out a name for me?'

'I did,' she said proudly. 'It's going to cost you, though.'

'I expected that. Nowt's free in this life. Nor in the next one, probably.' He took a coin from his pocket and gave it to her. 'What's his name?'

'Joshua Davidson. Strange man with a limp. He has two lasses. Says they're his sisters, but I don't know.'

'How do you mean?'

She looked up at him with eyes full of hurt. 'Mr Sedgwick, what kind of man would turn his sisters out for whores?'

'More than you'd imagine. You look after yourself,' he told her.

'And you look after your Lizzie and that little girl, Mr Sedgwick.'

He took the name back to the jail. The Constable raised his eyebrows when he heard it.

'I'd better go and have another talk with Mr Davidson.'

'You want me to come with you, boss?'

'No,' Nottingham answered slowly. 'I might have misjudged him once, but I won't do it again.'

Although morning had passed the shutters were still closed at the small house by Shaw Pool. He hammered heavily on the door and waited, then knocked again, rattling the wood in its warped frame. Finally he heard footsteps and Davidson appeared, barely dressed in shirt and breeches, blinking and yawning.

'Constable,' he said in sleepy surprise. 'What brings you back here? Nowt wrong, is there?'

'You'd better let me in,' Nottingham said stonily. 'I've some questions to ask.'

Davidson limped heavily away and the Constable followed him to the kitchen. There was coal in a bucket but no fire burned in the room and he felt the chill in the air. An old table had been scrubbed clean, three chairs pulled up close to it. The floor was beaten earth, worn down by generations of feet.

'Sit thisen down,' Davidson said with a smile. 'There's some ale if you like.'

Nottingham remained standing and shook his head. 'You've been lying to me.'

The man cocked his head and gave a gentle, bemused smile. 'Me?' he asked.

'You.'

'What have I lied about?' Davidson scratched his head.

'You said you only run two girls.'

'Aye, that's right enough. Me sisters, like I told you.' He

poured himself a mug of ale from a tall old jug that stood by the window.

'What about Lucy Wendell?' the Constable asked.

The man chuckled. 'Is that what this is about, then? Little Lucy?'

'It is, Mr Davidson. She's missing, and the last time she was seen was when she was whoring for you.'

'That were all of one night,' Davidson said, shaking his head sadly. 'She didn't bring in any money, anyway. The way she looked and all, and her getting heavy round the belly, I told her it wasn't the life for her.'

'So you beat her when she didn't earn anything.'

'I bloody well did not.' The man crashed the mug down hard on the table, eyes blazing. 'I'll not have it said I hit lasses.'

'No?' Nottingham asked, his eyes cold, watching the pimp's face carefully. 'Who did, then?'

'Someone who had her and didn't pay.'

'And why should I believe you?'

'Ask me sisters if you like. They'll tell you.'

'Where are they?'

'Out earning, I expect. They were both gone when I woke up.'

He'd find them later and ask his questions.

'Why did Lucy come to you?'

The man wiped the back of his hand across his mouth. 'I don't know, and that's the truth, Constable,' he answered with a shrug. 'Happen I was the first she saw. We'd not been here too long ourselves when she came around.'

'What did she say?'

'Said she needed work, and would I look after her. I couldn't understand too much of what she told me, mind, it was hard to make it out. She wasn't a pretty lass to start, and then there was that lip. When you saw that . . .' He shook his head.

'What else? There must have been more than that.'

'She said she'd been dismissed and she couldn't go home. One look at her with the belly starting to bulge and you could see why.'

'Was that all she said?'

Davidson scratched his head again, a fingernail digging into the scalp for lice.

'Aye, there was summat odd, I suppose. She said he'd find her if she went home.'

'Who?'

'I didn't ask. It didn't seem to matter.' He took another drink then poured himself more of the ale.

'If you didn't think anyone would want her, why did you take her on?'

'I told you, we'd just come to Leeds ourselves. I thought she might bring in a little. Besides, our Sarah felt sorry for her.'

'And are you always so kindhearted, Mr Davidson?' the Constable asked.

The pimp stared at him. 'Mebbe I was a bit when I came here. Not now. It's a cruel place, is Leeds.'

'What happened when she was hurt?'

'The lasses brought her back here and cleaned her up. Whoever he was, he'd done a right job on her face, it were all bloody and swollen up. Sarah looked after her, sat up with her all night.'

'What about the next day? Was she willing to go out again?'

Davidson shook his head. 'She didn't want to. She was scared. Offered to stop here and clean for us instead. Look at me, Mr Nottingham.' He opened his arms appealingly and glanced around the room. 'Do you think I'd know what to do with a servant girl? So she went back out with our Sarah and Fanny.'

'But she didn't come back.'

'No. When they were done they went looking for her, but she'd gone. Not seen her since.'

'You didn't search for her?' Nottingham wondered.

Davidson shrugged. 'What for? I thought she'd decided I were right and she wasn't made to be a whore. Best to let it be.'

The Constable stared at the man. His leg might stop him moving fast but he had a large pair of fists that could damage a girl. His tale seemed plausible enough but he still wanted to talk to the girls.

'You'd better be telling me the truth,' he said finally.

'I am, Constable. I told you, ask me sisters.'

He found them down by the bridge, standing close to the old chantry chapel. He could hear the yells of the men from the barges out on the river, loading cloth from the warehouses that would end up in more countries than he could name.

The girls were easy to spot, with the same pinched, hungry faces as Davidson, looking as if youth had been drained from them too early. They were standing together and talking, warily eyeing the men who passed. A few weeks before they'd probably had an air of innocence but it had already been rubbed off them, leaving their mouths and eyes hard. He walked up to them and the taller one turned, appraising him quickly.

'We're only looking for gentlemen today, love,' she told him.

'I think you'll talk to me,' he said with a friendly smile.

'Oh aye?' she asked cockily. 'Why's that, then?'

'Because I'm the Constable of the City.'

The girls looked at each other with the kind of quick, silent conversation only sisters could manage. He'd seen it in his own daughters when Rose was alive.

'We heard you said this was all right unless we caused trouble,' the girl said.

'It is,' he agreed, keeping his voice light. 'But I need to ask you some questions. You're Sarah?'

The taller one hesitated then gave a brief nod.

'I need to know about a girl called Lucy.'

Sarah sighed. 'What about her? She were hardly with us long enough to draw breath.'

He asked what he needed to. Everything they answered echoed Davidson's words. Lucy had been a timid little thing, hadn't talked much. With her face and the signs of a baby on the way they knew not many would want her, but she might have made enough to keep body and soul together. They'd looked after the girl when she was hurt, bathed her face and tried to ease her tears.

'She said she didn't want to go home?'

'Aye, that's right,' Fanny said. 'She said he'd find her there.'

'Who would?' Nottingham asked.

The girls shrugged together.

'Her business,' Sarah said. 'If she'd wanted to tell us, she would have.'

'Who beat her? Was it your brother?'

The girls glanced one to the other and started to laugh.

'Mister,' Sarah told him, 'it weren't our Joshua. He wouldn't dare raise his hand to a lass. I'd kill him mesen if he tried. I know what he seems like, but he's soft as summer butter.'

'It was someone she was with,' Fanny interrupted. 'Hit her all round the face. Thought it should have been free wi' her. Poor thing cried half the night.' She paused. 'She weren't made for this. I'm not sure she were made for anything.'

'What do you mean?'

'Well, she had the lip.' She stared at him to be certain he understood her. 'And mister, she were simple. Didn't know what you meant half the time, you had to show her. And then there were the babby. No lass should have all that,' she said seriously. 'It were like God hated her.' She blushed and looked down.

'What about when she left?' he asked gently.

'She came out with us the second day,' Sarah said. 'She didn't want to, not after what had happened, but it's like Joshua told her, you have to make money to eat. We left her here and that was it. She never came back.'

'You didn't look for her?'

Her eyes widened, surprised by the question. 'Why? She weren't one of ours.'

Davidson's tale hadn't fully convinced him. It had slid too glibly off his tongue. This was different, though. He'd no doubt the sisters could lie with the best of them when it suited them, but what they'd told him had the stark, spare ring of honesty. And it left him little further along.

Rob had watched the dark blue of evening turn to thick black on the western horizon. He'd already made his first rounds with the men, seeing everything quiet in the inns and alehouses. It was still early in the week and people didn't have enough money left to cause trouble. That would come after they were paid on Friday or Saturday.

He knew the smells of Leeds at night now. They weren't as strong as in daylight, the shit of carters' horses worked hard into the street and dried, the harsh steel tang of blood around the Shambles fading with nightfall, the rank stink of unwashed bodies now locked behind closed doors.

He made his way down to the river, hearing the water flowing and seeing a pair of fires glowing on the bank, looking for all the world like an entrance to hell. The sight made him think of tales of the gabble ratchets his governess had scared him with when he was young. Looking around, he half expected to see the eyes of the dogs made by the devil from the souls of children who'd died before they could be baptized. Instead he saw faces: people who had arrived a month or so before with the first warmth of spring. He'd met them on their first night, just men and women who had nothing, keeping each other safe in the darkness and looking for fitful work in the city or the country that surrounded it.

There were more of them now, maybe forty in all, a mix of the wounded and the weary, the hopeless and the defeated. The trust had vanished from their eyes, and the love from their hearts. They left with the dawn, only coming back when dusk fell.

They kept the fires burning all through the night, sleeping close to the flames for warmth and protection. The men kept cudgels close to hand to fight off the drunks who came for sport or rape.

One man stood as Rob approached. He was slight, his hair lank, but he stood out from the others, wearing clothes that had he kept carefully clean, his boots shiny from spit and effort. His right arm was withered, wasted and useless, life's dark joke that would always be with him.

'Mr Lister,' he said.

'Evening, Simon.'

Rob joined the others in the circle around the blaze. He saw some eye him suspiciously, wary of any authority. But Simon Gordonson was the one who seemed to speak for them all, a smiling man who persisted through a life that had done him no favours.

He'd made his way as a clerk for a shoemaker until the sleeping sickness had taken his wife and children at the tail of the previous summer, just as the nights grew chill. In his grief he'd given up his home, the things that no longer had meaning to him, and taken to wandering. He'd come back to Leeds a few weeks before, bringing the others who'd joined him, a strange, dispossessed band.

The men passed a jug of ale around and Rob took a short swig before handing it on. A pan of something bubbled over the fire. The women sat further away, almost in the shadows, babes and small children asleep on their laps, their bodies warmed with coats or threadbare blankets. Dogs rested nearby, raising their heads occasionally to sniff something on the breeze.

'Crime keeping you busy, Mr Lister?' Gordonson asked. He was an affable soul with a ready smile. Only rarely did it slip, but Rob could see the bottomless sorrow beneath the mask.

'There's no danger of ever being out of work,' he answered.

Gordonson laughed softly. 'God's kingdom's never so peaceful as he'd like it to be. I thought I saw you out with a lass the other day. Courting, are you?'

'I suppose I am,' he answered with a small laugh.

'Pretty girl,' Gordonson said quietly.

'She is,' Lister agreed. 'But my father's warned me I'd better not marry her.'

'Not marry?' he asked in surprise. 'Why wouldn't he want that? A man needs a wife and bairns to complete him.'

'You tell him that.' Rob couldn't keep the bitterness from his voice. 'He doesn't want me to marry her because her father's the Constable.' He saw the other man's confusion. 'She's not good enough for me, evidently.'

'Good enough is what rich folks can afford.' Gordonson stared at the ground then looked up. 'Are you rich, Mr Lister?'

'No,' Rob replied slowly, then said, 'Middling, maybe.'

Gordonson leaned forward. 'In that case I'll tell you something for free. Nothing's better than love.'

'It won't fill your belly, though, will it?' Lister asked.

'Maybe not, but food won't fill your heart, either.'

Rob looked at Gordonson carefully. 'And what about if the love goes? What then?'

Simon tapped his head. 'Memories, Mr Lister. Memories. They can keep a man warm for many a long night.'

Rob sat and considered the words. A wind soughed lightly through the reeds and the tall grass by the water. Finally he stood.

'I should get back to my work,' he said. 'Tell me, did you have a girl down here with a harelip? It would be a few weeks ago now.'

'You mean that Lucy?' Gordonson asked.

'Yes, that's her name.'

'She stayed with us for a few days. You'd need to talk to Susan, she was the one who looked after her.'

Rob scanned the faces almost lost in the darkness. 'Where is she?'

Gordonson shook his head. 'Not tonight, Mr Lister. She's off working. You come back tomorrow and I'll see she's here for you.'

Rob nodded. 'Do you remember when Lucy was here?' he wondered.

'Not really,' Gordonson told him with a gentle smile. 'Time's the one thing we have plenty of here. Maybe that's why we don't pay it much heed. Ask Susan tomorrow, she might know.'

Eight

'So we know she whored for one night after Cates dismissed her,' the Constable said. He sat behind the desk, hands playing with the quill pen as he talked. 'And she was down with these folk by the river.'

Rob nodded. He stood close to the door, breeches and hose still dripping from wading into the water to pull out a body below Leeds Bridge. The corpse sat in the cold cell they used as a mortuary.

'That's the start of a picture,' Nottingham continued, pushing a hand through his hair. 'We need more. You find out what this woman knows, Rob. John, I want you to talk to the servants up at the Cates house. Lucy was there a few months, she must have become friendly with one of them.'

'Yes, boss.' The deputy sat on the other chair, longs legs stretched out in front of him.

'Either of you have any idea where else she could have gone?'

Neither of them spoke. This was a story they'd need to piece together, a puzzle they'd need good fortune to complete. But the Constable was determined that they'd continue until the picture was finished.

'According to Davidson and his girls, Lucy said she couldn't go home because he'd find her there. See if you can discover who the *he* is.'

They nodded.

'And there's one other thing,' he announced. 'Yesterday evening I had a note from our Alderman whose house was robbed. It seems that his property has been returned.'

Sedgwick sat up straight. 'What? What do you mean, boss?'

'If I had to guess, I'd say our thief taker has a hand in this,' Nottingham said 'For a fee he arranges the return of the property.'

'What about the thief?' the deputy asked.

'He's paid for his efforts and probably makes more than he might if he sold the items to someone like Joe Buck. And with everything returned and the householder satisfied, no one will testify to a crime.' He threw down the quill. 'I'll be talking to Mr Walton later. It looks as if his advertisement might have paid for itself already.'

'It's wrong,' Rob said.

'Of course it's wrong,' the Constable agreed angrily. 'But the law of the land says it's legal, as long as Walton didn't arrange the burglary himself.' He shook his head in frustration. 'Right, you go home, Rob. John, see if you can give our drowner a name.'

Sedgwick was the one to talk to servants. The Constable knew that. He had the touch, the mixture of charm and easy banter that gained their trust and opened them up to say things they might never utter otherwise. They seemed to understand he was one of them.

Today, though, all he felt was a brittle weariness in his bones, as if he might snap into pieces at the lightest touch. Isabell had had another bad night, Lizzie up every hour to tend to her, feeding and soothing. And he'd lain awake, wondering what to do about James. He could take his belt to the boy, the way his own father had done often enough. But he knew it would do no more good now than it had then. The lad might be young but he was already like his father, bull-headed. As soon as the pain wore off and the tears dried James would be more determined than ever.

What sleep he'd managed had come in brief snatches, and now the skin on his face felt tight and his eyeballs gritty. He'd identified the dead man quickly enough as Jacob Miller; the deputy had known his face for years. There were no signs of violence, so he'd likely tumbled in the Aire when he was drunk. God knew that enough managed it as a way to die, by accident or design.

The Cates house was up at Town End, just beyond the Head Row. It was barely a few years old, its genteel, plain front as broad a notice of money as any. But that entrance was for the gentlemen and ladies who'd come to call on the family. He looked around until he saw his way to the back, where the servants and those in trade could come and go without the master having to notice them.

The kitchen door was open, the room steamy with the smell of cooking and the heat from the fire. A young girl was chopping onions, stopping to wipe at her eyes with the back of her hand, her apron ill-fitting and stained. He could hear the cook yelling her orders. He knocked and walked in. The room went silent.

'Who are you?' the cook asked finally. She was a heavy-boned woman, short and squat, hair pushed awkwardly under a cap, face red and flushed with sweat.

He smiled. 'I'm John Sedgwick,' he said. 'I'm the deputy constable. Have you got a moment?'

The cook had no time for gossiping, with a meal to prepare and have on the table for guests at noon, but she called down one of the serving girls to talk to him. Grace was a plain little thing; she looked thirteen but swore to three years older. She glanced nervously at the deputy, fingers working together nervously at having to talk to authority. He found a quiet nook where they'd be out of everyone's way, the dark wood around them smelling freshly of polish.

'Don't worry, love,' he told her, 'you've done nowt wrong. You're not in trouble.'

'Yes, sir.'

She bobbed her head quickly and he smiled.

'No need to call me sir, either. I'm just John. Did you know Lucy?'

Grace's eyes brightened. 'She was lovely, was Lucy.'

'You were friends, were you?'

'We shared a bed up in the eaves,' she said. 'But she didn't talk too much. She hated it 'cause the words all sounded funny. Once you got used to it, it were easy enough to understand her, really.'

'You know she was pregnant?'

Grace nodded seriously. 'I tried to tell her, sir, but she wouldn't believe me.' She paused and blushed. 'John.'

'Why not?'

'She didn't know how girls get babies.'

He raised his eyebrows slightly in disbelief. Still, if she was as simple as everyone said, it was possible.

'Do you know who the father might be?'

She shook her head, but it was too quick, too adamant.

'Do you?' he asked softly.

She lowered her head to hide her expression but he could see the livid colour rising up from her neck.

'Was it someone here? I won't tell anyone, I promise.'

'I don't know,' she answered in a voice so quiet he wasn't sure whether he'd imagined it.

'Do the men here . . . ?'

At first she was perfectly still and he stayed silent, waiting to see if she'd reveal anything. Then she gave a tiny nod.

'All of them?'

Grace glanced around hurriedly to assure herself no one could hear then whispered, 'Mr Cates and his sons.'

He kept his face blank and his voice steady. 'With you?'

'Yes.' She sounded resigned and hopeless.

'And with Lucy?'

'I don't know.' She looked up at him and he could see the tears in her eyes, thin shoulders shaking with the sorrow and secrets she'd been keeping inside for a long time. 'They didn't like her, they laughed at her. So maybe they didn't.'

'Didn't she say?'

The girl pulled at the hem of her apron. 'No.'

'Did she have anyone she saw when she had free time?'

'Just her mam and her brother.'

'Was she happy here?'

'Yes.' Grace smiled again briefly, her face lighting up, blue eyes bright and glistening. 'She was. We looked after her, you see. She felt safe here.'

'What was she like when she had to leave?'

'She cried. All the girls did.'

'Did she say where she was going?'

'No. She didn't know.'

'Not to her mam?'

'She said she couldn't, not now.'

'Did she say why?'

Grace looked confused. 'I just thought it was because she was having the baby.'

'Thank you, love. You've been very helpful.'

He stood and she looked up at him. 'You won't . . .?' she asked, then begged. 'Please.'

'I promise,' he assured her. 'Honestly.'

The Constable strode up the Head Row, his face set hard. A little before the impressive brick of the Red House he knocked on a door and waited for a servant to open it.

When one finally arrived, he gave his name and was shown into a withdrawing room that looked out on a tidy garden. No fire had been laid and he pushed his hands deep into the pockets of his coat to keep them warm. He listened for the sound of the servant's heels in the hallway.

He knew that Alderman Ridgely had dropped his case, and he was sure of the reason why: he was going to pay good money to the thief taker for the return of items that already belonged to him. But Nottingham wanted to look the man in the eye and hear the words from his own lips. It wouldn't be satisfaction, but it would be a small beginning.

When the servant finally returned, he looked abashed.

'I'm sorry, sir,' he said, 'but the master says he doesn't have time to see you.'

The Constable gave a small nod but said nothing. He picked up the tricorn hat from the chair where he'd left it and walked out. Word of this would run all around Leeds before the day was done, how the man had snubbed Nottingham. But who would look worse for it, he wondered? Men in Leeds would laugh at anyone fool enough to pay twice for his own property.

At the Talbot he asked for Walton, and a potboy was sent scrambling up the stairs to fetch him. The Constable sat at a bench, a stoup of ale and two beakers in front of him. When the thief taker arrived he motioned him to a seat and poured him a drink. The man was dressed in his grey suit, sponged clean now, his stock and the cuffs of his shirt rimed with dirt.

'Your business is off to a good start, I hear.' Nottingham raised his mug in a small toast. Walton smiled, showing the gaps in his teeth dark as the devil's word.

'I'll not say it is, since they say pride's a sin. But God willing, it'll prosper, Constable.'

'Only if you deal with criminals, Mr Walton.'

'I return items that have gone missing,' the man said carefully, his gaze straight and direct. 'I don't ask how they vanished.'

'Or how someone else now has them?'

'That's not my business,' the thief taker answered slowly. 'If someone's stolen them, it's for God to judge him, not me.'

'No doubt He will,' the Constable agreed. 'And it's a pious enough turn of phrase. But I'm concerned with the here and now, not what might happen at the gates of heaven.'

'That's your job,' Walton conceded. 'When a man pays me for the return of his property, that's all that matters to me. Not the criminal or the crime.'

'And my job is catching those criminals and seeing they're punished. I told you I'd let you work here if it didn't interfere with the law.'

'And has it, Constable?' Walton spread his hands on the table, the nails bitten short, the tips of his fingers dark with grime. 'Has anyone lodged a complaint?' he asked. 'Has anyone reported a crime I'm preventing you from solving?'

'Someone has withdrawn his report of a robbery.'

'So there's nothing outstanding?' The thief taker grinned. 'No cause for you to worry at me this way?'

Nottingham drank and slowly put down the cup. He stared at the other man.

'There's plenty of reason, Mr Walton. You're treading very close to the edge of my patience. Sooner or later you'll cross the line.'

'If that happens I might have some powerful people here in my debt. Have you thought of that?'

The Constable ignored the question. When the time was right, no friends would save the thief taker.

'The law is the law. Break it and you pay the consequences.'

'I've lived long enough to know that money can speak louder than law sometimes, Constable. I've found it to be a fact well worth remembering.' He stood. 'Good day to you.'

Nottingham finished his ale and left. Returning to the jail he decided it would be a good idea to have someone follow Walton. The man was going to cause trouble. With some care they might be able to stop it early.

'John,' he said, 'our thief taker's staying at the Talbot. I want a man following him day and night.'

Sedgwick stared thoughtfully into space for a few moments.

'We can rearrange the men,' he suggested.

'Who's best at blending into a crowd?'

'Probably Tom Holden. You can look at him and forget he was ever there.'

'Good. And among the night men?'

'There's no one, really,' the deputy admitted. 'Best to let Rob pick someone, they're his men.'

'True. I suspect we're going to see a few burglaries. Have everyone keep their eyes open.'

'This thief taker's involved?'

'If he's not yet, he will be soon enough,' Nottingham said with certainty. 'And once that starts, we'll have him.'

'Yes, boss.' He paused. 'What about the Cates men? What are we going to do about them?'

'I know what that servant girl told you, but they can deny it easily enough,' the Constable said in frustration. 'Who do you think most people will believe?'

'I'd believe the girl,' the deputy told him without hesitation.

'So would I, for all it matters. One of the men could have left Lucy with a baby and killed her.' He sighed. 'Trying to prove it will be close to impossible, though.'

'We still need to talk to them,' Sedgwick countered. 'I'll do it.'

'Are you sure?' Nottingham wasn't certain how wise that was. The deputy could be subtle with his questions, but he was at his best with the ordinary folk.

'Positive,' he answered with relish. 'I'll enjoy every moment of it.'

Finally the Constable nodded his agreement. It might not be a bad thing to shake them up a little.

'Start with Robert,' he advised. 'If he has religion the way everyone says he should be quick enough to admit his sins.'

'What about the father?' Sedgwick asked.

'Leave him for last. You'll need to be very careful with him. The same with Will. He's a smart lad, by all accounts. But if he's expecting anyone, it'll be Rob, not someone he doesn't know. You'll be able to press him harder.'

'When should I go?'

Nottingham considered.

'Tomorrow morning, I think. Start down at the warehouse. At least one of them should be there. If they're not, go up to the house. I doubt you'll get a confession but there might be something. And it could scare them enough to keep their hands off the girls for a while,' he added.

'Why not today?' Sedgwick asked.

'Do it when you're fresh.' He put on his coat and the tricorn hat. 'I'm going over to talk to Joe Buck and find out what he's heard about our thief taker. I think he'll have a few things to say.'

'If it's taking business from his purse I'm sure he will,' the deputy laughed. 'Tight as a squeaky farthing, is Joe.'

'And he'll probably hear about some of the burglaries that won't reach our ears. It could be a good way to catch our man.'

'So you'd be willing to work with him?'

Nottingham smiled.

'I'll use a very long spoon to sup with that devil, but yes, if needs must, I will. It's in his interest, too.'

'You know Joe, he's not going to do anything that doesn't help him.'

The bell at the parish church tolled midday, the sound dying softly.

'Come on, boss,' Sedgwick said, 'let's go to the White Swan first. I don't know about you, but my stomach thinks someone's slit my throat.'

★   ★   ★

Joe Buck lived on the south side of the Aire, among the tangle of small, ugly streets that were tucked out of sight behind of grand merchant palaces of Meadow Lane. Most of the houses were poor and faded, run down, a few even gutted, everything useful taken. There was rubbish against the walls, left where it had been thrown, and the stink of piss and shit. Packs of stray dogs roamed and growled and bony feral cats slunk quietly into the dark ginnels. But Buck's house was spotless on the outside, the windows clean and shining, blue paint fresh and sparkling on the door. Nottingham knocked and waited.

The servant arrived quickly, a large man with a small, powdered periwig on top of his head and sleeves rolled up to show muscled forearms. His skin was so dark it seemed to glow, his wide smile showing white teeth. Few would have believed he was Buck's molly boy.

'Constable,' he said, giving a brief bow. Only when he opened his mouth did the sense of the exotic drop away; his accent was broad Yorkshire. ''Ant seen thee in a while. Tha's here to see the master?'

'Yes, Henry, I am.'

'He's in t' back, same as he always is. Tha' knows where to go.' The servant stepped aside, his bulk almost filling the cramped hallway.

The parlour was immaculate, everything lovingly dusted, the way it always was when Nottingham visited. Buck was sitting at a rosewood desk and stood as soon as he saw the Constable. He was dressed in a suit that showed the tailor's art, the cut of the coat and waistcoat hiding his thickening belly, the breeches tight enough to display a strong pair of thighs. The hose, shirt and stock were all dazzling white, the shoes well-buffed, and a full-bottomed auburn wig was combed out to lie flatteringly on his shoulders. The business of selling stolen property paid well, Nottingham thought. Never mind that the Constable knew what Buck did, in ten years he'd never been able to connect the man with anything, not to the point of arrest.

'Mr Nottingham,' he said, extending his hand. 'Sit down, sit down. Do you want something to drink? A glass of wine? Small beer?'

'No, thank you.' The Constable settled in the chair and looked at the other man.

'So what can I do for you?' Buck asked. 'Although I've a feeling I know,' he added with a small smile.

'The thief taker.'

'I thought so,' he said with satisfaction. 'Our friend Mr Walton.'

'No friend of yours, I'd imagine,' Nottingham said.

'You're right there,' Buck admitted wryly. 'If I were in business — which I'm not,' he added cautiously, 'he'd be taking trade away from me with his little scheme, and I wouldn't care for that at all. You know about the robbery up by the Red House?'

The Constable nodded.

'There are rumours there was another last night.'

'I hadn't heard that,' the Constable admitted.

'People talk,' Buck said idly. 'So nothing's been reported to you?'

'No.'

'Which means they're relying on Mr Walton to retrieve their goods.' He frowned.

'That would touch an honest business in the pocket,' the Constable said, and Buck glanced up sharply.

'And it could turn people away from the law.'

Nottingham knew that. If he didn't hear that a crime had been committed he couldn't find the people who'd done it. They could conduct things any way they wanted in London and elsewhere, but he wouldn't stand for it in Leeds.

'What are we going to do about it?' he asked.

'Our friend could just disappear,' Buck suggested thoughtfully. 'It could be arranged easily enough.'

'No,' the Constable told him firmly. 'I can't condone murder, Joe. If he's going, he needs to be discredited. Caught with stolen goods or arranging a robbery. We'll do it the right way. It'll discourage anyone else from trying the same thing.'

Buck smiled and nodded in acknowledgement. 'Whatever you wish, Mr Nottingham.'

'You know the thieves in Leeds.'

Buck raised his eyebrows. 'Me?'

'I'm not going to play words with you, Joe,' the Constable told him, shaking his head slowly. 'I need your help. What I'm saying is we need to work together on this. When you hear what's going on, that someone's been in a house and taken things, you tell me, and I'll go after Walton.'

Buck sat quietly, hands steepled under his chin as he weighed the idea. The house was so quiet he could hear the longclock ticking softly in the hall.

'And you'll not come after me?' he asked eventually.

'I won't. You have my word on it.' He paused. 'Not until all this is over, anyway.'

Buck gave a slow smile. 'Anything more would have been too much to ask, wouldn't it?'

'Far too much, Joe,' Nottingham agreed with a grin. 'Now you'd better tell me about last night's break in.'

'All I know is one happened. I can find out for you.'

'Do that,' the Constable said, 'and send word to me.'

'I don't want you saying anything about this arrangement, Mr Nottingham,' Buck warned him. 'It wouldn't look good for me if people heard.'

'Nor for me,' the Constable said as he rose. 'Remember that, Joe. I need it quiet, too. The fewer people who know, the better.'

'There'll only be me and Henry.'

'And I'll tell Mr Sedgwick. You know you can trust him.'

'Yes.'

'Do we have an agreement?'

Buck stood and shook his hand. 'We do, Mr Nottingham. For now, at least.'

He returned to the jail with a feeling of satisfaction only to find a note summoning him to the mayor's office. It had happened before, and he knew it would occur often enough again, but this was the first demand since John Douglas had taken office. He brushed the worst of the dust off his coat, straightened his old, stained stock, took a swig of ale and strode up Briggate.

The Moot Hall seemed hushed after the roar of the street, clerks moving quickly and quietly, the only sounds voices from behind thick wooden doors and the scratch of a quill on paper. He knocked on the mayor's door at the end of the corridor and entered.

Douglas stood at the window, his back to the room, staring at the people below. When he turned his face was drawn.

'It's a big responsibility looking after all of them,' he said slowly. 'I don't think I realized it before I agreed to all this.'

'I can believe it,' Nottingham said.

'You know those quilts the women sew from scraps of fabric?' he asked and the Constable nodded. 'Running a city's like that. You make one law, then another and another and you try to fit them all into a pattern. Be glad you just have the crime, Richard.' He settled into his chair, the seat padded with a thick cushion. 'I'm expected to look after everything. For the poor as well as the rich.'

The Constable waited. By now he was used to the way Douglas liked to air his thoughts. He liked the man, he was a good, honest mayor, one of the few he'd known whose concerns went beyond the merchants and business.

'A couple of the aldermen have talked to me about this thief taker.' He searched the desk and brought out a copy of the *Mercury*, the advertisement circled in ink.

'I already know all about Mr Walton. One of your aldermen is already using his services.'

'Oh?' Douglas jerked his head up. 'Who?'

'Mr Ridgely had several things stolen from his house. I went and looked, but before I could do much he told me he'd been contacted and his items were being returned. Without a complaint there's nothing more I can do.'

'And you think the thief taker's returning the property.'

'I'm sure of it,' Nottingham told him. 'For a fee, of course. The only problem is that it's legal.' He glanced at Douglas. 'If the aldermen are complaining, you should advise them to tell their friends not to use his services.'

Douglas nodded. 'They hadn't told me that.'

'I've heard there's been another burglary, too. That one hasn't even been reported.'

They mayor stroked his chin. 'So what are you doing about it, Richard? Legal or not, it has to stop.'

'It's in hand,' the Constable assured him. 'It might take a little time, but I'll have Walton.'

'We don't want others following him here.'

'They won't.'

'Good. I won't ask what you plan to do.'

'That might be best, your Worship,' Nottingham said with a dark smile.

'Just get the bugger out of here as quick as you can.' He sighed and rubbed his cheeks. 'I love this city, I don't want people coming in and trying to ruin it.'

'I won't let them.'

'I know you have no love for the men in power, Richard. Sometimes I can't blame you. But this is where I grew up, too. We all want Leeds to grow rich.'

'With the riches for some.'

'The wealthier the city becomes, the more it helps everyone,' the mayor countered.

The Constable cocked his head. 'Perhaps.'

'I'm not really made for all the connivances of politics,' Douglas admitted. 'At least in trade there's an honesty to all the venality. You get in this and half the time they're so sly that you don't even think they're carrying daggers until they're buried deep in your back.'

'Your year as mayor will finish soon. September's only five months away.'

'It can't be soon enough for me. Believe me, I'll walk out of this office and never look back, and good luck to William Fenton when he takes over.'

'He'll be the next mayor?' Nottingham asked.

'He will, and may he have great joy from it.'

The Constable knew Fenton. As young boys, before Nottingham's father had thrown his wife and son from the house, the pair of them had gone to school and played together. They'd been firm friends then. Afterwards the tale had become twisted.

Fenton had eased smoothly into his life, taking money and position in Leeds as his due, serving his apprenticeship as a merchant before going to work for his father, then taking over his business.

Nottingham's path had been rockier. When they'd met again, after he'd become deputy Constable, Fenton had treated him with disdain, reminding him of his fall from grace and fortune at every chance. Working with him for a year was going to be difficult.

'I'm sure he'll relish it,' he said.

'Aye, he's that kind of man,' Douglas admitted with a long sigh. 'Do what you must about this thief taker, as long as it's above the law. Let's see the back of him as soon as possible.'

Nine

Rain was falling as John Sedgwick walked down to the river, the clouds hanging so low he believed he could reach up and touch the sky. A little dampness was nothing, he'd dry out later, once evening arrived and he was home where the fire was warm in the hearth.

Before the bridge he turned, taking the new path that led past the buildings downstream. Cates and Sons had joined many of the other merchants in building a warehouse on the bank, the better to load their goods on to the barges. He felt certain he'd find at least one of the family there.

The brick was new, its red glow still warm, the paintwork glossy and the glass of the windows clean and clear. Inside, three clerks bent over their desks, heads rising together as he entered.

'Can I help you, sir?' one asked.

'I'm looking for Mr Cates,' the deputy said.

'Yes, sir,' the clerk said pleasantly. 'Which one were you looking for?'

'Which one's here?'

'Mr Robert, sir.'

'Good,' Sedgwick said with a grin. 'Just who I want.'

The clerk slid from his stool and scuttled off into an office, his back slightly bent from too many years at his work. Within a minute he'd returned with Robert Cates, a tall, solemn young man with a long, quizzical face. His hair was receding, leaving him with a large, ugly dome of a forehead. His legs were scrawny; however good the tailor's skill, no breeches would ever flatter him, and stockings hung baggy on his calves.

'Can I help you?' he asked, his tone distracted and condescending.

'I'm John Sedgwick, the deputy Constable.'

'Yes?' He seemed astonished by the statement.

'Can we talk in private, Mr Cates?' He inclined his head towards the office.

'I suppose so,' the merchant agreed grudgingly.

The room was spare, the desk covered in papers, bills of lading, letters of credit and correspondence. Cates sat, leaving the deputy to take an old, worn stool. Pearl light fell through a tall, open window but the man still had a candle lit. A pair of spectacles sat next to a quill pen.

'Now,' he said briskly, 'what do you want?'

'You had a servant named Lucy in your house.'

'We did,' he acknowledged with a short nod, his mouth frowning with distaste. 'My father dismissed her.'

'She was pregnant,' Sedgwick said.

'So I was told.'

'We found her body. Someone had killed her.' He'd talked with the Constable earlier that morning and they'd decided to use the knowledge and see what it brought. He could see the shock jump into Cates's eyes and the colour leave his face.

'I'm sorry,' he said. 'The girl might have been a slut but no one deserves that. Do you have whoever did it?'

'Not yet. We think whoever was the father of her child might be responsible.'

'That makes sense,' Cates said quietly. 'It's terrible that Lucy's dead, but I don't see why you need to talk to me. Whatever happened to her was after she left us.'

'It was,' the deputy agreed mildly. 'But I've been thinking about time.'

'Time?' Cates asked.

'Consider it,' Sedgwick told him. 'She became pregnant while she was in service with you.' He waited, letting the merchant understand all the implications.

'What are you saying? You think it could be one of us?' he blustered. 'Is that an accusation?'

'It's just a thought, sir. From what I hear, you, your brother and your father all take advantage of the servants.'

'And who told you that?' Cates asked, anger simmering in his voice and the veins bulging in his thin neck. 'It's a lie.'

'Is it?' Sedgwick said, watching him carefully. 'The servant girls are there and available. They're too scared to refuse any of you. Your brother's already said he uses them.'

'Has he?' Cates said with a dry laugh. 'I suppose he would, given half the chance. But I won't have you slander my father that way.'

'And what about you? How many of the servants have you tupped?'

Cates eyed him with venom. 'I'd be very careful what you say. You're nobody, we're a family with influence in this city. You'd do well to remember that.'

'I know that,' the deputy told him with a bland look. 'So it would seem bad if word spread that all the men in this family of influence were using the serving girls, wouldn't it? Doesn't matter how common it is, it wouldn't seem good as general knowledge. Especially when one of them claims such Christian ways.' He paused to allow the truth of his words to sink home. 'Now, shall we start again, Mr Cates? How many of the servants have you tupped?'

Cates stayed silent and Sedgwick knew he'd have his admission soon.

'A few,' he admitted finally, his voice low, his eyes avoiding the deputy's stare.

'Was Lucy among them?'

'No,' Robert Cates answered quickly.

'You're sure?'

'Of course I'm sure,' the man hissed. His hand gripped the arm of the chair, knuckles white.

'And why not Lucy, then?' Sedgwick wondered. 'Wasn't she willing?'

'I didn't want her.' Cates glared. 'With that harelip, no one would have wanted her. It was like a devil's mark on her. She couldn't speak properly because of it.'

'You mean you weren't tempted to fuck the devil out of her, Mr Cates?' the deputy asked.

'No, and you mind what you say.' He raised his head high. 'I'd never be tempted by the likes of her.'

'Seems like someone was.'

'Well, it wasn't me,' he said, his voice hard. He leaned forward, planting his elbows on the desk. 'Whoever had her must have been a fool or blind drunk.'

'And what makes you say that?' the deputy asked with interest.

'Because she was as ugly as God's own sin and she was stupid,' Cates blurted. 'You'd tell her to do something and she'd just stand there with that twisted smile.'

'And did you often tell her to do things?'

'Just to do with her work.' He could see that Cates was sweating, the sheen thick on his forehead in spite of the window that drew in the cool breeze and noise from the Aire.

'Someone killed her, Mr Cates,' Sedgwick told her. 'And her baby along with her. Why don't you think about that?'

'It wasn't me,' Cates said again. 'I never touched the girl. I wouldn't.'

'But you'd touch others. And more.'

'When the temptation's too much.' He lowered his head at the admission.

'And was it with Lucy?'

Cates brought his hand down hard, the slap on the desk filling the room.

'I told you, I never had her. I didn't want her. It made me sick just to look at her. The girl was an abomination.'

The man was close to tears, the deputy thought. He believed him, though; Robert Cates was racked with enough guilt to fill the Parish Church by himself. He hadn't been the one to seed Lucy, although God only knew how many others he had. He stood slowly.

'I'll give you a word of advice, Mr Cates. The next time the devil's on your shoulder, urging you to take one of the serving girls, brush him away. Remember that they might not want it.'

He left Cates staring into space and closed the door quietly.

The walk up Briggate to Town End didn't take long. Ben Cates had joined so many of the other merchants up there, a little removed from the stench of the city. There were fields close by, the smell of wild flowers mingling sweetly with the scent of money. Somewhere close by, doves were cooing in their cote.

Will Cates wasn't at home, the servant told him coldly. He was meeting someone at the Talbot. That place again, Sedgwick thought as he retraced his steps. It seemed as if half the bad things in Leeds happened there. If he had his druthers, he'd tear it apart, brick by brick. But no one was going to grant him that wish.

The place was a warren, a cockpit in the back, rooms for whores and private gambling up the stairs. He wasn't surprised that he couldn't spot Cates when he entered. He found a place on a bench close to the door, ordered a quart of ale and waited.

Much of the talk had stopped when he came in, and over the next half hour he was gratified to see many of the customers leave. He allowed himself a small smile at ruining trade for a while. One of the few remaining, half hidden in a shadowed corner, was another of the Constable's men, watching for the thief taker. The deputy didn't acknowledge him, but stayed alert for a glimpse of Cates.

When the man finally emerged he was adjusting his coat then stooping to wipe some dust off the silver buckle of a shoe. A wig stood slightly askew on his head and he took the time to straighten it. As he walked towards the door Sedgwick stood and said,

'Mr Cates? I'd like a word with you, if you'd be so good.'

Taken by surprise, Cates raised his eyebrows, scrutinizing at the deputy's old clothes and wild hair.

'And who are you? Looking for charity?'

'I'm the deputy constable of the city, sir,' Sedgwick replied, emphasizing the title. 'We can talk here, or we can go to the jail. Or to your house, if you prefer.' He allowed the threat of the words to hang in the air.

'I've already talked to Rob Lister,' Will Cates said impatiently. 'Didn't he tell you that?'

Sedgwick smiled. 'Of course, but there are some more questions I need to ask. Where do you want to talk?'

Cates let out a frustrated sigh and sat, snapping his fingers for the potboy to bring ale. Finally, when they were alone, he said,

'I hope this is important. There are places I need to be.'

'Just a stop for a doxie on the way?' the deputy wondered with a smile.

'None of your business,' Cates told him.

'You knew Lucy Wendell, the serving girl at your house?'

'Bloody Lucy again?' Cates raised his voice. 'Haven't you found the girl yet?'

'Oh yes, sir, we've found her,' Sedgwick said.

'Then what's the problem?'

'She was dead. Someone had killed her and her baby.'

Just like his brother, the colour vanished from Cates's face and his hands trembled as he took a drink.

'And what do you think?' he asked. 'That I had something to do with it? Is that it?'

'Did you?'

'Of course not. Don't be so stupid. I told Rob I wouldn't have fucked her with another man's pizzle.'

'Someone did.'

'Don't look to me.'

'But you've had other serving girls.'

Cates started to laugh, the confidence of position and money returning.

'For the love of God, man, what's the point in employing a pretty girl if you can't enjoy her?'

'Doesn't matter if they want to or not?'

Cates stared. 'Of course they want to. If they wish to keep their jobs, that is.'

'And Lucy?'

Cates shook his head. 'Not me,' he said firmly. 'Try asking my brother, she might have been to his tastes.'

'I have,' Sedgwick said. 'He denies it.'

The man halted with the mug halfway to his mouth and inclined his head.

'You have your answers, then.'

'I have some answers,' the deputy corrected him. 'I still have to see if they're honest ones or not.'

Cates seemed amused. 'You don't believe me?' he asked.

'There's a great deal in this world I don't believe until it's been proved.'

The man shrugged and took a sip of his ale. 'I can't prove I never tupped the lass. I've been honest enough, I've told you I had others, and that I didn't want her.'

'The others aren't dead,' Sedgwick observed. 'That's a good reason for a man to deny something.'

'Maybe you should ask my father,' Cates said with a chuckle. 'I think he's had almost every serving girl. He likes anything female. Except my mother, of course,' he added with a smile. 'He hasn't wanted her in years.'

'I'll be talking to him,' the deputy promised.

'You do that.' Cates stood. 'See how happy he is with your questions. I can guarantee that he won't be pleased your stupid little bitch is causing us trouble in death.' He nodded his farewell.

Sedgwick sat and slowly finished the drink. He believed the brothers when they said they'd never touched Lucy. Their disgust seemed too genuine. He'd been lied to by better men than them, and he felt they'd given him the truth. If they thought twice before lifting the skirts of another serving girl, then some little good would have come from the questions. But he doubted that; it would pass from their minds soon enough. And he still had to deal with Ben Cates; that would be a different matter. He wasn't young and callow. He was a man who'd made his mark in the city, with wealth and power, and important friends. Still, it was the job he'd wanted and he had to do it.

He walked back up Briggate in the drizzle, the collar of his coat turned up, the smell of wet wool in his nostrils. The day seemed muted, the buildings in shades of grey, the ginnels leading through to the courts filled with deep, dark puddles. At least the rain had cleared some of the shit from the street, he thought, as the turds moved slowly down the runnel on the road, grabbed at by stray dogs crowded around the Shambles. Their ribs showed through their fur, and they snapped and barked at each other as they hunted the scraps from the butchers.

This time he marched to the front door of the house in Town End. He'd barely finished knocking when it swung open and he was looking at Grace the maid.

'Hello, Grace,' he said. 'I'm looking for Mr Cates. Is he in?'

'Yes, sir.' She looked flustered, glancing around her, eyes fearful. 'I'd like to see him.'

Grace took a breath and closed her eyes for a moment to gather herself before showing him through to a parlour.

'I'll see if he's available, sir,' she said. In a whisper, she added, 'Please don't say anything about . . .'

'I promised you,' the deputy told her. 'Not a word.'

'Thank you.' Relief flooded her face. 'I'll tell Mr Cates you're here.'

He waited a quarter hour by the clock until the door opened again and Cates entered, a frown on his face.

'The girl said you wanted me.'

'That's right,' Sedgwick said.

'She said you're the deputy constable?'

'I am,' Sedgwick acknowledged.

'And what's the reason you're here?'

'Lucy Wendell.' He spoke the name loud and clear, looking for a reaction.

Cates snorted. 'The Constable here a few days back, you today. Who's it going to be next, that lad you have?'

'She's dead,' the deputy told him. 'Someone killed her.'

'So you thought you'd come back and hound me?'

'We're looking for anything that can help us find her murderer,' he said evenly. 'Or perhaps you think she's better off dead, Mr Cates?'

'You watch your tongue with me, boy,' Cates warned. 'I already told your master everything. There's nothing to do with her death here. He should know better than to send his dog round.'

'So you and your sons don't take your pleasure with the serving girls?'

Cates rounded on him, anger in his eyes. 'What we do or don't do in this house isn't your business. Or maybe you'd prefer me to talk to the mayor and the aldermen?'

Sedgwick returned the stare, his head high, taller than the merchant.

'You can talk to whoever you want, Mr Cates. But I'll tell you this – if what happened here led to her death, then it's our business. Or perhaps you don't feel the law should apply to you? I'm sure the aldermen and the mayor would like to know if that's the case. Sir.'

'Is that a threat?'

'No.' The deputy drew the word out slowly. 'I never threaten, Mr Cates. And I'm sure there'd never be a need here, would there? Now, we can begin again if you'd like, or I can take you to the jail and ask the questions there.' He knew he was on dangerous ground, but he was damned if he'd be cowed by someone who stood on his money box to speak.

Finally Cates shook his head in frustration. 'I'll tell you what you need to know if it'll get rid of you. I never had that girl. Never wanted her. I didn't even want her in the bloody house, but my wife thought it would be a charity. How does she repay us? Gets herself with a baby.' He gave a shrug. 'You want to know the truth? I was glad to be able to dismiss her. I hated seeing her ugliness around my house every day. Between that and her stupidity, the world won't miss her.'

'Some people will,' Sedgwick said quietly. 'Her mother, for one, and her brother. Perhaps you'd like to think of them.'

The man waved the idea away with a shrug.

'She wasn't pregnant when she began work here,' the deputy said.

'What the servants do on their own time is their business,' Cates said brusquely. 'I told the Constable that. As long as they don't bring this family into disrepute, I don't care what they do. Do you understand that?'

'Yes.'

'The girl was a simpleton. She was stupid. Anyone could have had her.' His voice tightened. 'I'll say this for the very last time. I didn't have her, and I doubt either of my sons did. Now, do you understand that?' The final words came out as a furious hiss.

'Thank you.' Sedgwick put his hand on the doorknob, then turned back. 'You've had other serving girls.'

'What of it?' Cates said with a snort.

'Unless they agree, that's called rape. Sir.' He left the room, closing the door quietly, and made his way out into the fresh air. Away from the house, back across the Head Row, he made for the Rose and Crown. What he needed more than anything was a long drink of ale to wash the taste of the last few hours from his mouth.

Would Cates say anything to his cronies, he wondered? Probably not; even quiet words would make him seem ridiculous in front of his friends. He took a deep sip from the mug, feeling the liquid flood through him with a sense of relief. In the end it was just as well that Cates had backed down. Parading him past the

Moot Hall to the jail would have been one step too far. As it was he'd made another enemy for the Constable and himself.

But he felt certain that none of the Cates men had been responsible for the baby. He disliked all of them, each in his own way, yet their revulsion when he mentioned Lucy seemed too real to be a lie.

It had felt like a long day, one of endless frustrations. Richard Nottingham was glad to feel the softness of evening gather around him as he walked home over Timble Bridge, listening to the birdsong in the trees and the sound of cattle being driven home from the fields for milking.

The house was warm from cooking, and he hung his coat on the nail inside the door. In the kitchen he could hear Mary and Emily talking quietly.

'It's just me,' he shouted and settled in his chair with a loud, weary sigh. Soon enough, he knew, someone would come bustling through on an errand and supper would be ready, the chatter of the family together before sleep.

Until then, though, he had time to think. They were no closer to finding Lucy Wendell's killer than they had been when he'd discovered the body. With some luck Rob might learn something when he talked to the woman by the river, but that would only take them one step closer. He wanted the murderer. Someone who could be so callous and cold with life needed to hang, and for his crimes to be known. Alice Wendell deserved justice for her daughter.

Then there was the business with Walton. The alliance with Joe Buck should pay dividends, although it would require a little time. But he was determined to do things properly, legally, so word would spread and no one else would come to try the same tricks. Enforcing the law was difficult enough without having to deal with people like the thief taker.

He stretched out his legs and closed his eyes, but before he could sleep footsteps ran through the room and clattered up the stairs, followed by the slam of a door. Emily, he thought, and went into the kitchen.

'Is she in a mood?' he asked. Mary was standing by the table, head bowed, her palms pressing down on the wood. When she lifted her eyes, he could see the start of tears there, and he took her in his arms. 'What is it?'

'I don't know,' she answered in a small voice. 'She won't tell me.' He stroked her back gently, her fingers clutching tight at his shirt.

'What do you think?' he asked. 'School? Love?'

Mary pulled back and looked at him, wiping her eyes with the back of her hands.

'All I know is that she was upset when she came home. She was crying. It's nothing to do with school, I'm sure of that. She'd talk about that.'

'So it must be love,' he said calmly. 'An argument, maybe? Did Rob meet her from school?'

'He always does, you know that,' she told him with a small smile. 'But he didn't come in,' she added with a frown. 'That's not like him.'

'I could talk to her,' he offered.

She shook her head. 'Don't, Richard. It'll probably end up being something and nothing. You know what she's like, she flares up. Better to let her be for now.'

'I could have a word with Rob.'

'Do you think he'd talk to you about it?' Mary wondered. She'd regained her composure. 'He might not want to.'

'I'll leave that up to him,' the Constable promised. But he needed to know what was behind all this. Emily had been so happy since she'd begun teaching at the Dame school and taken up with Rob. He'd been able to see a settled life mapped out for her, with marriage and children, and he knew Mary had her dreams of the same thing. For a moment he considered walking back into Leeds to see Lister, but thought better of it. The morning would be soon enough, a quiet word before the lad went off to sleep after his night shift.

'Maybe they'll make up quickly,' Mary said hopefully, reaching out and stroking the back of his hand.

'It'll be his loss if he lets her go,' he told her. 'She'll have no shortage of suitors. I've seen men looking at her when we're out walking.'

'She loves Rob,' Mary countered. 'And he loves her, it's obvious when they're together.'

'I know,' he agreed sadly. He was the girl's father, he wanted her courting to run smooth. But he'd seen enough of life to know that rarely happened. There would be many ditches and hills on the way, too many places to fall. All he could hope was that the pair of them would find their way past this, that it would be nothing important. 'Let's go for a walk,' he suggested. 'You might feel better if you're away from here for a while.'

Mary smiled, the brightness in her eyes as well as her mouth. 'Maybe she'll want to talk when we're back,' she said.

'Don't worry too much if she doesn't,' he warned, and held her close. 'Things will work out one way or another.'

'I know. But since Rose, I worry about her so much. She's all we've got.'

'She'll be fine,' he assured her. 'That girl's got enough spirit for five people.'

They walked out past Burmantofts, out by the road to York where riders and carts were still travelling in the fading light. They let the peace of the countryside envelop them, moving without words, just the touch of hands between them, allowing contentment to slowly seep in. The rain had passed and the air was still; no gust of wind, sounds faint in the distance, a hawk hanging magnificently above the horizon and swooping down.

Full dark had arrived by the time they returned, the moonlight peeking through scudding clouds. There was no light in Emily's window; the girl must already be sleeping. They stayed quiet in the house, eating hot pottage in the kitchen before climbing silently up the stairs to bed.

'I'll talk to Rob in the morning,' he promised.

Ten

Lister made his first circuit of the city as darkness came, walking with two of the men. His thoughts roiled and tumbled, troubled by everything his father had said and the way Emily had acted when he'd told her. He was damned if he'd lose her just to please some notion of society that his father possessed; he'd tried to explain that but she'd been too upset and angry to listen. He kept his hand firm on the cudgel, eager to use it at the least provocation. But everything was quiet, all the inns and alehouses subdued as men eked out their money until payday, stretching out their ale or gin over an hour or more, their faces as sullen as their spirits.

When they were done he wandered away, heading down to the river. The fires were burning on the bank and as he approached he could make out the shapes and empty faces of the folk gathered around them, cooking some food or simply taking in the heat. Eyes glanced up at him with suspicion and wariness before turning swiftly away again, bodies moving back slightly.

He stood silent until Gordonson came over, his withered arm gathered at his side, a smile on his face.

'Mr Lister,' he said, as if he had no cares in the world, 'I was hoping you'd come back. Susan's been waiting for you. Come on, come on, I'll show you to her.'

The girl was sitting outside the light from the blaze, her back resting against a tree, her hair pulled neatly under a cap and her skirt gathered primly around her ankles. He could hardly make out her face but she seemed young, her body barely developed.

'Susan,' Gordon said gently, 'this is Mr Lister. He wants to talk to you about Lucy. You can trust him.'

Rob sat down by her, giving a smile to try to put her at her ease. He took a deep breath, trying to concentrate.

'You knew Lucy?'

'Yes,' she replied, and he waited in vain for more.

'You know she's dead?'

Susan turned to face him. 'Dead?' she asked, as if it was a new word she'd never heard before.

'Someone killed her,' he told her softly. 'We're trying to find who did it. You might be able to help me. Will you do that?'

'Yes,' she nodded. In a flicker of light from the fire he could make out the start of silent tears trickling down her cheeks. 'Dead,' she said again.

'How long was she here?' He watched as her fingers nervously plucked at the grass. Her answer didn't come quickly.

'Nigh on seven days, I think.'

'Did you become friends?'

'Aye,' Susan said after a moment. 'I liked her. People thought she was strange, because of . . .' She raised a hand to her lip and he nodded. 'But she were nice. We used to hold each other to stay warm when we slept.'

He took a piece of mutton pie he'd saved from his dinner and passed it to her. Her eyes widened for a moment, then she reached out and snatched it.

'Did she say why she came here?'

'She'd told me she tried whoring but there were no one who wanted her. When she didn't bring in any money, the man who'd been looking after her hit her and made her go out again the next day, even though she didn't want to. So she didn't go back. She just walked around Leeds until it got dark. Then she saw the fires and came down here.'

'What did she do during the day when she was here?'

'We'd walk and try to find things people had thrown away. Old food, all sorts. Lucy even found an old dress once, but it wa'nt much and it was too big for her.'

'Did she talk much?'

'Nay, mister, not a lot,' Susan said, wiping awkwardly at her eyes. 'It were her mouth, you see. It made the words funny so she didn't really like to say a lot.'

'When she did, what did she talk about?'

'I don't know,' she answered with a small shrug of her shoulders.

'Her family? A boy she liked?'

'She said she used to be a maid in one of them big houses.'

'She was,' he told her.

'But they said she had to go because she were going to have a baby.'

'They did. But did she tell you why she didn't go home? Her mother loved her, she'd have taken her in.'

Susan shook her head. 'All she said was that she couldn't go back there because he'd find her there.'

'Did she say who'd find her?'

'No, mister. She never did.'

'Why did she leave here?' Lister wondered. 'Did she tell you she was going, or where?'

'We went out like we always did when she was here,' the girl began, 'and she said she had summat she needed to do. Wandered off merry as you please and never came back. If I'd known . . .' Even in the dull light her could see the tears forming again and she lowered her head.

'You don't know where she might have gone?'

'No.' She shook her head adamantly. 'She never said owt. I kept looking for her after but she never came back. People leave all the time here.'

He looked around. It was company, it was safety, but it was a hard, hard life out in the open.

'How did you end up here?' he asked and he looked at him, surprise in her eyes at his interest.

'Me parents died, so me brother was looking after me. We'd been sleeping out past Town End until some men come and . . .' She let her words tail away for a moment. 'Then we come down here when he heard about it. A few days later he said he was going to 'list for a sailor. Said at least he'd eat and he might make his fortune. Promised he'd come back then and look after me. He will, won't he, mister?'

'I'm sure he will,' he assured her, although he knew the chances were slim. In this life you had to look out for yourself first. He stood, took some coins from the pocket of his breeches and handed them to her.

'Thank you, mister.'

'Thank you, Susan. How old are you?'

'Fourteen,' she said.

The night had ended but day hadn't yet arrived; the sky was the flat colour of old pewter as he walked up Briggate. A thin layer of mist lay over the river like magic. Behind the high walls of the grand houses he could hear the first servants at work, drawing water and lighting fires.

At the jail, Lister was sitting at the desk, quill scratching on paper to write up his brief nightly report as the Constable arrived.

He looked tired, Nottingham thought, not just in his face and eyes but in his soul.

'Did you see the girl last night?' he asked.

'Yes, boss.'

'Anything worthwhile?' Nottingham sat and Lister pushed a hand through his thick hair.

'Not really. Lucy told her she couldn't go home because he'd find her there, but still no mention of who *he* is. She was with the riverbank people for a week, then she just left. She was out with the girl I talked to, said she had something to do and never came back. Didn't talk much, evidently.' He paused. 'One more thing, boss.'

'What's that?'

'That pimp Lucy had claimed she'd been beaten by someone who didn't pay, didn't he?'

'Yes. His sisters said the same. Why?'

'The girl said Lucy told her the pimp had beaten her when she didn't make any money. She'd have no reason to lie.'

'True,' Nottingham agreed.

'And it would explain why she ran off.'

Nottingham sat and thought.

'I think I'll go and see Joshua Davidson again today.' He gave a dark smile. 'Let's see if he remembers the truth this time.'

'But it doesn't help us find out what happened to Lucy.'

'No.' The Constable gave a deep sigh. 'We'll get there, don't worry.'

Sedgwick arrived, his face creased in a smile.

'You look happy,' Nottingham said.

'Isabell only woke twice, James has been behaving and I slept,' he announced proudly.

'Anything from any of the Cates men?'

'They didn't have her, I'll wager on that. None of them liked her, I doubt they'd have touched her with someone else's pizzle. You might be getting a complaint about me from the father, though,' he warned. 'He didn't seem too happy at my questions.'

'I'll take care of it if it happens,' the Constable told him. 'We still need to know who she was scared of seeing if she went home. Any ideas?'

'Her brother?' Lister suggested.

'I don't see why she'd be scared of him,' Nottingham answered. 'He's her family and her mother said he looked after her. You said he seemed insistent on finding her himself, John.'

'He was,' the deputy agreed slowly. 'He's an odd one, though. Might be worth talking to his girl when he's not around.'

'You'd better do that, then. I'm going to see our friend Davidson and then keep on the thief taker business. Anything from the men who've been watching him?'

'Nothing unusual,' Lister said.

'Keep someone on him,' he ordered. 'And make sure he doesn't know he's being followed.'

They started to leave but the Constable said, 'Rob, can you stay for a minute?'

Nottingham watched the others exchange glances then Lister sat down again as Sedgwick walked out.

'Emily was upset last night, and she won't say why,' he said plainly, and stared at the younger man. 'I was wondering what you knew about it.'

'Boss . . .' Rob began, then the words wouldn't come to his mouth. He pushed his head down to the desk and raised it again. 'It's my father.'

'What about him?'

Nottingham could see the reluctance in the youngster's face. He waited, giving him time to frame his thoughts.

'He doesn't want me to marry Emily.'

'Oh?' he asked, trying to keep the surprise from his voice. 'I didn't know you two had even talked about it. Emily hasn't said anything.'

'We haven't. But we love each other.'

'I think all of Leeds knows that by now, lad,' Nottingham said kindly and watched Lister blush. 'So why doesn't he want you to marry her? Is she too young?'

Rob shook his head. 'It's not that.' He paused, then blurted it out quickly. 'He said . . . he said your family wasn't good enough. I'm sorry, boss.'

'I see,' the Constable said slowly.

'I told Emily and I tried to explain that what he wants won't stop me. But I don't know how much of it she really heard.'

'Now she's angry at you?'

Lister nodded.

'She'll come around. Meet her after school,' he advised. 'Talk to her again. You know what she can be like. You need to make sure she understands.'

'Yes, boss.' He hesitated. 'And I'm sorry about my father.'

'I'm not going to blame you for what your father believes,' Nottingham said with a small smile, making sure that none of what he was feeling crept into his tone. 'It's understandable, I suppose. After all, I'm the son of a whore, that's true enough, and I'm proud of her. There are plenty of people in this city who've never forgotten that. Your father's just one of them.'

'But it's not right,' Lister insisted.

'You and I both know that, but you can't change the way people think. I'm used to it by now.'

'What do I do?' Rob asked helplessly. 'I think he's wrong.'

Nottingham sighed and pushed the fringe off his forehead.

'I don't know,' he answered. 'He's your father and I know you don't want to cross him. But sometimes you have to do what you think in your heart is the right thing. Don't go marrying Emily just to spite him, though. If the pair of you really want to, that's one thing, and my wife and I will give our blessing—' Lister's eyes lit up briefly. 'But remember, you stand to lose a great deal with him if you do that.'

'I know. That's what I was trying to tell Emily yesterday.'

'Then my advice is don't give up until you make her see it. She can be stubborn, though.' He winked. 'No idea where she gets that from. Now, you go home and sleep.'

'Yes, boss.' He stood, then stopped. 'And thank you for not being angry about it.'

The Constable shook his head gently and Rob left. Alone, Nottingham could think, the fury simmering inside him. He'd always seen James Lister as a fair man and taken pleasure in his company. He'd never given a sign of what he truly believed. He felt betrayed, cut by the words. Still at least Lister had had the grace to hide his knife when they'd met. It had been years since he'd heard anyone say his family wasn't good enough; he'd believed those days were done. He'd loved his mother and hated the man who'd fathered him. His father had thrown them out and taken everything, left them to rot, to starve, to die without thought, care or regret. His mother had done what she could so they'd live. He still felt proud to have come from her.

If the words had been about him, they'd have hurt. But they were being visited on his daughter and that was what caught on his heart and made him bitter and angry.

He could go and see Lister's father, of course, but what good would that do? Nothing he could say would change the man's views; hard experience had taught him that. All he could see in the future was heartbreak for Rob or for Emily, and he'd do everything he could to protect his daughter.

But the one thing he couldn't save her from was love, the thing that was supposed to bring her the greatest joy. He gave a long sigh. None of this would be resolved today. Rob was going to have to make some choices and whatever his decision it would be painful.

Now he was in the right mind to see Joshua Davidson again.

Eleven

He brought his fist down hard on the door, feeling it shake in its frame. No one stirred in the house, the shutters closed, no puddle of night soil in front of the step. He banged again, hitting the wood over and over until he heard a muffled shout from inside.

When the lock turned he was ready, pushing hard and forcing his way inside. He closed the door behind him and saw Davidson sprawled on his back, the shirt hanging over his old, torn breeches, surprise and fear in his eyes.

'I don't like people lying to me,' the Constable said. The pimp tried to scuttle away, dragging his bad leg, but Nottingham stood over him. 'And you lied to me twice.'

'What did I do?' Davidson asked helplessly. 'I told you the truth.'

'You said you wouldn't cause any trouble.'

'We haven't,' the man insisted, sounding desperate. 'What have we done?'

'And you said you didn't beat Lucy.'

'I didn't!' Davidson yelled. 'I told you what happened. You asked my sisters.'

'And the three of you put together a fine pack of lies for me.'
He stared down at the man.

'We didn't,' Davidson said, but the outrage had worn thin in
his voice.

'Lucy told someone the real reason she'd left you.'

'And you believe that?'

'I do,' the Constable told him. 'She had no reason to lie.'

'I told you the truth,' Davidson said again.

'And I don't believe you,' Nottingham answered coldly. 'I'm
going to give you a choice. You and your sisters can leave Leeds
today, or I can come back tomorrow and put you all in jail. It's
up to you. If I see any of you in the city again I'll arrest you. Is
that clear?'

'Where will we go?'

'That's up to you, Mr Davidson. I really don't care as long as
you leave my city.'

He turned and left, slamming the door loudly behind him.

The deputy made his way back to Queen Charlotte Court. A
fragment of sunlight caught the corner of one building to show
off the stained, crumbling limewash. The stench of rotting rubbish
filled his nostrils, mounds of it piled against the cramped, tumbling
houses, the paw of a dead dog showing, covered by flies that
buzzed away as he approached.

He knocked on the door of Wendell's room, hoping the girl
would be at home. The lock turned, and she opened just enough
to glance out.

'Hello, love,' Sedgwick said with an easy grin, 'I was here the
other day, do you remember? I'm the deputy constable. Do you
have a few minutes to talk?'

'He's not here,' she said, her voice hoarse, barely above a
whisper.

'I know. It was you I wanted. Can I come in? It's better than
everyone knowing why I'm here.'

Reluctantly she let him in, standing back against the wall as if
she wished she could disappear into the plaster. He looked at her,
seeing she was little more than frail bones and thin skin. There
were fresh bruises on her forearms and more blossoming on her
face and throat. The old dress was too large for her small chest

and the shawl she hugged around her shoulders was faded and threadbare. Greasy hair hung around her face.

'What's your name?' he asked kindly. Her eyes were haunted, and he could feel the fear coming off her. 'Don't worry, I'm not going to hurt you.'

'Anne.'

'Anne, did you know Lucy?'

She nodded slightly, keeping her head down, eyes looking at the floor.

'Did you like her?'

She looked up at him as if she didn't understand the question. 'What?'

'Did you like her?'

She shrugged. 'He loved her, she were his sister.'

'Your man must miss her.'

'Aye.' She turned away again, as if she couldn't keep her mind on one thing for more than a moment.

'And she was never here after she left her job?'

Anne shook her head briefly.

'You didn't see her after that?'

'No.'

'How long have you been with Peter?'

She thought for a little while. 'A year, close enough.'

'Do you love him?'

'He's better than some,' she admitted flatly. 'We eat.'

He knew he wasn't going to get much from her, and she'd never dare say anything against her man; she was too scared of him. She'd probably had batterings so often in her life that it seemed the normal way to her. He smiled.

'Thank you, Anne, you've been very helpful.'

'Are you going to tell him you were here?' she asked, and he could hear the terror under the words.

'Not a word,' he promised, and her face relaxed a little.

The Constable sat adding figures, making sure the men would be paid, when there was a timid knock on the door and a boy of about eight entered, looking around wide-eyed at being in such a terrifying place.

'Sir?' he asked in a high voice. 'Are you the Constable?'

'I am,' Nottingham told him, smiling with his eyes.

'A man told me to give you this. He said you'd give me some money if I did.' He held out a small fist containing a folded piece of paper.

'Did he now?' he asked. 'And did he say how much?'

'He said you should give me a penny.'

The Constable laughed and dug into his breeches pocket for a coin.

'Who was this man?'

'I don't know, sir,' the boy answered, his eyes still moving around the room, full of curiosity. 'But his skin was black. Was it paint?'

'No. He was born like that. Some people are.'

The boy nodded sagely. Nottingham passed over the coin and took the note.

'Thank you,' the boy said. 'The man told me I should thank you.' He left quietly, and Nottingham opened the paper. It was from Joe Buck, in his thin scrawl: *Another house last night. Mr Collins.*

He knew Collins, a merchant who never seemed to find great success, still living in the old house on Briggate that his father had left him. The Constable rubbed his chin. It could be worth a visit to shake the man a little and see what happened. If it helped to catch the thief taker it would be worthwhile.

The house was down towards the river, almost opposite the office of the *Mercury*. Glancing across the street he saw Rob's father bent over his desk, stopping only to put more ink on his quill. A sour taste filled his mouth and he swallowed it away, turning his attention to the merchant.

The house needed a new coat of limewash. The mullioned windows were warped in their frames, the glass thick, a few small panes missing and never replaced, rags stuffed in their stead by a man who couldn't afford the repairs. It wasn't the home of someone rich, but rather someone who had little to lose.

He knocked and was shown in by a serving girl, the skin on her hands red and raw. She showed him into a parlour where the fire was laid but not lit, the room chilly and unwelcoming. Dust on the mantle showed a couple of objects missing since it had last been cleaned.

Collins arrived quickly. He was a small, thin man, barely reaching to Nottingham's shoulder, with startled eyes and a questioning mouth. His clothes were middling, the breeches of fair cut and style, the jacket older but clean, the material made to last.

'Constable!' he said. 'Milly said it was you, but I can't think why you'd come here. What can I do for you?' His voice sounded strained, the skin tight on his face.

'I heard that someone had stolen some items from you.'

'Really?' The surprise was so forced it wouldn't have fooled an infant. Nottingham raised his eyebrows.

'I hear quite a few things, Mr Collins. Your father was on the Corporation, if I remember.'

'He was.' The merchant eagerly nodded his agreement, happy to move on.

'It was the Corporation that created the post of Constable,' Nottingham continued. 'They needed someone to take care of the crime in Leeds. That's what I do. But if I don't know a crime's happened, I can't help, can I?'

'No.' Collins started to blush.

'I believe some people have been looking to this thief taker, the one who's new here, to help them. Everything returned for a small fee, I believe, and everything kept quiet. But I'd like to think that good people in Leeds would rather have the thief caught and tried.'

'Of course, of course.' Collins agreed quickly, staring intently at the ground.

'I'll leave you to think on it,' Nottingham told him mildly. 'You might discover some items missing that you want to report to me.' He moved to the door. 'I'll bid you good day.'

Collins would be at the jail later in the day, red-faced and tongue-tied, the Constable was certain of it. He left the house, glanced across the street to the *Mercury* again and walked away, bunching his fists.

It was a short stroll to the Talbot. He sent word up to Walton and sat in the corner with a beaker of musty ale that had sat too long in the cask. The thief taker came down the stairs yawning, his clothes dishevelled, raking a hand through his hair.

'You wanted to see me, Constable? I hope this is important. I was still asleep.'

'There have been four burglaries in Leeds within a week, Mr Walton.'

The man raised his eyebrows. 'In London that's no number at all.'

'I've told you before, this isn't London. And four is too many for this city. But there's an odd thing.'

'Oh?' Walton asked without interest.

'Two of them haven't even been reported and the third withdrew his complaint.' He glanced up at the thief taker. 'You won't mind if I look at your room?'

'And why would you want to do that?' Walton asked with a small grin.

'Just to be certain that everything there belongs to you,' Nottingham said.

'What if I refuse?'

The Constable stood.

'You don't believe I'm an honest man, do you, Constable?'

'I don't trust you, Mr Walton.'

The thief taker's smile was like an adder's. 'And if you find nothing in my room?'

'We'll see,' Nottingham said warily.

'Then shall we go?' the thief taker suggested. 'You can see for yourself.'

Following the man up the stairs, the Constable felt dismayed. He'd hoped Walton would have been careless, too proud of his little tricks, and left things openly around. But he must have been wrong; the man wouldn't have let the law in otherwise. Still, it had been a gamble, something worth doing in the moment.

Walton made a performance of unlocking his door, turning the large, heavy key and ushering Nottingham inside. It was a sparse, small space, the shutters thrown wide, the window open to the yard behind the inn. A small chest stood in the corner, its lid up, empty inside. There was a candle, holder and tinder on the shelf, and an old bed. Nottingham rummaged over the straw mattress and through the blankets and pillow, but it was just for the sake of appearance. There was nothing to be found here and they both knew it. Walton leaned against the wall, looking smug.

'I told you,' he said. 'Everything that's here belongs to me. There's precious little of it.'

'You asked if I thought you were an honest man, Mr Walton. I'll give you your answer. I don't believe you are.'

'Be careful what you say,' the thief taker warned. 'Slander's a crime even in these parts.'

Nottingham smiled. 'But the truth isn't. I'm sure I'll be seeing you again, Mr Walton.'

He frowned as he walked back to the jail. The thief taker had made him look foolish, but he wasn't the first and he wouldn't be the last. For all that, it had been worthwhile; he'd learned something from the room.

At his desk he scribbled quick notes to Sedgwick and Lister with new instructions for the men. With God's good grace they'd have Walton soon enough. He steepled his hands over his mouth, feeling the roughness of bristles against his fingertips. Sometime soon he'd need a shave.

He sat back, wondering what he could do to ease Emily's pain and realized there was nothing. What happened depended on Rob, and he felt sorry for the lad. Whatever he chose he'd lose something. If he followed his father, he might well believe he had to leave the job, just when he'd learned how to do it well. Nottingham sighed. No good would come of any of this.

He was still thinking when the door opened and Alice Wendell entered. Her back was straight, her clothes clean, hair neatly hidden by an old cap washed pure white. But her face had aged over the days; sorrow haunted her eyes, the lines so deep in her flesh they might have been put there with a chisel.

'Sit down,' he offered, pulling out a chair and pouring her a mug of ale from the jug. She drank politely, then set the beaker on the edge of the desk.

'I need to find out what you've learned about my Lucy's death,' she said, and he knew it had been the only thing in her mind since he'd given her the news, stealing her sleep and tearing at her waking hours.

'We've been trying, but we haven't managed to find much yet,' he admitted, knowing he was really saying nothing at all.

She stared at him. 'Please?' she asked. 'Tell me what you know.'

He sat down slowly. He shouldn't say anything to her, but how could he refuse the woman's request? Hard as it might be, the knowledge was all she'd have left of her daughter.

'She tried her hand at whoring for a night, but she didn't have any luck. Then we know she was staying with a group who camp down by the riverbank at night. It seems she was there for a week. After that we simply don't know. I'm sorry. We're trying to find out.'

'Thank you.' She made to get up and he said,

'She told people she couldn't go home because *he*'d find her. Do you know what she meant?'

Alice Wendell shook her head sadly. 'There's nobbut me there, and her brother when he comes to visit. Just family who love her.'

'No man who's been interested in her?'

She snorted. 'How many of them you talked to would have wanted her? Eh?'

He nodded his head slightly in acknowledgement.

'I've heard about you,' she said. 'They say you're not like them as run Leeds. You care about us.'

'Everyone deserves justice, Mrs Wendell.'

She held her head up. 'Get the bastard who did this to my Lucy, then. You can do that for her. I want to see him hang up on Chapeltown Moor.'

'If I can, I will.'

'I'll have to live for that, then.'

Alone again, Nottingham rubbed his eyes. How many women had come to the jail over the years wanting news of husbands, sons and daughters? He'd lost count long ago. He'd been able to give good tidings to a few, but for most there were no happy endings. He hoped that in time he'd be able to tell Alice Wendell who'd murdered her daughter, but for now the path had ended and they'd managed to account for little more than one of the three weeks before the fire. She'd been somewhere in Leeds. Someone would have seen her face, maybe even known her name. The city wasn't so big that they couldn't find out. A few thousands souls, so many of them pushed together in the cold, crowded spaces of the poor: faceless, anonymous folk, all working for the few who tasted luxury each day without thought. He'd discover where she'd been. The image of her in the cellar, the half-formed child on her belly, would remain in his mind forever; no one in this world deserved to die that way. She'd had precious little voice in life, and he was damned if he'd let her be silent in death.

Rob had dressed in his best suit and breeches. His hose were spotless, his shoes lovingly polished so the steel buckles shone. He'd washed and run his hands through his hair, staring at himself in the looking glass until he was satisfied with what he saw.

He waited outside the school, standing aside as the girls ran out into the city. He felt as nervous as a child called in to be disciplined, his eyes anxiously darting to the door, knowing she'd be there soon.

When Emily came out, she was talking to Mrs Rains, and he caught his breath. He knew she'd seen him; she had turned her head pointedly away, letting the conversation drag out, making exaggerated gestures with her small hands. But sooner or later she'd have to pass him and then he'd have his chance. Unable to sleep, he'd spent the day formulating the words, grinding them deep into his memory.

Finally she finished and walked towards him. He stepped away from the wall, right into her path.

'Please,' he begged quietly, 'hear me out.'

She tilted her head and said nothing, but stopped and crossed her arms, her face expressionless. He took a breath.

'What I told you was just what my father had said to me. Please, you have to believe me, it's not how I feel about things. He can find me a hundred women to marry and I'll turn them all away.'

Emily looked at him. A curl had escaped her cap to hang down her cheek. He wanted to reach out and push it behind her ear but was too scared to touch her.

'Have you told him that?' she asked.

'I tried.'

'Then you'd better tell him again and make sure he understands.' She moved around him and started to walk away.

'Your father even asked about it this morning.'

She stopped and turned. 'What did he say?'

'He said I should talk to you.'

'He's proud of my grandmother, did he tell you that?'

'Yes,' Rob said.

'What she did took a lot of courage,' she said, admiration in her voice.

'I know,' he agreed.

'I'm not sure I could be that strong,' Emily admitted.

'Then pray God you never have to find out.'

'If I had to, what would you do?' she asked. 'Would you be proud of me?'

'Yes,' he answered without hesitation.

She moved closer and looked deep into his eyes. 'And what about your father? What do you think he'd say?'

'You know exactly what he'd say,' he told her and she nodded sadly.

'But I'm not him,' Rob protested desperately. 'That's what I've been trying to tell you. Since I became a Constable's man I've seen things he couldn't begin to understand.'

'He's still your father.'

'He can't make me think like him.'

'He has money, Rob, he has influence,' she said sadly. 'Sooner or later he's going to try and make you do what he wants. Can't you see that?'

'He won't succeed,' he promised. 'Trust me.'

'I want to believe you.' She took his hand. 'I really want to believe you. But I daren't love someone who might hold my family's past against me some day.' She walked away, leaving him standing, torn and hopeless.

The deputy arrived home in the early evening. He'd made his final round of the day and passed the keys over to Lister, along with the Constable's note. Collins had arrived in the afternoon to report his robbery.

'What does it mean?' Rob asked. Sedgwick had shrugged.

'The boss knows what he's doing. Just put your man on the yard instead of the front entrance of the Talbot and see what happens.' He paused. 'What's wrong with you, anyway? I've seen happier looking corpses.'

'It's nothing.' Lister turned away and sorted through some papers.

If the lad wanted to talk about it, he would, the deputy thought. It was his business.

'Right, I'll leave it all with you, then.'

He made his way home through the streets, most of the houses already shuttered and locked for the night, keeping the robbers and evil spirits at bay. The inns and alehouses glistened with noise and music, lights shining in the gathering darkness but they held no appeal for him any more. He'd rather be with his family at his own hearth.

He opened the door of the tiny house on Lands Lane and walked into a room full of the rich scent of cooking meat. The day before one of the butchers on the Shambles had given him some beef as thanks for a small favour and he'd been looking forward to it all day.

Lizzie stood over the pan, stirring the stew with an old wooden spoon. Glancing across he could see Isabell asleep in her basket, eyes pressed firmly together, fat little hands showing above the blanket, black hair beginning to grow in thickly across her scalp. He bent down close enough to see her chest rise and fall in the slow pattern of breathing, then kissed Lizzie.

'Has she been down long?' he asked softly.

'About an hour. Slept well this afternoon, too. It's starting to get better.' She stretched, pushing her hands against her back to straighten it, then put her arms around him and gave him the smile he loved. 'And before you ask, James is upstairs asleep. I fed him when he came home from playing.'

'How was he?'

'Just the way he used to be,' she said with a bemused shake of her head. 'Sweet and loving. Settled down when I told him and went straight off. I don't understand what gets into him sometimes.' She ladled hot stew into a bowl and put it on the table for him, along with a beaker of ale and a crust of bread. 'That should see you right.' Lizzie watched happily as he spooned the food into his mouth, scarcely stopping to savour it, only slowing down as he sopped up the gravy.

'That was grand,' he said finally, reaching out and taking her hand. 'Thank you.'

'Don't thank me; that butcher of yours did you proud. It's better than we could afford. Plenty of meat and it wasn't even spoiled. There'll be enough for tomorrow, too. What did you do for him, anyway?'

'Just showed him how his apprentice was stealing from him. Nothing much.'

Lizzie glanced over at the sleeping baby. 'We could have an early night ourselves,' she said coyly, her fingers twining in his.

'We could,' he agreed.

'Then you'd better get up those stairs sharpish, John Sedgwick, and make sure you're quiet so the little one doesn't wake.'

Twelve

There was no more than a band of pale light on the horizon when the Constable walked up Kirkgate but already the day felt oppressive. The thick clouds in the sky seemed weighted and full, the air heavy. He could feel sweat in his armpits, and his hair was damp when he ran his hand through it.

Lister had the window open wide, but there was no breeze to flow and cool the place. Rob's jacket hung on a nail, his long waistcoat unbuttoned and the sleeves of his shirt pushed up.

'Morning, boss,' he said. 'It's close out already.'

'If it keeps up like this, tempers are going to flare sooner rather than later. People don't take the heat well here.' Nottingham poured himself a mug of small ale and drank it down quickly. 'Anything worth knowing about? Did putting the man on the yard of the Talbot help?'

Lister sat back and laughed.

'As soon as it was dark Walton climbed down the kitchen roof and was off down the back way. Johnson was on him. He said the only time he's seen anyone move faster was when a husband's come back without warning.'

Nottingham grinned with satisfaction. 'Where did he go?'

'A place off Currie Entry. There's a small court there.'

'I know it. About as wide as your arm to get in, then just a few houses back there. Was Johnson able to see which one he went into?'

Rob nodded. 'He did a good job. Walton stayed there almost half an hour by the church clock, he said, then went back and climbed up to his room. Johnson found me and showed me where Walton had gone.'

'Good. I think we'd better take a look at this place. Somehow I doubt our thief taker was just visiting an accommodating widow.'

The Constable carefully avoided the other subject that hung between them. He'd talked to Mary the night before, waiting until Emily had gone to her room to work after arriving home in a flustered, sour mood. They'd discussed it in low voices, Mary's anger at Rob's father brittle and bitter, his own sadder, tempered by experience. But finally he'd convinced her that there was nothing they could do. Everything depended on the decisions Rob made. He'd put no pressure on the lad. He wouldn't even hold it against him if he caved in to his father. The lad needed time to make up his mind fairly.

By the time Sedgwick arrived, yawning and stretching so his fingertips almost touched the ceiling of the room, Nottingham knew what he wanted to do about Walton.

'The three of us are going in together,' he told them. 'If we do it soon they'll still be asleep. Look for anything of worth. Those houses are poor, so it'll stand out. John, you watch whoever's in there while Rob and I search.' He opened the cupboard and took out three swords. 'Let's hope we don't need them.'

Full light had arrived as they left the jail, the clouds low in pale shades of grey. They entered the court one at a time, the Constable in the lead, alert for any noise, treading carefully on the packed down dirt.

The house was old, the wood of the frame rotting and sagging so the windows couldn't close. It only took a single kick to push the door back, and they walked in, weapons drawn.

The couple was asleep. They sat up as Nottingham entered the room, the man with one foot already on the floor, the woman pulling the sheet up to cover herself.

'Stay there,' he ordered. 'What's your name?'

The man stayed silent. He was older, the hair on his head thin and a dirty, greasy grey, with more sprouting heavily from his nostrils and ears. The bed was straw resting on planking, roughly covered with a sheet.

'I'm the Constable. What's your name?' he repeated.

'Matthew.' The man's voice had the rough edge of someone who drank too much, too often. He coughed and spat into a bowl on the floor.

'John,' Nottingham called, 'come and watch these two while I look around.'

'No need, boss. They have everything out. You'd think they were running a shop here.'

The Constable waved his sword. 'Up, the pair of you, and get dressed. You're either thieves or fences, and either one will get you both hanged.' Neither of them moved. 'Come on.'

Slowly they stood. The woman was of an age with the man; she turned her back to hide her thick body under her shift. He waited until they were clothed then looked through into the other room.

Sedgwick had piled items on the table, good plate, jewellery, some lace and coins.

'They've been busy, boss. The hangman will love them.'

The Constable could see the fear in their eyes, the dread of death coming so soon.

'What's your surname, Matthew?'

'Trill.' The man coughed again, took a dirty kerchief from the pocket of his coat and spat.

'And how did all this end up here? Don't give me any stories, either,' he warned.

The man glanced at his wife and took her hand in a small gesture of comfort. Tears were tumbling down her cheeks and she pawed at them.

'Well?' Nottingham asked, his patience running thin.

'We keep them here for someone,' Trill said, his voice flat.

'Who?'

'He says his name's Walton. He pays us.'

'How did you meet him?' the Constable asked.

'I was in the Talbot and we started talking. He asked if I wanted to make some money.'

'How long ago was this?'

'A few days,' Trill replied morosely.

'And what did he want you to do?'

'Just hold all that for him,' the man said. 'He told me it was all above board.'

'And you didn't ask any questions?'

The man shrugged and coughed again. 'It was money.'

'It's not any more,' the Constable told him. 'Was he here last night?'

'Yes.'

'And when will he be back again?'

The couple looked at each other.

'Tonight,' the man said finally. 'He'll be coming to collect some things to take back to their owner.'

'What time?'

'Once it's dark,' the woman answered sadly. 'I told you,' she said to the man, and he simply shook his head, looking straight ahead.

Nottingham was silent, leaving them to think, letting their imaginations feel the rope tightening around their necks.

'I'm going to make you an offer, Mr Trill,' he said finally. 'You can have your lives if you help us get Walton.'

He saw the woman's hand clutch tightly at the man's fingers.

'How?' Trill asked, hope in his voice.

'All you have to do is be here when he comes. I'll have someone hidden in your other room, and men outside.'

'What else?'

'Just do what you would. Then we'll take him.'

Trill nodded his agreement wearily.

'Do that and you'll escape the noose,' the Constable told him. 'Don't try and send word to warn him.'

'I wouldn't,' the man answered, his voice low and hoarse. 'Let the bugger come. As long as you save us.'

'I will,' Nottingham promised. 'If you do what you're told.'

'Aye,' Trill said with a sigh.

'Good. Then I'll have my man here before the sun sets. And,' he warned them again, 'no word to Walton. You'll be watched all day.'

Out on Currie Entry, the air heavy around them, Rob asked, 'Who's going to watch them?'

'No one,' the Constable told him with a grin. 'They're scared enough, they won't do anything. I just wanted to keep them fearful.'

'What about tonight?' Sedgwick asked.

'You'll be in the house with them, John. Keep yourself hidden. Rob and I will be out here. We'll let Walton do his business and leave. You follow him out and we'll take him in the yard. He won't be able to escape from there and if he has any sense he won't try to take on three men.'

'Yes, boss.'

'Lucy Wendell,' he said, changing to the topic that kept worrying at his mind. 'She was somewhere for two weeks and we haven't found where yet.' Nottingham looked at the others. 'What do you think? Rob?'

Lister spoke slowly, putting into words what he'd been wondering.

'From what the other girl, Susan, told me, she seemed happy enough down by the river. I think someone found her, the man she was scared of.'

The Constable nodded slowly. 'That's possible. John?'

'I agree,' the deputy said. 'There must have been some reason she never went back there. Something happened.'

'I believe the man she feared was the one who made her pregnant,' Nottingham said. 'He's the one we need to find. We need to start asking around again. Someone will remember her. Go hard on them.' He paused. 'You get started on that, John. Rob, we'll meet at the jail just before sunset. I'll go and see everything's well at the cloth market.'

The bell for the start of the market sounded as he arrived on Briggate, conversation turning to whispers as the merchants moved with purpose through the crowds. The cloth was laid out on the wood to show length and the quality of the colour. The weavers stood with coats off against the heat, deep circles of sweat showing under their armpits.

By habit the merchants always dressed well for the markets, displaying their wealth and finery, no matter how uncomfortable the weather. It was a matter of pride, it kept them apart, a reminder of the wealth to be made in wool for the right people.

He exchanged nodded greetings with a few of the men and

watched bargains made and sealed with a quick shake of the hands. The cloth was folded, ready to be moved later to the warehouses. This was the real business of Leeds, fast and certain, where fortunes were founded and added to. Nottingham knew that full twenty thousand pounds could change hands over the next hour. And there would be more in the afternoon at the White Cloth Hall, where the only sounds would be the echo of heels on flagstones, the voices as hushed as if they were in church.

He remembered the Hall being built, the stone clean and golden, the large area inside, the pillars as impressive and grand as any cathedral, where commerce stood as a god equal to any in heaven.

Nottingham turned and caught Ben Cates glaring at him. The man stood with his sons, giving quick, whispered instructions. Robert was concentrating, nodding furiously, while Will glanced around, bemused, standing apart.

By the time the bell sounded again to finish trading most of the cloth had gone. Only a few sad lengths remained, material of poor quality, weeks of work wasted and families going hungry.

He stopped at the White Swan and drank a mug of small beer. The closeness was still pressing down on the city. If it remained, violence would abound tonight. Tempers would quickly shred, fists would become knives, men would bleed and die and women would weep.

By the Moot Hall the traders were setting up for the Saturday market, chickens already squawking loudly in their wicker baskets, fearful as the tang of blood rose from the Shambles to fill the air, sweet and sickening, mixing with the stench of shit and piss along the street.

Wives and servant girls crowded round the stall selling old clothes, small purses clutched tightly in their fists as they pulled and rummaged, drawing out dresses and shifts to hold against their bodies.

Girls had come in from the farms carrying butter, fresh that morning, and churns full of milk. The street was bustling, voices raised to be heard, a clamour of people moving, pressing to one side as carts tried to pass. A woman wandered through the throng shouting herself raw as she tried to sell bunches of lucky heather.

The Constable moved among the sellers he knew, asking if any of them recalled Lucy. Some thought they recollected a girl with a harelip but none could remember when they might have seen her. Too much time had passed, too many faces seen at markets in the towns all around.

He was wondering what to do next, who to ask, when a hand tugged at his arm. The woman's face was tight and frantic.

'You're the Constable, aren't you?' she asked. 'Can you help me? My son's gone missing.'

Thirteen

He straightened, immediately alert and attentive.

'How old is he?'

'Just six,' she said, the tears beginning to stream. She wiped at them with a hand that had seen plenty of work, her knuckles raw and red. 'He wandered off a few minutes ago. The clock had just struck.'

He placed her now, the wife of Morrison the chandler down on Swinegate.

'What's your son's name?' he asked.

'Mark.' She fumbled in the pocket of her old dress for a kerchief and blew her nose. She was perhaps thirty and she'd been pretty once, the faint traces of beauty still around her eyes and mouth. But time and children had taken their toll, and now her skin sagged and her hair was limp.

'Where did you see him last?' He tried to keep the urgency from his voice.

'Up by the cross. I was going to buy a chicken, I turned round and reached for him and he'd gone . . .' Panic filled her and her face crumpled again.

'What was Mark wearing?'

For a moment she looked as if she couldn't recall, then said, 'His blue coat and breeches. They're too big for him, they belonged to his brother and he hasn't grown into them yet.'

'How tall is he? What colour is his hair?'

She held her hand at her waist. 'About this high. He's very fair.'

Already Nottingham was looking around, but any boy that size would be almost invisible in the press of people.

'You stay up by the cross,' he told her. 'I'll start looking.'

He squeezed his way through the crowds, moving down to the Moot Hall, searching rapidly. Children were lost at the market every week. A woman would let go of a small hand to pay for something and the young one would be pulled away, as if out to sea. They'd be found a few minutes later, crying and terrified.

He gave the boy's description to one of the stallholders, knowing it would quickly pass among them all, more eyes looking for the lad; it was what they did. He pushed between people, watching closely for small movements at the edge of his sight. Slowly he worked his way back up to the Market Cross, crossing and re-crossing every inch.

Mrs Morrison was there, standing as tall as she could, shouting out the boy's name, the words lost in the tumult of the market.

'I haven't found him yet,' he told her, seeing the terror grow in her eyes. 'Don't worry. All the sellers know by now, they'll be watching for him.' She reached for his hand and he took it, patting it gently. 'We'll find him. You stay here.'

He plunged back into the crowd, glancing at the stallholders who all shook their heads. Nothing. He could feel the first twinge of fear, the sense that something was wrong, creeping up his spine.

Someone should have spotted the boy by now. He kept looking, checking all the nooks and hidden areas he knew so well, hoping against hope that he'd see the flash of a blue coat or the wail of a tiny voice.

Around him people were beginning to drift away, their baskets full, the sellers slowly packing up their wares. Soon the bell would ring noon and the market would end. He walked back to the cross, where Mrs Morrison stood twisting a kerchief in her hands, still yelling her son's name, her voice growing hoarse and desperate.

'I'm sorry,' he told her. 'I can't see him.'

The tears brimmed from her eyes and tumbled down her cheeks.

'I'll get the men out and searching,' he told her. 'We'll find him. Go home. You have other children, don't you?'

She nodded dumbly.

'You go and look after them,' the Constable said; it would give her something to do. 'I'll come as soon as I know anything.' He waited. 'Please. We'll look everywhere.'

Finally she gave another nod and set off slowly down Briggate, walking as if she was in a dream, head darting hopefully from side to side.

He strode into the Rose and Crown, shouting to be heard over the crowd there.

'There's a boy missing. He's small and fair, in a blue coat and breeches. His name's Mark. Who can help?'

Several of the men drained their mugs and came to him. He divided them up, telling them where to look, then moved down the street to the Ship. More men volunteered. It was the same all along Briggate, until a small army was out looking for the lad.

He returned to the jail, thinking quickly. The boy must have wandered off somewhere. There were enough men to find him in a few more minutes, an hour or two at most.

Sedgwick was sitting at the desk, eating bread and cheese, a full mug of ale at his side.

'We've got a missing lad, John.'

'How old?'

'Six.'

He could see the deputy thinking of his own son as he stood and pushed the food away.

'Who's out there?'

'Some men from the inns, about thirty of them. I sent his mother home. She's Morrison's wife, the chandler. Get everyone organized. I want him found quickly.'

'Yes, boss.'

'Come and tell me as soon as you know anything.'

'I will.'

Alone, behind his desk, Nottingham remembered the last time a child had vanished and not been found. It had been eight years before, a girl who hadn't arrived home from the charity school.

Men had searched through the evening, into the night and all the next day. They'd found her body, cold and long dead, in the orchard by the old manor house. Her mother drowned herself in the river a week later, weighted down by the heaviness of her heart, leaving a husband and two babies. He couldn't allow that to happen again.

Anxiously he heard the bell ring each quarter hour, and with each minute that passed he understood that the chances of finding the boy were growing bleaker. Twice he took up his hat to go and join the search, then put it down again. He needed to be here, where people could find him.

The time passed slowly as he sat, measuring it in heartbeats. Outside he could hear the clamour of Kirkgate, people busily passing, the clop of hooves and the squeak of a carter's wheel as it turned the corner on to Briggate.

It was late afternoon when the deputy returned, his clothes dusty and his face drawn.

'Well?' Nottingham asked.

Sedgwick shook his head. 'Nothing. There's about fifty of them out there now, and we've looked everywhere. We've already been through all the yards, out in the fields, down by the river . . .' He sighed, poured himself some ale and drank it down quickly.

'What about the other side of the Head Row?' the Constable asked. 'He could have wandered over there.'

'We've searched there, boss,' he answered with a tone of resignation. 'We went out past the grammar school, walked the fields. Most of them are willing to keep looking, and there should be more to join them later.' The deputy sat and stretched out his legs. 'It's as if he's vanished.'

'Or someone's snatched him,' Nottingham said darkly. He steepled his fingers under his chin.

'No one would do that,' Sedgwick said. 'Not a little boy.'

'Let's hope not, John, for everyone's sake. Unless you want to see real panic in Leeds.' He sat forward. 'I still want to take Walton tonight.'

'Do you think he'll go with everyone around?'

'I don't know,' Nottingham admitted, 'but we need to be ready. Be at Trill's before sunset. Keep yourself out of sight in the other room. I'll bring Holden with me and we'll cut off the yard. Then we'll have him.'

'Who's going to lead the search for the boy?'

'It'll have to be Rob. I'll give him instructions. Once we've got the thief taker in a cell we can go out and help. You'd better send word to Lizzie that you might be late tonight.'

Sedgwick gave a small, sad smile. 'Already done it. I told her why.'

'Good. Now go and get yourself something to eat and pray it doesn't turn into a long night.'

'What about you?'

'I'm not hungry,' the Constable said.

At five he was in the mayor's office with no good news to tell. Douglas looked a month past weary. His eyes were hard and he needed a shave, the dark bristles on his face shadowing his skin.

'How many are out looking?' he asked.

'Scores,' the Constable answered. 'Everyone wants to find him.'

The mayor nodded thoughtfully. 'Tell me what you think, Richard,' he said, and before Nottingham could reply, he held up his hand. 'I don't want it sweetened or hopeful. I want the truth.'

'I believe someone's taken him.'

'Why? Morrison's a chandler, for God's sake,' Douglas said angrily. 'He's not rich, he doesn't have any power in the city.'

'I don't know,' Nottingham told him with an exhausted sigh. 'Probably because the boy was off by himself and he was easy prey.'

'So what do we do?'

The Constable raised his eyes and stared at the mayor. 'The only thing we can do is keep looking and hope we find him. I'll have men out all night. We look and look and hope he's alive.'

'Do you think . . . ?' Douglas began, but couldn't voice the thought.

'It's happened before. You know that.'

The silence in the room was full of memories. Nottingham stood.

'I need to get back,' he explained. 'We're arresting the thief taker tonight.'

The mayor raised his eyebrows. 'With all this?'

'With all this,' Nottingham confirmed.

'Do you want me to go and see the lad's parents?' Douglas asked.

The Constable gave a brief smile. 'That would be a kindness. I'm sure they'd appreciate it. Just tell them we're doing everything we can.'

By the time Lister arrived, news of the missing boy had spread throughout the city. Close to a hundred men were out looking as dusk fell. The Constable had sent most of the night men to join them, keeping only two back to help him.

'Have you heard?' Nottingham asked.

'The boy?' Lister answered. 'Yes.'

'I need you to lead the search for him. Mr Sedgwick and I are going to arrest the thief taker.'

'Yes, boss.'

'Keep them going as long as they'll stay out or until the lad's found. Have people walk both banks of the river and look south of the Aire. Keep combing the places where we've already been.' He ran a hand through his hair, pushing the fringe off his forehead. 'Find some lanterns somewhere, that'll help.'

'My father thinks someone's taken him.'

Nottingham stopped. 'What makes him think that?'

'He says we'd have found him otherwise.'

'Has he said that to anyone else?'

'Only to me. He's at home.'

'And has he been out searching?'

Lister shook his head.

'Then go and tell him he'd be a lot more bloody use outside than airing his opinions in the parlour,' the Constable said sharply, then paused. 'I'm sorry, it's not your fault.'

'He's right, though, isn't he?'

Nottingham sat on the corner of the desk, his mouth tight, hands pressing on his thighs.

'He might be, but I don't want you breathing a word of it. Once people start to believe that they'll be looking for a culprit, and that's when innocent men can die. Get out there, Rob, keep them going. And see if you can get your father off his arse to do something useful.'

Lister grinned. 'Yes, boss.'

Nottingham took the sword from the cupboard, tested its edge against his thumb and buckled the weapon around his waist. Evening was closing around the city. The deputy would be in place, watchful and quiet. Walton would probably make his move once darkness fell; with so many folk around he'd probably imagine no one would notice him.

Tom Holden, the Constable's man watching the thief taker, had found a small space that offered a view of Walton's window and the yard at the Talbot.

'Anything yet?' Nottingham asked.

'Just pacing a few times. He'll not be out while it's full black.' He paused. 'Have they found that lad yet?'

'Not yet.'

The man clicked his tongue softly. 'I know them, the Morrisons. Used to drink wi' him sometimes. She's a good woman, always looked after that boy well. Poor lad.'

'Plenty of people are looking for him.'

'Aye, I'll be on it myself later.'

They waited, letting the night slowly slip around them. In the distance the sounds of the search retreated, moving out from the heart of the city. Finally the man stirred, his voice a husky whisper.

'He's coming out of his window now.'

They stayed deep in the shadows as Walton emerged from the yard. The man began to follow, but the Constable held him back.

'Wait. I don't want him hearing us.' A few heartbeats later he released his grip. 'Quietly now.'

The thief taker walked without any fear, striding out, never glancing back. He vanished into the court off Currie Entry.

'We'll go in there,' Nottingham ordered. 'Stay off to the side, over where he can't see you. We'll take him as soon as he comes out.'

It wouldn't take long, he knew that. His palm was damp where he held the hilt of the sword and he flexed the hand slowly, eyes firm on the door.

Finally it opened with a sharp creak and a thin sliver of light and the thief taker stepped out, a sack in one hand. He was part way across the court when the Constable said,

'Stand there, Mr Walton. Drop what you're holding.'

The man turned as if to start back to the house, but Sedgwick stood behind him, his weapon drawn.

'Mr Nottingham said drop it.'

The thief taker let go of the sack. It fell in a brief clatter of metal.

'Stolen goods, Mr Walton, some of the things Mr Collins reported missing. Items that can make a man dance from the noose.' He advanced, taking out his weapon. 'Search him, John, make sure he's not armed. Look in his boot for a dagger.'

Walton stayed silent, his body tense, his breathing low. He stared at the Constable, fury black in his eyes.

'Two knives, boss.'

'Nothing to say?' Nottingham asked. 'No clever London words for the provinces?' He knew he was waiting for an answer that would never come. 'You shouldn't have thought we were fools,' he said, shaking his head.

Walton spat and the Constable moved slightly aside, letting the spittle land on the ground.

'Holden,' he said, 'take him to the jail. Watch him carefully. If he tries to escape, you know what to do.'

He moved between the groups of searchers, asking what they'd found and encouraging them. It was hard going in the night; the men were growing disheartened and tired, ready for their beds.

The Constable rubbed at his eyes, feeling them gritty with exhaustion. He should have felt satisfaction in taking Walton, but instead it seemed like a small thing, insignificant when held against a missing boy and a dead girl.

Lanterns were burning all over and men moved through the night, sticks pushing through the undergrowth, the cry of voices in the distance. It was close to midnight and they'd still found no trace of the lad. If there was nothing by dawn they'd have to admit he'd been snatched. Then everything would change.

The only way he knew the time was from the church bell. At two o'clock plenty were still out, going over everywhere again. Lights burned in some of the houses, and wives came out with ale and bread for the searchers, aware that it could easily be their child that was missing.

By three, deep in the heart of the dark, there were fewer of them. He understood. They'd searched hard, they were tired, they'd need a few hours' sleep before working. He ached with tiredness, but he knew he'd have no real rest until the boy had been found. Lucy was dead; pray God the lad was still alive.

He'd just turned on to Boar Lane when he heard the noise. There were shouts of joy and laughter. He turned and without thinking began to run. It was coming from the bridge. When he arrived, a group of men was standing by the parapet, others coming quickly. He pushed through, his heart beating fast. A man was holding the lad. It was definitely him, with fair hair and blue coat and breeches that looked almost black in the torchlight. The boy looked dazed, as if he'd just woken. Nottingham let out a long, silent breath of relief.

'Who found him?'

'We did,' a man said proudly. 'Me and Ezra were coming back over the bridge and he were just standing there at the other side.'

'Was anyone with him?'

'No, it was just him.'

They couldn't have missed him all this time, Nottingham thought. Too many feet had tramped across the Leeds Bridge in the last few hours. The boy seemed too unsteady to have walked. Someone had put him close by, wanted him to be found.

'Has anyone gone for his parents?' he asked

'Aye, his father's on his way,' a voice told him.

'Bring that light closer,' the Constable said. Very carefully he checked Mark for injuries, feeling along the bones, examining the flesh for cuts and finding nothing. He brought his face close to the boy's mouth, and caught the scent of wine on his breath mixed with something he couldn't identify.

Drugged, he thought. That would be it.

'How do you feel, Mark?' Nottingham asked gently. He knew he only had a short time before the boy's father arrived. The lad didn't answer, looking around fearfully, scared by the press of faces that surrounded him. 'You're fine now,' the Constable assured him. 'You're safe. Do you remember how you got here?'

Mark shook his head.

'That doesn't matter. You're here now, that's all that counts.'

He picked the boy up, holding him for the searchers to see and they started to cheer. As he let Mark slide down his body he felt something in the pocket of the blue coat. While the others talked he slipped his hand in and took out a piece of paper, sliding it into his waistcoat before anyone could notice.

'Where is he?' a desperate voice cried, and Morrison forced his way through the crowd and dropping to his knees.

'He's fine,' the Constable told him. 'Don't worry. Take him home and let him rest. I'll come by tomorrow.'

Morrison's hands were shaking as he slid them under his son and lifted. In the light Nottingham could see tears of relief coursing down his cheeks as he pulled the child close to his chest.

'The city thanks all of you,' Nottingham said, raising his voice. 'You've given your time and we've found Mark. We're grateful, and I'm sure his family is, too. Now let's go home and sleep. You've all earned it.'

He waited until they began to disperse and made his way back to the jail. As he turned on to Kirkgate the clock struck four, the first line of dawn on the horizon. He checked to be certain Walton was locked in a cell then lit a candle and settled into his chair, stifling a wide yawn.

He remembered how, just a few years before, he'd often go two days and a night without sleep. It hadn't worried him then; a few hours' of rest and he'd be ready to work more. Now he knew he'd doze off during the sermon in church. The place would be full of people giving thanks for the safe return of Mark Morrison, the way it always was after events like this, reminders of the rare goodness God could give.

He reached into the pocket of his coat and drew out the paper he'd found in Mark's pocket. He smoothed it out on the desk and brought the flame closer and read the words.

'This is what we can do. Next time no mercy.'

Fourteen

Sedgwick and Rob arrived together, laughing and loud, their voices echoing up and down the street like a dawn chorus.

'Good news for once,' the deputy said, pouring ale and easing himself into a chair.

'I'm glad my father was wrong,' Lister said.

'He wasn't.' The Constable pushed the note across to them. 'Someone had dosed the lad with something. He could hardly stand when they found him. That was in his pocket.'

'Next time?' Sedgwick asked after he'd read the words.

'Next time,' Nottingham echoed darkly. 'We've been warned.' He looked at the others. 'The first thing is, not a word of this outside here. Understand?'

They both nodded.

'It's just luck that I was there and took this. You can imagine what would happen if people heard about it.'

'So what can we do?' Rob said.

'We've got to find whoever's behind this before they can do it again.'

'How?' the deputy wondered.

'I don't know, John.' The Constable shook his head in frustration. 'I really don't know. I'll go over to Morrison's today and talk to the lad, but I doubt he'll remember anything.'

'Where do we even start?' asked Lister. 'If we begin asking if anyone saw this boy with someone, people will become suspicious.'

Nottingham ran a hand through his hair.

'True,' he acknowledged wearily. 'I'll talk to the mayor after church. Just keep your eyes and your ears open for anything. Anything at all. You know how many children there are around.'

Silence filled the room.

'John, see that the thief taker goes over to the prison at the Moot Hall today. And check that Joshua Davidson and his girls have gone. The house is by Shaw Pool. I gave them their marching orders. If they're still there, arrest them.'

'Yes, boss.'

'Both of you think what we can do about Lucy Wendell, too. I'm not going to let her killer escape. Anyone who can do that is an affront to God.'

He stood, feeling his back ache and his knees protest at the weight as he rose.

'And remember, not a word to anyone.'

'Did you find him?' Mary asked anxiously as he walked into the kitchen.

'We did,' he said with a weary smile. 'Alive and fine.' He brought her close, happy to feel the warmth against him. 'I think half the city must have been out looking.'

'Are you going to church this morning?'

'I'd better. I need to see the mayor after.' He cut some cheese and tore off a hunk of yesterday's loaf. 'I feel like I could sleep for a year.'

She kissed him.

'At least there was a happy ending,' she said. 'That's reason enough to give thanks.'

'This time,' he told her, and she glanced at him curiously. 'I'll wash and put on my Sunday suit.'

At the top of the stairs he could hear Emily moving in her room. For a moment he considered telling her about the child snatcher so she could try to protect the girls she taught. But if one person was told, the word would spread on the wind. Within an hour all Leeds would know.

He stripped and splashed cold water from the ewer over his body. The lye soap made a harsh lather on his skin, but after a few minutes he felt cleaner, more awake and ready to face the day.

Mary had sponged his good suit and laid it out on the bed. It was excellent material, a gift from a merchant a full ten years ago. Now the cut was long out of date and the breeches were uncomfortably tight at the waist and in the thighs. But for a few hours each week it was fine. He didn't have the money to waste on a new one. This one would last for as long as he needed it.

As he locked the front door the bells at St Peter's began to peal for the early service. With Mary on one arm and Emily on the other he walked proudly down Marsh Lane and over Timble Bridge.

He knew the mayor would be in his office. It was a post that gave no respite, a mistress that demanded complete devotion for a year. Nottingham walked down the hallways, the rich Turkey carpet under his heels, no sound of voices behind the closed doors today. The dark wainscoting was polished to a high sheen, the portraits of the rich men who'd run the city looking down on him balefully.

He knocked on the door and entered. John Douglas glanced up, a quill in his hand as he worked through the pile of papers in front of him. His coat was draped over the chair back, his long waistcoat unbuttoned and his stock undone, the costly wig tossed on to the windowsill.

'Something must be important to bring you here on a Sunday, Richard,' he said, leaning back in the heavy chair.

'Morrison's boy,' the Constable said.

Douglas raised his eyebrows.

'You found him,' he said. 'The lad was safe and unhurt. His parents are grateful and the churches were full this morning.' He nodded at the chair and Nottingham sat.

'We didn't find him,' the Constable answered. 'He was left for us to find. He was barely awake. Someone had taken him and drugged him.'

The mayor studied him before asking, 'Are you certain about this?'

The Constable drew the note from his pocket and put it on the desk. 'That was in his pocket.'

Douglas remained silent for a long time after reading.

'What can we do?' he asked finally.

'I don't know,' Nottingham admitted, shaking his head. 'We daren't let people know that someone's taking children. There'll be panic all over the city.'

The mayor nodded soberly. 'But if we don't say anything there could be more children snatched,' he pointed out.

'I know.'

Douglas filled two beakers from the jug on a table and passed one to the Constable. 'How do we find these people?'

'I don't know that, either. If I start asking questions folk will become suspicious. It doesn't take long for a wisp of rumour to become fact here, you know that as well as I do.'

The mayor studied the liquid in his mug. 'Who else knows about this note?'

'Just two of my men. They won't say anything.'

'No one else?'

Nottingham shook his head. He could hear the sounds of the day outside, couples making their way up Briggate to St John's, the cacophony of bells from the city's three churches.

'Do whatever you have to do, Richard,' Douglas said with a grimace. He took a long drink of the ale. 'I don't care what it takes to find whoever did this.'

'And when we do find them?'

The mayor didn't reply.

Nottingham stood and walked towards the door.

'You'll have my full backing in everything,' the mayor told him.

He walked along Swinegate. For once the street was quiet, the businesses all closed for the Sabbath, no carts clattering along the road to disperse the puddles and clumps of stinking night soil tossed from the windows. Horses whinnied in their stable at the ostler's and smoke rose lazily from the chimneys. Like all the other shops along the row, the chandler's was shuttered.

The Constable slipped into the passageway that ran by the building and through to the yard behind. The ground was filled with buckets and basins, tools of the chandler's trade, the smell of lye heavy and acrid in the air.

He knocked on the door and waited. It was Morrison himself who came, all the pain and tension eased from his face.

'Constable,' he said.

'How's Mark? Awake and well?'

'Aye, he is that, praise God.' The chandler smiled, showing the nubs of brown teeth in a wide mouth. He was a stout man, his knuckles gnarled and misshapen, two fingers gone from his right hand. 'Come in, come in.'

The chandler and his family lived above their business in a

series of small, untidy rooms. He could hear the wife in the kitchen, giving orders to the maid and the sound of children behind another closed door.

Morrison led him up another flight of stairs, the rail trembling under his touch, and into a small room under the eaves. The floor was swept and a window looked down on the street. The boy lay in clean sheets on a pallet of fresh straw, a spotless shirt over his scrawny body.

'This is the Constable, Mark.'

The lad turned and Nottingham could see his eyes were alert and the colour had returned to his face.

'Hello,' he said, squatting down and smiling. 'How do you feel, Mark?'

Mark glanced at his father then back at the Constable. 'Fine, thank you, sir,' he replied, his voice clear and strong, although Nottingham could see the faint traces of fear lingering in his expression.

'You had us all worried yesterday, you know.'

'I'm sorry, sir.'

Nottingham grinned and ruffled the boy's hair. 'You're back and safe now, that's all that matters.' He turned to Morrison. 'I'd like to talk to your son alone, if I might.'

'Of course,' the chandler agreed with an eager nod. 'Just come down when you're done.'

He waited until the footsteps had faded before speaking.

'What do you remember about yesterday, Mark?'

'I don't know,' the boy answered slowly. 'It's all mixed up inside.'

'Do you recall being at the market with your mother?' he prodded gently.

Mark nodded.

'What happened after that?'

'I was holding her hand and then I was on my own. I tried shouting but no one heard me.'

He could see the tears of memory welling in the lad's eyes.

'Did anyone help you?'

'Yes. There was a lady. She said she'd take me to my mam.'

'And did you go with her?'

He nodded. 'But we went the other way, down Briggate. I asked if she was taking me home.'

'What did she say?'

'I don't remember,' the boy admitted with a blush of embarrassment. 'She gave me something to drink. It tasted funny but she said I had to drink it all. Then I don't remember anything after that until I was back here. I'm sorry, sir.'

Nottingham smiled and patted the boy's hand.

'You're doing very well,' he said. 'What did the woman look like? Can you close your eyes and see her?'

He waited as the boy concentrated, careful not to rush him.

'She had a blue dress.'

'Very good, Mark, you're doing well. Anything else?'

'Her hair was dark.'

'What was her name? Did she tell you?'

He said nothing.

'I'm sorry, sir,' the lad apologized, 'that's all.' He turned to stare at the Constable. 'Was she a bad lady?'

'I don't know,' Nottingham told him. 'You're safe now and that's the only thing that matters. But you probably shouldn't say anything about the lady to anyone. Can you keep it a secret?'

'Yes, sir,' Mark answered seriously.

'Even from your parents?' he asked quietly. 'Just between us? You promise?'

The boy nodded.

'Good lad.' He stood, feeling the ache in his knees. 'You just rest today, you'll be fine tomorrow.'

Wearing his best clothes, his hair combed, Rob stood outside the Constable's house. He'd managed a few hours of sleep, broken by the church bells, then he'd determined to come down here, the way he had every Sunday afternoon for months. Maybe Emily would refuse to see him, but he had to try. His father might want to marry him into society but he was going to follow the course his heart set.

He had no great experience of girls but he knew enough to understand that she was different. She enchanted and nonplussed him in equal amounts with the way she looked at the world, a girl who spoke her thoughts fearlessly without caring who heard them.

What he felt for her wasn't the bloodless love his parents

professed. It was passion, not propriety. Maybe it was ridiculous, maybe it would come to naught, but he'd fallen into it without hesitation.

He stood straight and knocked. Almost before he was ready, Mary Nottingham was standing there, a woman with greying hair and a kindly face. Beyond her he could see the boss sitting in his chair, rubbing his chin with his hand as he thought.

'I've come to see Emily,' Rob said.

'Come in, I'll shout for her.' She climbed the stairs and he waited in the room, the Constable staring at him and smiling.

'I'm glad to see you're persistent,' he said.

'I love her,' Lister answered, as if it explained everything.

'She knows that, I'm sure.'

He turned as he heard footsteps and saw Emily, her expression as unsure as his own. She was still in her church dress, the dark colour showing off her pale skin, her hair loose and tumbling over her shoulders.

'I thought we could take a walk,' he suggested.

He watched as she glanced briefly at her father then back at him.

'As long as it's not far,' she agreed cautiously. 'I still have to prepare work for school tomorrow.'

'Just to the river and back,' he said, feeling as nervous as if they'd barely met.

'You go and enjoy yourselves,' the Constable said. 'Stay for supper if you like, Rob.'

He saw the minute shake of her head.

'I can't today, boss,' he answered.

Outside, under the high clouds, he wanted to reach for her hand as they crossed the tenters' fields, the wooden frames standing stark, empty of cloth. But she kept a discreet distance, too far for a casual touch.

'I wasn't sure you'd come today,' Emily said hesitantly.

'Why not?'

She glanced at him. 'After we talked the other day.'

'Did you really think I'd just give up?' he asked.

'I don't know,' she sighed.

'I told you, I love you.'

He listened to the silence until they reached the riverbank and sat on an old log where generations of lovers had carved their initials.

'But I said I didn't know if I could love you,' she continued as if there had been no gap. 'Not unless I can be sure of you.'

'If we don't see each other and if we don't talk to each other, how can you ever know?' Rob let the words rush out. He stared at the water moving lazily past. 'If we stop it's the same thing as my father winning.'

'Is it?' she wondered.

'Yes,' he replied with certainty, and she looked at him.

'Why do you love me, Rob?'

The question took him aback. He tried to dig down, to find the words that could capture his feelings for her.

'Because you're you,' he answered eventually. 'You're not afraid of anything,' he added.

'That's not true,' she told him, sadness in her voice. 'I'm afraid of lots of things.'

'But you don't show it,' he insisted. 'You care about people . . . about things.' He knew it hardly made sense, but it was all he could manage.

Her fingers touched his and he felt a pull of hope as he put his hand over hers.

'I do love you,' he said.

He waited, holding his breath for her reply.

'I know, and I love you. It's just . . .'

'What?' he asked quickly.

'I don't know,' she admitted and shook her head. 'I really don't know; I wish I did.' She looked down at her feet. 'I'm scared of what your father might do if you refuse him. I'm scared that you'll give in to him and break my heart. Or if you don't, I'm scared you might resent me some day.'

'I won't,' he told her, knowing it was true.

'But I have to be certain and I'm not.' She stood and smoothed down the dress. 'Let's go back. I really do have work to finish.'

They held hands, meandering slowly, letting idle words cover their feelings until they were outside her house.

'It's not over,' he said. 'I don't ever want it to be over.'

She smiled and gave him a small, quick kiss.

'Neither do I.'

John Sedgwick had almost finished his day's work as the sky clouded over in the late afternoon and a light drizzle began to fall. He perched the battered tricorn hat more squarely on his head, turned up his coat collar and made his way back to the jail.

The only thing remaining was to take Walton over to the prison below the Moot Hall. He'd wait there until the Quarter Sessions reached the city then stand trial for his crimes. There was no doubt of his guilt; they'd caught him with the loot from a burglary. Within days of the verdict he'd be dangling from the noose up on Chapeltown Moor and the crowds would jeer and roar as he danced in the air.

He'd let the thief taker sit all day without food or water. They could look after him at the prison. There had been more pressing business. He'd gone over to Shaw's Well and seen that Davidson and his whores had gone then asked around casually to see if anyone had noticed Morrison's boy when he'd been missing.

After this he'd finally be able to go home. All day he'd been scared of James wandering off again, of the child snatcher taking him. He was small, he'd be easy to grab for anyone with determination. Minute by minute the fear had eaten through him and he knew he'd embrace his son tightly when he walked through the door and saw him there.

He needed to talk to him, to make him understand that he needed to stay close to home, close to Lizzie, close to safety. How could he make a boy of his age comprehend all the dangers life held? All he could do was try. If necessary he'd lock him in the house and keep him there.

Maybe the boss was right, and there'd be panic if word of someone taking children spread through the city. But maybe panic was better than another child gone and parents grieving, he thought. With everyone watching and wary the bastard would have a much harder task.

Walton was sitting in his cell, eyes closed as if he was asleep. The deputy turned the key in the lock and said,

'On your feet. Hands out in front.'

The thief taker obeyed without a word and Sedgwick snapped the shackles on his wrists, the iron weight pulling his arms down.

'Sit down. Legs out.' He moved deftly, locking the ankle rings and chain in place. They'd make walking difficult, but the distance was short and he'd learned long ago to take no chances. A desperate man could run fast and he had no taste for the chase right now, not with his own hearth calling him. Before they left he armed himself with a sword and pistol, loading and priming it as Walton watched. 'Try to escape and I'll put the load in your brain.'

Briggate was quiet, only a few people out, courting couples and girls parading arm in arm, eyes darting around for any eligible young men. The deputy walked slightly behind the thief taker, one hand lightly gripping the hilt of his weapon, the handle of the gun in easy reach. What could he say to James that would make the boy listen, he wondered? How could he bring back the happy child who'd been there before Isabell was born?

As they approached two serving lasses who giggled at being so close to danger, the thief taker slid quickly to the side and turned. In one swift movement he lifted his arms, looped the chain around the neck of one of the girls and pulled it taut.

He smiled, showing his black teeth, his eyes dark and empty, edging backwards, keeping the girl as a shield in front of him. Her face pleaded with the deputy, her small fingers scrabbling helplessly at the metal.

'Stay back,' Walton said, taking a step back and pulling the girl along with him.

'Let her go,' Sedgwick ordered. He had the sword in his right hand, the pistol extended in his left. The other servant was backed against the wall, screaming, but he hardly heard her. 'Let her go now.'

Walton took another pace backward, the girl's heels dragging. One shoe came off, standing alone and empty on the flagstone.

Breathing deeply, the deputy raised the pistol, aiming at the thief taker's head. Slowly, keeping his arm straight, he squeezed down on the trigger. The noise filled his brain as he fired.

Fifteen

'I'm sorry, boss.'

The deputy was sitting with his head in his hands, an empty mug of ale in front of him. Nottingham was in his chair, hands together under his chin. He'd been asleep at home, stretched out in his chair in just shirt and breeches, when one of the men had pounded on the door.

He'd dressed hastily and walked to the jail. Walton's body lay in the cold cell they used as a morgue, part of his skull gone, the ball buried behind empty eyes. The apothecary said the girl would live; the bullet had only grazed her head. He'd bound the wound and given her something to make her sleep before letting her go home with her friend. She'd been trembling, too fearful to speak, bursting into tears every time she tried to open her mouth.

'Just be glad she wasn't really hurt,' the Constable said. 'For the love of Christ, what were you doing, John?'

Sedgwick raised his eyes and shook his head.

'You weren't paying attention. You let him get away from you and a girl was almost killed.' He sighed and pushed the fringe off his forehead then poured himself some more ale. 'You know better than that.'

'I was thinking about this child snatcher and James.'

'I don't care that Walton's dead,' Nottingham continued, slamming his palm down on the desk in anger. 'I don't give a fuck about him, it's just sooner rather than later. But you took a risk with someone's life.'

'What else could I do, boss?' Sedgwick asked. He stood up and began to pace around the room. His long legs seemed constrained by the small space. He looked hard at the Constable. 'What?'

'You shouldn't have let it happen in the first place and you know it,' Nottingham answered coldly. Before the deputy could reply he held up his hand. 'I know. It did happen. But you should at least have waited until you could get a clearer shot at him or used your sword.'

'I was trying to fucking save her!' Sedgwick shouted. 'She was terrified. What should I have done?' He stormed out, letting the door slam behind him. The Constable started to rise from his chair and follow then sat back. Sedgwick needed some time. He knew full well what he should have done, that he should have been alert and watching the prisoner every second. It was one of the first things he taught all the men. He understood what the man was thinking, that he was blaming himself and his own stupidity, and feeling relief at not killing or badly injuring the girl. He knew the deputy had had no choice once Walton had taken the servant. Finally he stood and sighed loudly. It was time to go home. There was nothing more he could do here.

Sedgwick needed to be alone, to walk and calm himself before going back to the house on Lands Lane. James would be asleep, Isabell too, or fretting at her mother's breast. He knew Lizzie would still be awake, starting at every noise, waiting, worrying about him.

He strode up Briggate, past the patch of blood smeared over the flagstones where the thief taker had died, up to the Head Row, then out past Burley Bar and down the hill away from the city. There was a nip to the night air and he breathed deeply, taking in the scent of grass and animals.

But there was no silence out here, no peace in nature. Owls hooted and creatures scurried, branches creaked and leaves rustled. In the distance he could hear the bleat of sheep and the soft lowing of cattle from a barn up the hill.

He waited as the anger stopped throbbing in his head, standing still in the darkness, fists clenched and pushed deep in his coat pockets. He'd been wrong and he knew it; that was why it galled so deeply. He'd made the simplest of mistakes and then he'd panicked.

He wouldn't have blamed the boss if he'd let him go on the spot. He should never have done what he did, not with the girl in the way. But he'd been so scared that Walton might escape that he'd just pulled the trigger at the first opportunity.

He could feel himself beginning to shiver from what had

happened. He'd killed men before, when there'd been no other choice, and with Walton all he'd done was save the city the cost of a trial. Those other times, though, it had been him or them, with no one else in the way. He could have found another way with the thief taker if he'd only thought calmly. He pulled the coat more tightly around himself and saw the eyes of the serving girl pleading and praying as he aimed the pistol. He'd never forget that look, the terror as she stared helplessly at him.

He was no believer but he silently thanked God for saving her. Maybe he shouldn't be doing this work, he thought, not if he acted like that. Even Rob knew better. He could find something else to bring in a wage and support his family.

But even as everything cascaded through his mind, he knew it was just guilt and fury with himself. He loved being the deputy constable and hoped that some day he could replace the boss. Not if he was that stupid, though. He stood still until the shaking passed.

As soon as Walton fell he'd been on him, freeing the girl, pulling her away, watching in horror as the blood flowed from her scalp. Her friend was still screaming, the sound seeming to come from miles away. He'd pulled out his kerchief and dabbed at the wound, praying it was nothing. But the blood wouldn't stop.

He looked around, noticing the people stopped and staring, keeping their distance from death and danger.

'You,' he said, picking a man's face from the crowd. 'Go and fetch the apothecary.' When the man didn't move, he yelled, 'Now!'

The kerchief was soaked in moments. The girl was breathing, but her eyes were closed, her hands limp and chilled, all the colour gone from her face. He could feel prickles of cold sweat on his back as he knelt, the fear she might never wake.

He had no idea how much time passed before the apothecary arrived, a wheezing, fat old man carrying his medicines in a large bag. Only as he began to examine the girl did the deputy look at the thief taker. The ball had smashed a hole in his scalp, and flies already covered the edges of wound. Dead and no loss to the world.

He felt as if something was separating him from everyone else.

The people gathered around, almost thirty of them, rumbled with speculation on the servant girl, betting on whether she'd live or die, or casting glances at Walton, carefully making the sign of the evil eye after looking at the corpse. No one stared at him; it was as if he wasn't there.

Finally he tossed a beggar boy a coin and sent him for the coroner, watching as the boy limped away.

'Mr Sedgwick,' the apothecary called, rousing him from thoughts that travelled nowhere. 'She'll be fine.'

The girl had her eyes open, although she seemed to struggle to focus. The man had stopped the bleeding and wiped her face clean. He took her hand.

'I'm sorry,' he told her, not sure whether she even understood him. He looked up and saw her friend. 'I had to do it,' he explained, even though the words seemed weightless, vanishing in the air. 'I had to do it. Please, tell her that. There was nothing else I could do.'

Before the clock struck the hour it was all over. Willing hands lifted the girl and helped her home; she'd only be left with a scar and a memory of terror. Brogden the coroner pronounced the thief taker dead and Sedgwick sent one of the men for the Constable and then fetch an old door to carry the body to the jail.

He felt weary, his shoulders bowed as if the world had thrown its whole weight on to him. He slowly made his way home. A dead cat clogged the runnel in the middle of the street, water and piss puddling around it. He stepped over it and unlocked his door.

Lizzie sat slumped by the light of a candle stub, stirring as he walked in. Her face was in shadow, and as he moved closer he could see she'd been crying, the salt marks on her cheeks, her eyes brimming.

'John,' she said. Her voice was no more than a raw, husky whisper. 'They said someone was dead. I thought it was you.'

He pulled her tight to him, her tears falling freely as she sobbed. Tenderly, he wiped them away with his fingertips, kissing her forehead, her hair, her lips.

'I'm here,' he told her, his lips close to her ear. 'Everything's fine, love. Everything's fine now.'

She rested her head against his shoulder. Her fists grasped his coat tightly, the spasms slowly leaving her body. He could feel her warmth, her breath soft on his neck.

'Come on,' he said, 'let's go to bed.'

The Constable was late to the jail. The sun was full risen, carters arguing for right of way in the streets, servants out shopping or working in the heavy steam and harsh lather of the Monday wash. Lister sat at the desk writing his report and Sedgwick paced the room anxiously, pushing a hand through his wild hair.

Finally Nottingham arrived. His face was serious as he removed his coat and the tricorn hat and picked up the note addressed to him, then put it aside.

'I've been to see the girl and the mayor,' he said. 'She's well enough, she's recovering and making sense. Another day or two and she'll be back at work.' He glanced up to see the relief on the deputy's face. 'The mayor wasn't happy. It's bad for the city to have a man killed on Briggate.'

'I'm sorry, boss,' the deputy said. He shook his head shame-facedly. 'I just didn't know what else to do. He'd got the girl.'

'That's what I told his Worship. He accepted it, finally.'

'Thank you,' Sedgwick said. 'I know I was wrong yesterday, boss. I just wanted to say—'

The Constable held up his hand. 'It's done, John. But I'd go and see the lass, if I were you. She works for Alderman Wilkins.' He smiled as the deputy's face fell. 'Don't worry, the mayor will look after anything he might say.'

'Yes, boss.'

'Right. Anything on the child snatcher?' He looked between their faces as they shook their heads. 'Rob, I'm going to need you to work as much as you can for now. We need to find whoever's doing this before she can take someone else.'

'She?' Lister wondered in astonishment.

'Mark Morrison said it was a woman in a blue dress with dark hair who said she'd take him back to his mother when he was lost. She gave him something to drink. That was all he remembered.'

'So it's a woman behind it all?' Rob asked.

'It looks that way.'

'It could be a pair working together,' Sedgwick offered, and the Constable sighed deeply.

'That's possible,' he admitted.

'So where do we look?' the deputy said.

'Mark was found at the south end of the Bridge,' Nottingham answered slowly. 'There were plenty of us out on this side of the river. I've been wondering if he was kept over on the far side.'

'Enough folk over there,' Sedgwick observed.

'Then go out and ask them. See if anyone's just moved into the street, if there were any strange sounds on Saturday. You both know what to do. I'm going to keep looking for whoever killed Lucy Wendell. Now go on. And John,' he added, waiting until the men were at the door, 'try not to kill anyone today, please.' He winked as they left.

Once he was alone he broke open the seal on the letter. Inside it read simply, 'Good job. Buck.'

He walked through to the cold cell. Walton's body was still there, covered with an old, dirty sheet. There were stains by the head where blood and brains had leaked. Later today he'd be gone and buried in a pauper's grave outside Leeds. At least that problem had been resolved. And, as he'd told the mayor, the city had been spared the expense of the hangman's fee. For a few days the talk would be of the man shot on Briggate, but even more of how he'd tried to grab the girl. And the deputy would be able to go into any beer shop or inn and have drinks bought for him by men whose own courage would have failed them.

The Constable had hoped for the spectacle of a trial. He'd wanted to see the thief taker in the dock, confronted by his evidence and by testimony, all his pride stripped away. He'd thought that being from the capital would let him outwit the provincials. For once he'd looked forward to the obscure words of lawyers and judges. The verdict would have warned off others who thought Leeds an easy place.

In the end, though, there'd been justice. He hadn't managed that for harelip Lucy yet. The more time that passed, the less likelihood that people would remember her; he knew that all too well. If it dragged on much longer her killer might never be found, and he couldn't allow that to happen. The picture of her body, the small, charred mound of the foetus on her belly, was fixed clear in his mind. He'd never be able to put it aside. God alone knew that he'd seen plenty of brutality, men murdered, even the skin cut from their backs, but this horrified him even more. She'd done nothing, hurt no one.

With nowhere else to turn, he decided to talk to her mother again. There might be something, some small idea, some thread he could follow that would lead somewhere. First, though, he needed to make his own visit to the dead.

At the churchyard he realized he hadn't been to Rose's grave as often since the stone had been set in place. His heart was still full of her, he could hear the quiet sound of her laugh and see her smile, but the memories were growing gauzy and fainter as time passed. He knelt, placing his hands on the ground where grass had grown in full, deep green and breathed slowly, ashamed of himself for letting her go but knowing he could do nothing else.

He moved between the memorials, over to a space by the wall. A flat slab lay on the ground, placed there just a month or two before. It was simple, giving nothing away. Only the name Amos Worthy, and the years of his birth and death. Another connection to his own history severed by time. The man had been a criminal, a pimp, violent. But a long time before he'd also been the lover of Nottingham's mother, something the Constable had only discovered two years before. It had created an odd bond between the pair.

Finally he shook his head to rouse himself and walked down the Calls. The builders had almost finished work on the house where Lucy had died, a new front wall in place, the timbers light and clean, the limewash standing out in brilliant white. He could hear the workmen inside, laughing and joking. Soon someone else would live there, and in time none would remember the fire or Lucy's killing.

Alice Wendell answered the door as soon as he knocked, almost as if she'd been expecting him. The room was scrubbed spotless, each of the few pieces she owned precisely in its place. He knew it was her way of giving order to a world that had collapsed around her. And part of her nature. The air smelt of vinegar and her knuckles were red and raw from cleaning.

'Tha'd best come in,' she said and waited until he was in the only good chair by the window. The woman he'd met just a short time before seemed withered now. Her hair was grey, wiry, her cheeks sunken, the flesh of her face almost translucent, as if she was slowly fading from the world. On her arms the skin had become wrinkled and her dress seemed to hang even more loosely on her bony frame. 'Have you found him?'

'No,' he told her, 'and I don't know where else to look. I need your help.'

'What can I do?' she asked bitterly. 'Finding them's your job.'

'Sometimes we can't do our job by ourselves.' He gave her a gentle smile. 'Who did Lucy spend time with? What about her friends?'

She shook her head.

'There were only me and her brother. We were the only ones cared about her.'

'Are there other relatives?'

'Nay mister, I had two brothers but they both died when the children were just bairns.'

'No cousins or anyone Lucy might have known?'

Alice Wendell snorted. 'Oh aye, there's plenty of them all right, not as they'd have owt to do wi' her. Who wants to know a harelip?'

'What about friends?' the Constable wondered. 'Lucy must have had some friends.'

The woman stared at him, her eyes empty and hard.

'Their mams used to tell them to have nowt to do with her, that she were bad luck. You ever heard a girl crying because the others told her she had to go away before she brought curses on them?'

'No,' he admitted, but he understood how he'd have felt if it had happened to his daughters.

'There were a time it happened over and over, back when our Lucy were still young.' She rubbed briskly at her eyes. 'After that she just stopped trying. It were her and me and Peter.'

'What about your son's girl?' he asked. 'How was she with Lucy?'

'Have you seen her?'

Nottingham shook his head.

'She's no more than a twig, that lass.' Alice Wendell stopped, as if she wasn't sure whether she wanted to say more. Then she took a breath. 'I'll tell you, I know our Peter isn't a good man. He spends his money on drink or he's off in the Talbot putting money on the cock fighting. And when he's in his cups or he's lost his brass he takes it out on her.'

'That happens,' he said.

'Aye,' she agreed sadly. 'My man drank but he were never like that. Never raised a fist to me or my children. He knew I'd have killed him if he'd tried. But Peter, he doesn't care, and he's strong from working at the smithy. I've seen her all bruises and bleeding. He broke her arm once.'

The Constable waited.

'But he loved his sister. He protected her. He'd never have done owt like that with her.' He lifted her eyes to meet his. 'Or wi' me, in case you thought. He stayed in line around me.'

'So who could Lucy have turned to?'

'Do you think I've not spent all my nights thinking about that?' she asked him, her voice desperate. 'Do you think I've not asked God why she couldn't come here and feel safe?'

'She said she couldn't come because *he* might find her,' Nottingham said. 'Do you have any idea at all who she meant?'

Very slowly she shook her head. 'Nay,' she answered. 'There's no one.'

'And you don't know who got her with child?'

'No,' she answered firmly. 'Unless it were one of them Cates.'

'I don't believe it was. I mean that,' he insisted. 'We've talked to them.'

'Only because Lucy looked like that.'

He said nothing, knowing she was right.

'Until we can discover more, we're stuck,' he explained. 'I told you, we traced Lucy for part of the time after she left Cates's, but then there's nothing. You see why I need your help.'

'I don't know more than I've told you.' She paused. 'And what now? Do you stop looking?'

'No. I'll keep on,' he promised her, standing up. 'If I can, I'll find whoever did this and make sure he hangs.'

He was at the door when she spoke again.

'If I had money and lived in one of them big houses do you think all this would have happened?'

'I don't know,' he answered her.

'Then tha' dun't know much, dost tha'?'

She was right, the Constable thought as he walked back along the Calls. Money could keep life's evils at bay. With money Lucy would never have gone for a servant. She'd have had nurses and folk would have liked her in spite of her disfigurement. Poor was a hard trick of fate.

He'd have to talk to Peter Wendell's girl; the deputy had said she might know more than she'd said. It would be better if he went himself this time. If Sedgwick hadn't managed to draw the truth out of her, the weight of authority might make a difference.

He walked up Briggate towards Queen Charlotte's Court. He passed the Shambles with the bloody carcasses and cows and sheep on display in the butchers' shops, the stink of the offal and dead meat filling his nostrils.

In the court he picked his way beyond piles of rubbish, slowly rotting down and foul, and climbed the stairs to the room. He tested each step before placing his weight on it.

He had to knock twice before she answered, opening just wide enough to see who was there.

'You're Anne, aren't you?' he asked with a smile. Her face was thin and wary, eyes moving around as if she was hunted.

'Who are you?'

'I'm Richard Nottingham,' he told her. 'I'm the Constable of Leeds. Can I come in?'

The sheets had been quickly thrown over the pallet in the corner. The plates were dirty, flies hovering around them and crawling on the waste. She hadn't emptied the night soil and the smell from the bucket brought bile into his throat.

The girl clutched a shawl around her thin shoulders but it couldn't hide the bruises on her skin. They coloured her arms, some fresh, others fading into shades of blue and green and yellow. One eye was blacked, and when she opened her mouth he saw her two front teeth were missing.

'Do you know why I'm here?'

'It'll be about Lucy,' she answered, and he could hear the resentment in her voice.

'Yes, it is,' he said calmly. 'When my deputy was here, he

thought you perhaps didn't tell him everything. I'm trying to find out who killed her so I need to know it all now.' He kept his voice gentle and friendly, but glanced at her so she'd understand his meaning. Nottingham watched her, leaving her to say the next word or endure the silence.

'I never liked her,' Anne told him finally. There was curdling spite in her voice. 'She didn't look right. Made me shudder every time I saw her.'

He didn't need to ask what repulsed her.

'How often did you see her?'

'He'd make me go over to his mam with him whenever Lucy had a day off from that big house.'

'They were a close family,' the Constable said.

'Oh aye,' she agreed with a sneer. 'He doted on her. Couldn't do enough for her. And if I said owt he'd hit me. Wouldn't hear a word against his precious Lucy.'

'What about their mother?'

'She liked them all together. No one else wanted Lucy, did they? So the family was all they'd got. Not a surprise, the lass was so stupid.'

'Are you glad she's dead?'

The girl stroked the bruises on her arms. 'Does it look like I should be?' she wondered. 'All he does these days is drink and use his fists. Never really says owt.'

'Did you kill Lucy?'

'Me?' She began to laugh. 'If I was going to kill anyone I'd start wi' him, mister, for all he's done to me. I didn't like her but I'd not have hurt her myself.'

'If you hate Peter, why do you stay with him?'

She looked hard into the Constable's eyes. 'And where would I go? You tell me that. I don't have a mam and dad to run to. I don't have anything.' She waved a hand round the room. 'You see what's here, all the things he hasn't sold yet? They're his. I got nothing, mister. Any time I have a coin it's because he gives it me to buy food. So you tell me what I'd do if I left him, or where I'd go.' She paused to draw breath. He could see the fear in her eyes. 'I'll tell you summat else for nowt, an' all. He'd find me if he wanted to. He's told me often enough what he'd do.'

'What's that?'

'He'd kill me.'

'Do you believe him?'

Her voice was as steady as her gaze when she answered. 'You've not seen him when he's been drinking. Of course I bloody do.'

'When did he last see his sister?'

She shook her head and snorted. 'You think he tells me where he goes?'

The Constable paused, then said, 'When do you know he saw her?'

'When she had a day off. He went over to see her and his mam.'

'I thought you said he always took you. Where were you?'

'He'd done me so bad the night before that I had to stay here.' She nodded over at the bed. 'In there.'

'How was he after he learned she was dead?'

Anne shrugged, a small gesture that expressed nothing. Her fingers moved over the fabric of her dress, finding a stray hair and winding it tight around her finger.

'Was he worse?' the Constable asked. 'Better? What did he do?'

'He was just him,' she replied. 'Quieter, mebbe, I don't know.'

'He hasn't said anything?'

'To me?' She shook her head again. 'He doesn't talk to me, never has. Got his friends for that. I'll tell you summat, though, he's not been over to his mam's as much.'

'Why?'

'No Lucy, is there? And his mam just nags him about his drinking.'

'Is he at work today?'

'Aye, putting in his labour for the money he'll spend on drink later.' She sighed.

He stood slowly. 'Thank you,' he told her.

'If you talk to him, you won't say owt, will you? About . . .'

'Not a word,' he promised.

Could Peter Wendell have killed his sister, Nottingham wondered as he returned to the jail? It seemed unlikely, if he cared for her as much as Anne claimed, but certainly not impossible. He could be a man with a twisted sense of family honour, who decided her pregnancy had brought shame on the family.

But that didn't answer where she'd been for two weeks before the fire. Still, there were enough questions to warrant talking to the man.

'Where do we start?' Lister asked Sedgwick as they crossed the bridge. The river was flowing fast and free from rain up in the Pennines. Barges creaked where they were moored, and wood rubbed against stone as the water lapped on jetties and along the bank.

'Same as we always do. We just ask. Find out if anyone saw a woman with a lad that wasn't hers, if anyone new has moved in.'

'But where?'

The deputy pointed at the large new houses along Meadow Lane, where merchants had moved away from the city for cleaner air and more land to display their wealth.

'We can forget those. If anyone from them had been doing it the servants would have seen something.'

They walked into the poorer streets, courts where colour and light and hope seemed to have been leached from the air.

'We'll do it like we did on the Calls,' Sedgwick announced. 'You take one side, I'll take the other. And when we've finished here we'll move on to the next road.'

'Do you think it'll work?' Rob asked in an unsure voice.

'No idea, lad. But for now it's all we've got, isn't it?'

By afternoon they'd only covered five streets, repeating the same questions over and over. The dust had settled in their throats, their voices were strained, the answers they heard all too similar. No one had seen a woman with a child that wasn't hers. New people came and left all the time. The old women kept an eye on things and knew who was who and where they lived, but none of their hints or gossip had come to anything.

'I need to go,' Rob said finally. 'We're doing no good here and I'm working tonight.'

'Going to see that lass of yours first?' the deputy asked with a grin.

'I am, but . . .'

Sedgwick raised his eyebrows. 'Like that, is it?'

Lister shook his head. 'I told her that my father didn't want me to marry her.'

'You shouldn't be so daft as to think on marrying yet.' The deputy glanced around. 'Come on, there's a beer shop over there. Let's get something down our throats before we die of thirst. You've got time for a drink.'

Rob knew better than to refuse. And he was parched, it was true; some ale would go down well.

The place was almost empty, save for two old men in the corner, eking out their days over mugs of beer. They glanced up briefly at the newcomers then returned their stares to the bench.

Sedgwick banged on the trestle to bring the owner out of the back room, a small man with a face set in a sneer.

'What's the best you have here?'

'That,' the man answered without hesitation, pointing at a barrel. 'Fresh brewed, that is. Just ready to drink.'

'Two, then.'

At the table they drank deep, letting the ale wash away the grime and the words of the day. The deputy wiped his mouth with his sleeve.

'By Christ, I needed that. It's thirsty work, this.' He looked at Lister and shook his head. 'You're not really thinking of marrying the boss's daughter, are you?'

'I don't know.' Rob took another drink and sighed with frustration. 'I just told her what my father said and she thought it meant I didn't love her.'

'Why doesn't he want you marrying Emily? She's a grand lass.'

'He says she's not good enough.'

'What?' Sedgwick put the mug down hard. 'The Constable's daughter isn't good enough? Where does he get ideas like that?'

'He thinks I should marry someone with position and money.'

The deputy laughed. 'Aye, if she'd have you.'

'I don't want anyone else.'

'Have you told him that? Have you told Emily that?'

'I've told her.' Rob took another drink. 'She says she doesn't want someone she can't trust. She thinks I might give in to my father . . .'

'Well, you can't blame her there,' Sedgwick told him. 'But keep trying. Give her some time. She'll come around, they all do once they know you mean it.'

'I hope you're right.' He pushed a hand through his red hair. 'I don't want to lose her, John.'

'She's got her head on right, that one. She won't let you go, not if she cares about you. Have you told the boss what your father said?'

'Yes.'

Sedgwick let out a low whistle. 'What did he do?'

'Nothing. Just nodded, the way he does.'

'Aye, I know, and you wonder what he's thinking. What'll your father do if you don't go along with his idea?'

'I don't know,' Rob answered bleakly.

'Do you want some advice?' the deputy asked, his voice serious.

'I'll take anything that might help.'

'If you love that girl, you make sure she doesn't get away from you. If that happens you'll spend the rest of your life regretting it.'

Lister nodded absently and let the silence drift before saying, 'What did you think yesterday? When it happened?'

The deputy pushed the mug around the table.

'I wasn't thinking,' he answered eventually. 'That was the problem. Don't ever do what I did. I got scared and I reacted. I'm just grateful the girl wasn't badly hurt.'

'What did you do? After, I mean.'

'I looked to her first. The blood wouldn't stop coming out of her head. I thought I'd killed her.'

'What about Walton?'

'Who cares about him? He'll be forgotten tomorrow.' Sedgwick paused. 'I'm just lucky the boss stood up for me and didn't decide to get rid of me. He came as close to losing his temper with me as I've ever seen.'

'Mr Nottingham?' Rob asked disbelievingly.

'Aye, and you know what, that hurt as much as anything. I let him down by being so bloody stupid.' He took a drink. 'Go on, you'd better go and persuade that lass there's some good in you. You'll have an uphill task, mind.'

Sixteen

The deputy took time over the rest of his drink. He kept seeing the girl's face as Walton put the chain around her neck. The image had knitted itself deep into his sleep, waking him constantly during the night, the sweat chilled on his forehead, his muscles tight and aching, his breathing quick and shallow. When Isabell began to cry he lifted her from the cradle, taking comfort from the warmth of her small body and the joy of him in her eyes. He soaked a rag in sugar water and let her suckle on it until she slept again. He could hear James's breathing on the pallet in the corner and just make out Lizzie's shape, her hair all a-tangle on the pillow. He'd tried to sleep but the events of the day ran over and over in his head and kept rest away.

He made his way back to the bridge, dodging between women carrying their purchases home and the piles of horse manure in the road. In the distance he could hear the raw, strained sound of a violin playing a tune that had been changed by experience, scarred, full of weariness and the sadness of life. Its edges had been filed down, all the excess rubbed away until only the essence remained. Then he saw the blind fiddler by the old chantry chapel, working the strings of his instrument with a bow whose best years had passed decades before. He reached into his pocket for a coin and tossed it into the ancient hat that sat on the ground.

'Thank you, Mr Sedgwick.'

The deputy stopped. 'I thought you were blind, Con,' he said.

'That I am, Mr Sedgwick,' the fiddler answered with a grin that showed a mouth empty of teeth. 'You know that.'

'How did you know it was me?'

'Your footsteps. People walk in different ways, it's like a signature, like seeing them. Now you're a man with a long stride, and you bring your heel down hard. No one else does it quite the same way.' There was still a faint whisper of Ireland in his voice, a musical lilt that the deputy liked.

'Can you tell many people that way?'

'Some,' Con admitted. 'And I can tell plenty of things about people from hearing them move. And half of them seem to think that because I don't have my sight I must be deaf and dumb, too.' He laughed, a wheezing cackle in his chest. 'They say all sorts in front of me.' He lifted the instrument and played a fast jig for a minute, smiling at the jingle of coins in the hat as a man passed.

'You heard about that boy who disappeared on Saturday?' Sedgwick asked.

Con chuckled. 'Show me someone in Leeds who didn't hear about it. Bad business, though. Very bad.'

'If you hear anyone talking, let me know.'

'And what might they be saying, Mr Sedgwick?' the fiddler asked shrewdly, turning his empty eyes to the deputy.

'You'll know if you hear it, Con. There'd be some money in it, too.'

The man nodded. 'I'll keep my ears open, then. A few more pennies never go amiss, now do they?'

'Might be a bit more than that.'

'Might it now?' he said thoughtfully. 'That's interesting.'

'Just remember, if you hear anything, tell me.'

'I'll do that, Mr Sedgwick. And say hello to that lad of yours. He always has a kind word. You've got a good boy there.'

The deputy smiled. 'I'll do that, Con.'

He made his rounds, circling the city to see all was well, and finished at the jail. The Constable was there, laboriously writing a letter.

'Anything?' he asked.

'No,' Sedgwick answered with a long shake of his head. 'You didn't expect much, did you, boss?'

Nottingham put down the quill and the knife he used to keep it sharp.

'I'm always hopeful, John. Ask enough questions and eventually you'll get some answers.'

'Aye, but we need them fast before that bitch does it again.'

'I know that well enough,' the Constable said seriously. 'I'll go out myself tomorrow. I want you to talk to Peter Wendell.'

'You talked to his girl?'

'I did. He treats her badly.'

'We'd seen that. Did she give you anything?'

'Not really. But I think it wouldn't hurt to have another word with him. He might well know something.'

'I'll go and see him in the morning.'

Nottingham nodded. 'You go home,' he said. 'And try to forget what happened on Sunday. The girl will be fine and Walton's no loss.'

'Yes, boss.' Sedgwick gave a small, weak smile.

'I mean it. Give it a few days and folk won't even remember it.'

Rob watched the girls file out from the school then run off in a swarm down the street, laughing and grabbing at their freedom. A few more minutes and Emily would come out of the building and look around the way she always did. He brushed dust off his coat and breeches with his palm, tightened his stock and licked his fingers to try to tame his hair.

Then he leaned against the stone wall and waited. The sun was trying to push through high white clouds and the air was spring warm, full of promise, but all he could feel was the heady anticipation of seeing her. He ached to talk to her, to make what suddenly seem fragile solid again. He straightened as she approached, warmed by the way her pace quickened as she saw him and the smile on her face.

'I thought I'd come and walk you home.'

'Good,' she said happily. 'I'm glad you're here.' She slipped her hand into his and he held it lightly as they set off down the road. 'I've hardly been able to work today,' she told him.

'Why?'

'I kept worrying that perhaps you wanted to break from me.'

'Me? I've told you, I'm not going to do that,' he insisted.

'I know, but those are words.' She paused and blushed slightly. 'I'm sorry, that was wrong. I just couldn't concentrate. Mrs Rains wondered if I was ill.'

'I won't let my father bully me,' he promised.

'You haven't had to make that choice yet,' she pointed out.

'I've already made it up here,' Rob answered and tapped his skull.

'But are you sure?' she asked seriously.

'Of course I am.'

'A girl with money and position . . . it's what most men would want.'

'I want you.'

'I'm glad you do.' She squeezed his fingers.

'You're everything I need.'

She smiled again, glanced around to be certain no one was watching and kissed him softly on the lips.

'Just as I am?' she asked.

'Exactly as you are.'

She stayed quiet as they turned on to Kirkgate. His eyes moved to the jail, the office empty. He felt content, as if they'd manage to settle everything with just a few words.

'I love you,' he said as they approached Timble Bridge.

'I love you, too,' she replied. 'But what do you want us to do?'

'What do you mean?' Her question confused him.

She leaned on the parapet and looked down at the water.

'What do you expect?' she wondered. 'Marriage and children?'

'I suppose so, in time,' he told her warily. 'That's what men and women do. They marry.'

'Not all of them, Rob.'

'What do you mean?' He could feel fear rising in his stomach.

'Not everyone marries. Life isn't always as simple as that.' She turned, her eyes staring at his. 'Are you happy with me?'

'Of course I am. I said I love you.'

'They're not the same things,' she said with a small shake of her head.

'Then I love you and I'm happy with you,' he corrected himself.

'Good.' She kissed him again, moving closer, her lips lingering against his. 'Do you think everything is fine as it is, the way we meet like this, the courting?'

'Yes,' he grinned, tightening his grip around her waist. 'I think it's close to perfect.'

'What would you say if I told you I'd never marry you?' Her voice was quiet and wary.

'What? What do you mean?' He pulled back to watch her face, to see if this was a strange joke she was playing.

'You know what marriage means,' she told him. 'You'd own everything I have. And you'd own me.'

He opened his mouth to speak but she placed a finger over it to quiet him.

'Please, Rob, hear me out. I've been thinking about this, it's important to me. I can't ever let anyone own me like that. I'm not a chattel or goods. However much I care about you, no matter how much I love you, I'll never be your wife. Or anyone's wife. But I don't want to lose, you, either.' She gave a small, wan smile. 'So if it's a wife you really want, maybe you should do what your father asks.' She began to walk away across the bridge.

Rob took a deep breath.

'Don't go,' he said, and she turned to wait for him. Her words had been a shock, a blow to his belly. What she said went against everything he'd known, strained against all his upbringing. But he knew he'd rather have her on any terms than not at all.

'We don't have to marry. We can stay as we are.'

Her face glowed and she put her arms around him.

'You know, Papa will say I'm a foolish girl,' she said. 'He won't understand why I don't want to marry anyone. Mama will weigh it carefully in her mind. But in time they'll understand it's me, it's always been me.' Emily looked at him. 'What will your father say?'

'I don't care,' he told her, and realized he meant it.

They stopped outside the house on Marsh Lane and she gave him another long kiss. 'I'd best go inside,' she said. 'Mama will be waiting for me. Can you meet me in the morning?'

'Yes,' he agreed and watched as she walked away with small backward glances and smiles.

The evening was gathering as the Constable walked home, his footsteps raising dust in the dirt along Marsh Lane. Glancing ahead he could see a light in the window of the parlour and another from Emily's bedroom upstairs.

The glow of the tallow candle gave enough light for Mary to read, the greasy scent filling the room. He hung his coat on the nail by the door then bent to kiss her.

'You look tired,' she said tenderly.

'I feel like I'm a hundred.' In the kitchen he poured ale and scraped the remains from a pan of pottage for his supper. 'Some days I feel like I've been walking for miles and never arrived anywhere,' he said as he sat down with a sigh. He inclined his head upwards. 'How is she?'

'Much better today.' Mary put down the book. 'They must have talked after school, she came home happy and smiling. All's right with the world again.'

'For now, anyway,' he allowed darkly. 'I hope this doesn't mean they're getting married.'

Mary laughed. 'I think we're safe from that yet, Richard. She does have some sense, you know.'

'Sense leaves by the window when it comes to love,' he told her. 'You know that as well as I do.'

'If it had been a wedding she wouldn't have stopped talking,' Mary pointed out.

'Maybe,' he grunted and finished the drink. 'I need my bed. A week's sleep would be just about right.'

'And you'll still be up before the birds and off to work. I've known you too long, you can't change now.'

'True enough,' he admitted ruefully. 'Sometimes I wish I could.' He held out his hand. 'Coming with me?'

The morning was breezy, with clouds the dull colour of old lead scudding across the sky. Lister struggled to stay awake, Sedgwick tried to rub the sleep from his eyes as the Constable finished summing up.

'There's a market today,' he said. 'I'll take Holden with me and watch for women with dark hair and blue gowns. She might come back and try it again, there are always plenty of children.'

'What do you want me to do?' Sedgwick asked.

'Back over the river, John. After we go and talk to Peter Wendell. Since he seems to like using his fists, it might be better if there's two of us. And you,' he said to Rob, 'go on home and sleep so you're fit for tonight.'

'In a minute, boss.'

Nottingham grinned at the deputy. 'He must be back under Emily's thumb.'

'Young love, eh?' the deputy said with a broad wink to Lister.

'She'll be along soon enough,' the Constable said, 'but you see you rest today.'

★   ★   ★

The weavers were putting up their trestles and laying out cloth for the market as the Constable and Sedgwick strode down Briggate. The inns were busy with men eating their Brigg End shot breakfasts, plenty of beef and ale to fill their bellies for a couple of pennies.

Carters filled the road, delivering their goods, eager to leave before the market bell closed the street. The first merchants were out, walking around and smiling in anticipation of the profits they'd make.

Nottingham and the deputy turned on to Swinegate, the shops just opening as shutters were lifted. They moved to the side as a woman opened a window on a top floor and threw out the night's piss to splash in the middle of the street.

The smithy's forge lay at the back of a cobbled yard, the doors wide open, heat already roaring from the fire. The blacksmith was busy working horseshoes on the anvil, bringing his hammer down expertly on the red hot metal in a fast, ringing rhythm to shape it.

Wendell was feeding coal into the blaze, stripped to breeches and hose. His chest and thick arms were already shining with sweat and he wore a rag tied around his head to keep the moisture from his eyes.

'That's him?' the Constable asked and Sedgwick nodded. 'Let's get him out where we can talk to him properly.'

They entered the yard. The smith glanced up briefly, never breaking the stroke as he pounded against the anvil. Wendell stopped work, watching carefully as they came closer and picking up a hammer.

'Mr Wendell,' the Constable said, raising his voice above the noise, 'can you spare us a moment?'

Peter Wendell took a kerchief from the pocket of his breeches and wiped at his face.

'This about Lucy?' he asked.

'It is.'

'You found who killed her yet?' His tone was belligerent, anger boiling beneath the surface.

'Not yet,' Sedgwick told him. 'You told me you were going to look.'

Wendell shrugged his shoulders. 'And I've not found anyone. It's your job, anyway. Why are you coming to me at my work?'

'I'm just wondering if you know anything more that can help us,' Nottingham said genially.

'Me? No.'

'Are you sure, Peter?'

'Of course I'm bloody sure. What are you saying? You think I killed my sister?'

'Nothing like that,' the Constable replied. 'Why? Did you?'

Without warning, Wendell turned and drove his large fist hard into the deputy's belly, sending him to the floor, gasping for breath. Then he began to run.

Nottingham was in front of him, standing firm with his legs apart. Wendell swung the hammer hard. The Constable moved aside, but it still caught him on the thigh, tumbling him as he grunted, the pain sharp as a knife. He could only watch as Wendell dropped the hammer and ran off along the street.

Slowly he raised himself, barely able to hobble, and went to help the deputy. Sedgwick was on his knees, hands clutching at his stomach, still struggling to draw a breath. The Constable rolled him on to his back and pulled him by the belt, forcing the breath into him.

'Take your time, John, we won't catch him right now.'

He worked his leg slowly, feeling along the bone, but it was intact. He gestured for the smith to come over. 'Has Peter been acting differently lately?' he asked.

The smith looked at them emptily, running a large, scarred hand over his beard.

'Different how?' he asked.

'Quieter, maybe, more secretive.'

The smith shrugged. 'Long as he does his work I don't give a bugger whether he talks all day or says nowt. So what's he done to make him go for you like that? Why's he run off?'

'I'm not sure,' Nottingham told him, then helped the deputy to his feet. 'If he comes back, send someone for us.'

The smith gazed at the gate. 'Someone runs like that, he won't be back.' He shook his head. 'I'll need a new lad now.'

'Maybe you can find a more reliable one,' the Constable said.

They walked slowly back to the jail, Sedgwick still rubbing his belly and the Constable feeling the sharp ache where Wendell had hit against his leg.

'Christ, the bastard packs a good punch,' the deputy gasped finally, unable to keep a hint of admiration from his voice. 'I'll be feeling that for days.'

'I think we just found our killer,' Nottingham said thoughtfully. 'I can't see any other reason he'd run when I asked him that.'

'He doesn't like the law. He already told me that.'

The Constable shook his head. 'This was more than dislike. I was watching his eyes. When I asked if he'd killed her I could see the guilt in them. He did it.'

'How did you know?'

'I didn't,' Nottingham admitted. 'The words just came into my head. I didn't really believe it was him.'

'But why would he murder his own flesh and blood and then set her on fire?' Sedgwick wondered. It was beyond understanding, the work of someone who'd forsaken his soul.

'I've no idea, but I'm going to find out once we catch him.' The Constable's voice was dark and urgent. 'Take two of the men and go up to his room. I doubt he'll be there, but you'd better check. If you find him, use your cudgels.'

'Yes, boss.'

'Talk to that girl of his and find out who his friends are and where he'd be likely to go.'

'What about the child snatcher?' the deputy asked.

'I'll watch for her at the market. I'll have Holden with me. First, though, I'm going to see Peter's mother.'

He strode briskly over to the Calls, rapping on the door of the cellar room. He could hear the woman moving inside and the tap of her soles on the floor.

'You've found summat?' she asked. Her face had grown even more pinched. Her hose lay on the table with a needle and thread where she'd been darning under the thin light from the window.

'I have,' he told her. 'I went to see your son this morning.'

'Did he know something?' she asked with a catch in her voice. 'He's said nothing to me.'

'We wanted to talk to him about Lucy. But when I asked if he'd killed her he punched my deputy and ran off before we could stop him.'

Alice Wendell looked him in the eye. 'What's tha' saying?'

'That he's guilty, Mrs Wendell.'

'Could be summat and nowt,' she tried to tell him, but the fingers bunching her apron showed she realized the truth.

'Maybe. But you don't believe that, do you?' he asked gently.

'You really think he killed her? That he murdered my Lucy?'

'Yes,' he said. 'I do. I'm sorry.'

There were tears clouding her eyes as she spoke. 'I know my Peter's never been good, but he loved her well enough. He looked after her, he protected her.'

'What would he have thought about her having someone's baby?' he asked gently.

'He'd have killed whoever did it,' she answered simply. 'There's a bad streak in him.'

'Maybe he killed her instead.'

She shook her head again, more firmly this time. 'Nay,' she said, and raised her head, her words full of despair. 'I'll not believe my son would do that to his own blood.'

'If he comes here, bring him to me.'

'So you can hang him.'

'All I want is the truth,' he told her. 'If it turns out he didn't do it, if he had a good reason to run like that, I'll let him go. But I'm going to find whoever murdered Lucy.'

She took several breaths before nodding. She was still standing in the same place, fingers pressing down on the wood of the table, as he left.

'Keep your eyes open for women in blue dresses with dark hair,' the Constable instructed Holden. The cloth market had ended and traders were setting up their stalls at the top end of Briggate.

'Blue?'

'If you see someone like that, watch them carefully.'

'There could be dozens of dark-haired women dressed in blue, boss,' Holden complained.

'I know,' Nottingham agreed. Already people were drawn to the trestles, talking, gossiping, hunting through piles and clutter for the early bargains.

'So why are we looking?' Holden asked. 'And what are we looking for?'

The Constable stared at him. 'You'd better keep this to yourself. And that means not telling it later when you've had a drink. The chandler's boy was snatched by a woman in blue. You see anyone in blue reach for a child, follow them. You understand?'

'Aye.'

'I'll be looking, too. Move about and keep your wits clear.'

'Yes, boss.'

Nottingham wandered around the market, idly inspecting items, his eyes alert. The crowd had grown thicker, thronging the street, filling the air with a din of noise. He stayed around the fringes, picking out the women dressed in blue. Some wore dresses so ragged and pale the colour could have been pulled from the dawn sky, others had rich, deep velvet and every shade in between. They were old and young, thin and rounded.

He tried to spot Holden but the man was good, staying hidden from sight. Women were holding their children close, keeping tight grips on hands and wrists, giving quick smacks if the little ones tried to squirm away. But he knew it only took a moment for an infant to be gone.

After an hour he spotted a face that seemed familiar. She was in blue, a gown whose best days were long past, ill-fitting on the bosom. He tried to place the girl, but her name danced just beyond the edge of memory. He watched her drift between people, scarcely paying attention to the displays and patter around her. He'd seen her before and talked to her, he knew that, but try as he might he couldn't place her.

The Constable kept his distance, careful not to be seen, staying behind her. Whatever her reason for being at the market, it wasn't to buy anything. She moved around slowly for half an hour by the church bell, without pattern or purpose. Then she walked away, taking slow, idle steps back down Briggate.

He found Holden in the shadow of the Moot Hall.

'You saw the girl in blue who left the market a minute ago?'

'The young one going down the street?'

'That's her. Follow her,' Nottingham ordered. The man looked at him questioningly.

'Has she done summat wrong?'

The Constable shook his head. 'Find out where she lives. And make sure she doesn't see you.'

Holden grinned. 'The lass'll never know there was anyone behind her, boss.'

He slipped away, agile and anonymous and Nottingham made his way back to the jail. He'd just bought a slice of pie, the crust warm and crumbling between his fingers when he remembered the girl's name.

It was Fanny. And the last time he'd seen her, she'd been working down by Leeds Bridge with her sister, the pair of them run by their brother, Joshua Davidson. He'd ordered them all out of Leeds days before. So what was she doing here?

He waited anxiously for Sedgwick to return. He knew Wendell would be difficult to find; the man had lived his whole life in Leeds and he'd have friends to offer him comfort or shelter.

But the Constable knew the city, too. Sometimes he believed he could feel its pulse in his blood. He loved it, he held it close to his heart. He knew where to hide, where to find food; long ago Leeds had seemed like both mother and father to him. Wendell might run, but in this place Nottingham would find him. He'd make Wendell think that the city had turned into a false friend, an enemy. He'd hunt him.

'We missed him by five minutes,' the deputy said when he arrived. He poured himself ale and sat down. 'He took some clothes and all the money she had.'

'We'll catch him,' the Constable said with certainty.

'I left someone to watch the place but I doubt he'll be back.' He took a long drink. 'I think that girl of his is glad in a way. I think she was surprised by him, though.'

'Did she tell you where he might be?'

'I don't think she really knows his friends. But he spends most of his time and money at the Talbot.'

Nottingham raised his eyebrows.

'Have you been there yet?'

'I thought we should both go.'

He nodded. The law wasn't popular there, and looking for a favoured regular could mean trouble. But even so they'd think twice before attacking the Constable. He took a cudgel from the drawer and looped the thong around his wrist.

'Better to be safe,' he said.

As they moved down Briggate Nottingham asked, 'Did you check that Davidson and his girl had gone?'

'Yes, boss. The house was empty. Why?'

'I saw one of the girls at the market. Holden's following her. She was wearing a blue dress.'

Only the afternoon drinkers were scattered around the Talbot when they entered. The door to the back room, with its pit for cock and dog fighting, was firmly closed and locked. Bell the landlord stood behind the trestle, his arms folded, a forbidding expression on his face.

Nottingham walked up to him, just the wood between them.

'Peter Wendell,' he said. The landlord said nothing. 'You know him?'

The man gave a brief nod.

'When was he here last?'

'What business is it of yours?' He curled his heavy, scarred knuckles into fists.

'I'm looking for him. That makes it my business.' He slapped the cudgel down so it barely missed the other man's hands. 'I remember you told me you thought his sister was hard done by.'

'Aye,' Bell acknowledged.

'We went to talk to Peter about her death and he ran. You make of that what you will. I think you understand what I'm saying.' He paused to give the man time to consider his words. 'Now, when was he here last, Mr Bell?'

'Last night,' he said grudgingly. 'We had a cock fight, he's always here for those.'

'How much did he lose?'

Bell shrugged.

'I want to know who he drinks with.'

'Whoever's here,' the man answered. 'He's in most nights, people know him.'

'Names,' the Constable ordered.

'Daniel Scott, Luke Andrews, Solomon Smith.'

It was a litany of petty criminals, men often arrested for violence and drunkenness. Nottingham looked at the deputy.

'If he comes in here, send someone to the jail,' he ordered Bell. 'You want whoever killed Lucy found, don't you?'

The landlord nodded.

'Then do your duty for once.'

Outside, he put the cudgel in the deep pocket of his coat.

'Go and see those three, John. Take some men with you, just

in case. Tell them why we're looking for Wendell. The word will spread. If people believe he killed his sister, they'll shun him.'

'Yes, boss.'

'We'll find him soon. He'll be scared now. Let's make him terrified. I want every single door closed to him,' he said.

By the time he reached the jail he felt a grim satisfaction. It was only a matter of time until they'd have Wendell. He wasn't smart; he was a man who thought with his fists, not his brain.

Holden was waiting by the door, a deep frown on his face. As the Constable approached he stood straight and rubbed a hand across the bristles of his beard.

'Where did she go?'

'I lost her,' he admitted bashfully. 'She must have seen me.'

'Where?' Nottingham asked.

'She went up Lands Lane. I gave her a few moments and then I turned the corner. She was gone.'

The Constable kept his face impassive and his voice carefully even.

'Did you look for her?'

'Yes, boss.' Holden looked at the ground. 'I don't know where she could have gone, honest. You know me, I'm good at this, but I couldn't find her.'

Nottingham nodded. 'Go and see Mr Sedgwick. He needs some men to help him.'

Alone, he brooded. There could be a reasonable explanation for the girl vanishing. She might have a room on Lands Lane. She might have seen him at the market or spotted Holden behind her. But in a blue dress, acting the way she was, she could be the woman snatching children. They needed to find her.

Five minutes later he was still wondering where they could look when the door opened.

'Mr Nottingham,' the woman said, 'where's my John?'

Lizzie was wearing an old dress, its deep red faded to pink. Her hair was neatly tucked under a cap. She was holding Isabell close to her, the baby swaddled tight. But her face was filled with desperation, her mouth tight, her eyes frantic.

'What's wrong?' he asked. 'Is it James?'

'I can't find him.'

Seventeen

'Sit down,' he told her, and poured her a mug of ale. 'Now, what's happened?'

'The lad's not been the same since this one was born, Mr Nottingham.' She held the girl close and drank in timid little gulps, not looking at him. 'Says I'm not his mam, half the time he says he hates us, all sorts of things.'

The Constable rested against the edge of the desk. He pushed the blanket back from the baby's head and stroked the black down of her hair as she slept.

'Has he run off before?'

She nodded. 'Often enough lately. He'll stay out and go where we've told him he can't, things like that. He'll be starting at the charity school soon enough. We just hope that's going to help.' He could see her fingers pressing again the clay of the mug, hands shaking slightly. 'But with . . . you know, we've told him to stay at home.'

'When did you notice he was gone, Lizzie?'

'About an hour ago.' She reached up and wiped away a tear. 'I'd just fed this one and put her down to sleep, then I went to play with him, but he was gone.' She breathed slowly. 'I've looked all over for him but I can't find him. I'm scared. That's why I came down to find John, Mr Nottingham. He told me about the child snatcher. If anything happens to James he'll never forgive me.'

'Did you have words with James this morning?'

'He wanted to go out and I said no. I told him there were bad people out there and he had to stay inside today. He started shouting so I gave him a smack and told him to go upstairs.' She began to cry again. 'He must have gone out when I was busy with Isabell.'

The Constable took her hand and squeezed it reassuringly.

'You live on Lands Lane, don't you?'

'Yes.'

'I'll have someone find John for you,' he assured her, 'and I'll send a couple of the men out to look for James.'

'Thank you,' Lizzie said gratefully. She breathed deeply.

'What was he wearing?'

'A shirt, black breeches with a hole in the knee, grey hose and shoes,' she answered.

'We'll find him,' the Constable promised, making sure no note of doubt crept into his voice. 'You go home,' he advised her. 'Look after Isabell. James might come back on his own.'

She looked up at him, the sadness bedded deep in her eyes, clutching the baby.

'He never has before, Mr Nottingham, not since this one came. Why would he now?'

He sent one of the men to find the deputy and dispatched two others to search the area around Lands Lane, back into the orchards by the old manor house. That would be a good place for a boy to play and explore, he thought.

He paced the floor, waiting for Sedgwick to arrive, only stopping when the door banged open and he burst in, breathless from running.

'They said it was important. I'd just been to see Dan Scott.'

Nottingham cut him off. 'Lizzie was here. James has gone again.'

'I'll—'

'That girl of Davidson's, Fanny. I had Holden follow her. He lost her on Lands Lane.'

'Fuck.'

'John,' he began, but Sedgwick had already dashed out. The Constable sat down and ran a hand through his hair. James could just have run off and be hiding somewhere. Boys did that and returned when they were ready; he remembered doing it himself. But he'd have done the same as the deputy if it has been his child. Especially with Fanny so close . . .

They needed to find her, to find James, to find Wendell. And he didn't have enough men for all three jobs. A missing boy was the most important, there was no question on that. Best to hope he'd just wandered away to sulk and they'd find him hidden away somewhere. The girl close by could just be a coincidence. He'd have to pray it was.

He put on his tricorn hat and walked over to Lands Lane. Two of the men were there, looking in the doorways and small, dark courts that snaked back from the street.

'You start knocking on doors,' he told one of them briskly. 'Mr Sedgwick's boy is missing. See if anyone's seen the lad. You,' he said to the other, 'go and find three more men to help. We'll start here and work outwards.'

When they were busy he strode through to the orchard that lay beyond the houses. The trees were overgrown, gnarled, mossy branches splayed in all directions, much of the wood dead and rotten. But there were still apples in the autumn, drawing boys from all over the city; he'd come here often enough when he was young and hungry, greedily collecting the fruit. Once it had been part of the grounds of the manor house, but all that was left of the building was rubble. Everything useful had been taken and reused, wood and stone and tile, the past becoming part of the present.

The grass had grown high and wild, tangles of brambles with their sharp thorns, bushes grown into strange shapes that offered refuge away from the eye. He sighed and began to search, selecting a long stick to poke into the places he couldn't reach, raising his voice to call the lad's name. An hour passed as he laboured slowly over the area, finally sure James wasn't here.

There were so many places, that was the problem. Any lad who knew the city would have special places he never revealed, where he could run and feel safe and alone.

He knocked at Sedgwick's door, his breeches smeared with dirt, hose ripped and torn. Lizzie answered, fearful and quiet, Isabell crying loudly behind her in a basket, tiny arms and legs flailing at the air, her eyes pinched shut.

'Has he come home?'

She opened her mouth then just shook her head, as if she couldn't trust herself with words. Her eyes were red and her cheeks blotched from crying.

'We'll find him,' the Constable assured her. 'I've got men out looking, and we'll bring in other people.'

'John?' she asked, her voice choked.

'He knows, he's out there, too.'

She glanced over her shoulder to the baby.

'You stay here,' he advised. 'Look after her. I'll see someone tells you if there's any news.'

A few more men had joined the searchers, small groups working their way through the streets. Two men were knocking on doors, only to be met by women shaking their heads. But he didn't see the deputy.

He waved one of the men over. 'Where's Mr Sedgwick?'

'Haven't seen him, boss,' the man shrugged. He must have his own ideas of where to look, the Constable thought. For the rest of them there was no alternative but to carry on. He crossed Briggate, sliding through a passageway and into a court. Rubbish had rotted in the corners, the bloated body of a dead dog tossed aside, swarming with flies. He began in one of the houses that crowded into the space, working his way up stairs that were missing treads or where the boards were rotten. The lad wasn't in any of them. He poked through all the waste with no success then moved to the next small yard, meaner and dirtier than the last.

It was the same story, a place where little light had ever penetrated, the buildings all patchwork fabrics without hope. Just a short distance away he could hear the sharp sounds of the street, the cries of women selling lavender from their baskets, the clack of hooves as cattle were herded to the Shambles. Back in the yard there was only a dank, dead silence. He finished checking and moved back through the passageway, feeling as if he was returning from another, dark country.

He could see others searching, more of them now, their faces grim and determined, combing the corners and hidden places for the boy. They'd find him, Nottingham thought. They had to.

Sedgwick had gone straight down to the bridge. James loved to stand there, fascinated by the flow of the river below and the trundle of carts along the road. He darted between people, crossing the span, then coming back, but there was no sign of the lad.

His heart was beating fast and his mouth was dry. His eyes moved from side to side, praying to spot the small, familiar figure, but there was nothing, not even the others he'd play with or follow. He clattered down the stairs to the bank of the Aire, scared to look into the water for what he might see there but knowing that he had to check.

'James!' he yelled, and waited for a reply that never came. He was running along the path, out towards the New Mill, then into the trees, hearing his breath come hard and feeling the sweat on his face and palms. Every few seconds he'd stop, gazing around desperately for any movement, any sign of his son, the fear growing large in his belly.

Finally, after covering the ground four times and shouting himself hoarse, he had to admit that the boy wasn't here. He pulled his hands through his hair, wondering where the lad could have gone, where else he could look.

He couldn't allow himself to think that the child snatcher had the boy. James had gone off before and been fine. He'd wander home this evening as if nothing had happened.

The deputy knew that James resented his baby sister. She received so much of the attention that had once been all his. He knew it hurt him, and he'd tried to explain, but there was so much that didn't make sense to a boy. James couldn't see why Lizzie gave most of her time to Isabell, or that she loved him as much as she had before, and was just as much his mam. Slowly he made his way back, hoping over hope that someone would have found the lad, but knowing in his soul that no one had.

Eighteen

The night birds had begun their songs when they sat down in the jail. The deputy looked haunted, wild-eyed, distracted by every small noise, unable to sit still. Nottingham sat back thoughtfully, his coat hanging from a nail, the long waistcoat unbuttoned and his stock untied. Lister, fresh-faced from sleep, was alert and anxious.

'Have you been home, John?' Nottingham asked.

Sedgwick nodded absently.

'How's Lizzie?'

He shook his head, lacking words to describe the feelings.

'Rob, you take over the search. We've had plenty of volunteers, just like with the Morrison boy. Organize them, get them into the fields beyond Town End.'

'Yes, boss.'

'You should go home and sleep, John.'

'I can't,' he answered simply. 'Not while James is out there.'

'Then help the others,' the Constable said softly. 'Don't go haring off on your own. If you have any ideas where James might be, tell them so they can search properly.'

Sedgwick nodded again. Nottingham knew he needed to be back out looking for his son, that each moment away was rubbing his heart raw.

'Go on,' he said. 'I'll join you soon. And John,' he added, 'we'll find him.'

There were torches in the night, small points of fire that touched the darkness, spread across Town End, out beyond Burley Bar, along the side of the Aire and even past Timble Bridge.

Lister had volunteers spread across the fields towards the Grammar School, its shape a silhouette picked out by the faint light of a quarter moon. He'd heard about the boy being gone when he went to meet Emily after school, the talk slipping around the streets, folk wondering how it could have happened again, rumours beginning to spread.

But they'd still come out to help, dozens of men giving their time, women bringing stoups of ale and bread. With luck they'd find the lad. But if the child snatcher had him . . . It was a thought that stayed at the back of his mind as they worked, and he knew that each passing hour must be leaving the deputy in terror.

He paused as someone's wife handed him a full mug, and he drank deep. At least the night wasn't too cold; if James was out here he wouldn't freeze. Wiping the back of his hand across his mouth he thought about the whore the Constable had mentioned. Maybe she was the child snatcher, maybe not. If she was, and if she had the boy . . . he remembered the words *No Mercy* from the note left with the Morrison lad. They'd just have to hope she didn't have James.

The Constable had charge of people searching around the Parish Church and beyond. The mayor and two of the aldermen had come out to help, working as hard as anyone. They'd looked at Sheepscar Beck, some men even wading into the water, but they'd found no body.

Nottingham had managed to slip home for a few minutes, putting bread and cheese in the deep pockets of his coat. Mary had been in bed, and came downstairs in her shift as she heard him move around.

'John Sedgwick's lad is missing,' he told her.

'James? Oh, dear God. Emily said she'd heard another boy was gone.'

'There are plenty of us out searching.'

'What about Lizzie?' Mary asked, her voice urgent. 'Who's looking after her? She has the baby, too.'

'I don't know, love.' He sighed; he hadn't had time to give it any thought.

'I'll go over and sit with her,' she offered.

'What about Emily?'

'She'll be fine here for the night.'

'Take her with you,' he suggested; he didn't want the girl in the house alone. 'She can go to school from there in the morning. I'll have one of the men escort you.'

He held her, glad of the comfort of her warmth. It was what he needed, the sense of being loved. In a moment he'd be back out there, each hour growing more desperate. He couldn't even begin to imagine what the deputy must be feeling, or how he could keep from screaming.

'I'll have someone here in just a few minutes,' he said finally. 'I need to go.'

She kissed him. 'I hope you find him soon.'

'So do I,' he answered wearily. 'There's too much of this.'

Back outside, owls hooted as they hunted. He could hear the men moving and see the torches flaring. The night took him and he walked back to them. Mary's idea was good and generous. Lizzie would welcome someone else around, a woman to talk to, and help her with Isabell. And for Emily it would be a good lesson. She'd learn what it was like to be around a baby, and the darker, sadder side of loving someone.

Another hour passed and his faith in finding the boy faded. Over half the men had left, going to their rest before work in the morning, and the rest were struggling to stay alert after so long. Soon, he knew, he'd have to send them home. In the morning, once it was light enough, they'd begin again.

The deputy and his volunteers had begun on Boar Lane, searching the ground around Holy Trinity Church, then moving out and along, down Mill Hill, past Shaw's Well and through Swinegate. They'd hammered on the smith's gate until he opened up and let them in, examined the stables at the ostler's, moving slowly back towards the river. The tenters' grounds were open, with no place to hide, but the woods took them two hours.

They moved in a line, sticks out to sweep over the grass and into the bushes. Sedgwick had been in front of them, his throat so dry that all his words came out as nothing more than whispers. He tried to tell himself that they weren't searching for James, but just another missing lad. For a minute it would work, then the fears would flood back into his mind.

The weight pressed down on his chest so hard that it hurt to breathe. His legs ached from walking, and every step made his head pound with ringing pain. There were fewer men around him, some leaving quietly, others coming to explain that they'd need to work in a few hours.

He paid it no mind. Only one thing filled his thoughts: an image of James, the boy he loved more than the world, the boy he had to find. He knew the sweet beauty of the lad, the gentleness and kindness that would return. He was determined that James would become more than his father had ever been. He had to concentrate on finding the lad.

The deputy knew he should go and comfort Lizzie. He'd spent five minutes there, holding her, wiping away her tears, quieting her apologies. He didn't blame her for this. She'd been a mother to James, one he'd loved until Isabell was born. And he loved the baby, so helpless, so beautiful. They'd done all they could for the boy. Maybe the wildness that had grown in him was a sign of something, some madness. But he'd want to thrash the lad when they found him.

At dawn they were back sitting in the jail. The Constable rubbed his eyes with the heels of his hands, trying to ease the weariness away from them. Sedgwick looked blankly into the distance, fingers and feet making small movements.

They'd said little; words had no power. The silence pressed around them, heavy and oppressive.

'Go home, John,' Nottingham ordered finally. 'I'll keep the men looking. Lizzie needs you, and you need sleep.' When the deputy didn't respond, he said, 'Go. Come back when you've had some rest.'

The deputy left like a ghost, silent, drifting away as if he'd never been there.

'What do you think?' the Constable asked Lister.

Rob took his time in answering. 'We haven't found James yet. We have to believe the child snatcher has him.'

Nottingham nodded. 'I agree. If he was out there we'd almost certainly have found him by now.'

'What about that whore?'

'I don't know. She vanished in Lands Lane, then James was gone.' He raised his eyebrows. 'That's a coincidence, and I don't like coincidences.'

'How do we find her?'

'We look.' He sighed. 'There's nothing else we can do.'

'What about Peter Wendell?' Rob asked.

'He can't run too far. Leeds is all he knows. The rumours are out that he killed his sister. Do you think anyone will shelter him after that?'

'Are you sure he did it, boss?'

The Constable pushed the fringe off his forehead. 'Yes, I am. Those eyes of his were full of fear and guilt. And there's no other reason he'd run like that.'

'What do you want me to do?'

'Get the men searching. Then go and sleep. Come back early if you can.'

'Yes, boss.'

'Emily and her mother went to be with Lizzie. She won't be passing this morning.'

'Yes, boss.' Rob smiled.

As he entered the house, his father was already at work in the *Mercury* office, writing at his desk. He crooked a finger, motioning Rob in.

'Any word on the boy?'

Rob sat down heavily. 'He's still missing.'

James Lister shook his head sadly. 'Terrible. I don't know what's happening to this city.' He paused. 'Not seeing the Constable's daughter this morning?'

'Not today.'

'Have you thought about what I said before?'

'Yes.' He was tired, he needed sleep more than this argument, but he knew his father. The man wouldn't let it go until it was resolved. 'I'm not marrying Emily.'

Lister smiled. 'Your mother and I will find you a suitable wife.'

'No,' Rob said firmly. 'The only reason we're not getting married is because she doesn't want to. I'd marry her if she was willing. We'll still be courting.'

The older man sat back in his chair and studied his son with interest.

'Why court her if the lass won't marry you? What are you going to do?'

'I don't know,' Rob told him. 'But I'm not going to wed anyone else.'

'So you won't do what I want?' Lister's voice had grown harder.

'No, father,' Rob answered wearily. 'Not in this.'

'Don't be so bloody stupid. If I'd refused my father that way he'd have beaten me. Never mind that I was grown.'

Rob stood up. 'You're not your father, though. And I'm not you. I need to sleep.'

'And then he'd have disinherited me,' Lister said to his son's back.

Rob kept on walking.

The deputy stood outside his door and realized he was scared to go in. He didn't know what to say that could comfort Lizzie or how he might sleep. Around him he could hear the sounds as people stirred and smell the cooking fires starting to blaze.

He took a deep breath and turned the handle. Lizzie was inside, sitting on the chair, one hand gently rocking Isabell in her basket. The Constable's wife sat on the other chair, with Emily on a stool, watching the two of them.

Lizzie stood, questions and terror on her face. He held her

close, feeling her shudder, knowing she wanted to cry but that the tears had already all flowed from her; she had nothing left. Gently he stroked her hair for a long time.

Slowly he released her, keeping a light hold of her hand.

'Mrs Nottingham,' he said with a nod. 'Miss Emily.'

'No word?' Mary asked.

'Nothing,' he said emptily.

'You'll find him, Mr Sedgwick,' she told him. 'Keep your faith in that strong.'

'I will.'

'We should go now you're home. You need to eat and rest.'

He waited until they'd gone then held Lizzie close again. Isabell slept on, peaceful and quiet.

'I'm sorry, John,' Lizzie said. 'I should have watched him better.'

'You did everything you could. Don't blame yourself. He'd have gone whatever you did.' He pulled an old kerchief from his pocket, wet it with his tongue, and wiped away the traces of tears on her cheeks. 'Were they here long?'

'Most of the night,' she replied. 'I don't know what I'd have done without someone else here. She's a good woman, your boss's wife. Changed the baby, looked after things.'

'I had to keep looking,' he explained.

'I know.' She kissed him. 'I'm scared, John.'

'So am I,' the deputy admitted. He rested his head against her. There was so much he wanted to say, but none of the words seemed to have any weight.

'Can you sleep?' she asked and he shook his head slowly. He was exhausted but knew that if he closed his eyes rest would never come. He'd simply have pictures of James running through his mind, over and over, to prey deep on him. From the girl his bullet had grazed he'd gone to this, from nightmare to nightmare.

She moved away, busily cutting bread and cheese and pouring him ale.

'Eat,' she told him. 'You'd better sit and eat, John Sedgwick, you'll not have had anything for hours.'

'I'm not hungry.'

'Don't be daft. That isn't going to help. You need your strength.' She led him to the table. 'Eat,' she said again.

With the first bite he realized how hungry he was. She leaned over, kissed his cheek and said, 'I told you.'

The Constable walked over to the Calls, his face set, feeling exhaustion in every part of his body. His clothing was dirty, hose stained with grass, mud and dust coating his boots. He knocked on Alice Wendell's door and waited. James might be missing but he couldn't ignore Lucy.

She answered in a moment, her appearance neat, everything in the room scrubbed meticulously clean as usual, the acrid scent of vinegar filling the air.

'Come in,' she said. He sat at the table, and she stood, the lines deeper on her face, her expression impassive. 'Have they found that little boy yet?'

'Not yet.'

She clicked her tongue. 'His mam must be in hell.'

'His father is, too,' he said. 'Have you heard anything from Peter?'

'No,' she answered shortly.

'He'll come,' Nottingham said. 'There won't be many other places he can turn.'

She grunted.

'When he does I need you to tell me. I don't have enough men to go looking for him at the moment.'

'Are you sure he killed my Lucy?'

'He did it.'

'What if you're wrong, Mr Nottingham?' she asked plaintively. 'Have you thought about that? No man goes and kills his own sister.'

'Then I'll let him go and tell everyone I was wrong.'

'Aye, and the damage will have been done.' She stared at the Constable. 'Just give me one good reason why he'd kill her.'

'I don't know,' he admitted. He'd tried to find one and failed. 'The family honour? I'm sorry, I truly don't know, mistress. But I'm certain he murdered her.'

Alice snorted. 'Family honour? He was born before I married his father.'

'You'll have to ask him yourself. That's what I want to do.'

She considered what he'd said for a long moment.

'I'll believe you,' she said finally. 'If I'm going to tell you the truth I'd not put it past him to do it if he was drunk and angry enough.'

'Thank you.'

Nineteen

The Constable walked along the riverbank, watching the water for a few minutes, hearing the cries of workers loading cloth on to barges from the warehouses and the creak of carts as they squeezed past each other on the road, carters cursing, horses moving slowly.

He made his way back up Briggate, smiling when he saw the face he'd been seeking at the entrance to a yard.

'Hello, Jane.'

'It can't be good news if you're looking for me again, Mr Nottingham,' she said, but there was a small smile on her face. She was wearing gloves to hide her missing finger.

'I'm looking for someone.'

'But not me?' she pouted mischievously.

'Do you remember I asked you for the name of a pimp?'

'Aye, Davis or something, wasn't it?'

'Davidson,' he corrected her. 'He was running the girls, said they were his sisters. One of them was called Fanny. They worked down by the bridge.'

'Down by the Bridge? New, was she?'

'Fairly new.'

'They come and go so fast,' she shrugged.

'This one's stopped, but I know she's still around. Can you find out if anyone's seen her and knows where she's staying? I need to know.'

'Lovestruck, are you?' Jane grinned.

'There's money in it for you. Good money.'

'Must be serious.'

'It is. And I need answers soon. She wears a blue dress and she has dark hair.'

Jane nodded. 'I'll ask around, Mr Nottingham.'

'Bring word to the jail when you find out anything,' he told her. 'It's important.'

Down by the Bridge Con was playing his fiddle. A few stopped to listen for a moment, fewer still put a coin in the hat on the ground, too busy with their own business to pay the music much attention.

'Constable,' Con said as he heard Nottingham's footsteps, turning his sightless eyes to the sound.

'Morning, Con.'

'Have you found Mr Sedgwick's lad yet?'

'No.'

'He was by here, you know.'

'Who?' The Constable was suddenly alert, feeling the blood pumping. 'James?'

'Aye, yesterday, about the middle of the morning.'

'Was he by himself?'

'He was, and he had me play a jig for him the way he always does. He dances a bit and it brings in a few coins. We both like it.' The man smiled.

'Where did he go after that?'

Con inclined his head. 'Down the steps to the river there. He was angry when he arrived, but he was feeling better when he left me, Mr Nottingham.'

'Thank you, Con.' He drew out three coins from the pocket of his breeches and tossed them into the old hat, smiling broadly. 'That's the best news I've heard today.'

The fiddler raised his bow and began to play, a quick reel that sounded out across the water. The Constable walked back to the jail with a sense of relief. If James had been seen down by the river it looked as if the child snatcher hadn't taken him. They still needed to find him alive, but it removed the threat they'd all been dreading. He walked over to the house on Lands Lane and knocked quietly. Within a moment Lizzie was there, her hair unkempt, Isabell on her shoulder crying softly.

'Have you found him?' she asked urgently, the panic bright in her eyes.

'Not yet,' he said. 'Is John awake?'

'He's sleeping a little. What is it?'

'I've some good news. Con the fiddler saw James. They talked and your boy went to play by the river. So it seems as if he's just taken himself off. We'll find him.'

Lizzie closed her eyes and breathed deeply.

'I'll thank God for that, Mr Nottingham. I'll wake John and tell him.'

The Constable made his way back to the jail and sent one of the men to find the others and keep them searching along the riverbank. Further this time, though, beyond Dyers' Garth, out into the countryside beyond Leeds. If James wanted to hide, there were plenty of places out there.

He poured a mug of ale and drank it slowly. Now he knew that the boy hadn't been taken he felt calmer. They'd find him soon, he felt sure; a little lad might spend one night out in the open, but hunger and the cold would start to weigh upon him soon enough.

Nottingham removed his stock and opened the collar of his shirt. The surge of energy he'd felt when talking to Con was fading and the exhaustion was gradually creeping through his body.

There'd be time for sleep tonight, when he could crawl gratefully into his own bed, close his eyes and rest. With every year that passed he felt the long hours of the job more and more. He'd long since left his youth behind, and these days his body ached when he rose and his hair was almost as much grey as fair.

He could plot the time, count out all the weeks on his fingers, that had brought him here. None of it grew any easier with age, he knew that much. The city had changed around him, growing, booming, the wealth of the merchants becoming greater, their mansion houses like castles built on commerce, while the poor had no choice but to take what they could find.

He must have dozed; the sound of the door creaking open started him and he blinked his eyes.

'You were sleeping,' Jane said with a smile.

'Too many long days and nights,' he explained, stretching in his chair. 'Do you have anything for me?'

She frowned. 'That lass you're after, she's still in Leeds, right enough. Some of the girls have seen her and talked to her.'

'Whereabouts?'

She shook her head. 'T'other side of the river, that's all anyone seems to know.'

'What about her sister and the pimp?' Nottingham asked.

'No one said anything about them.'

He took out money, not even looking at its value, and put it on the desk. As ever, her hand moved quickly, hiding the missing finger, as she slipped it away.

'Thank you,' he told her. 'And if you find out anything more . . .'

'This is about the boys, isn't it?'

He raised his eyebrows. 'Why would you think that?'

Jane chuckled. 'I wasn't born yesterday, you know. You're looking for this Fanny and you want her now. The only reason I can see for that is the deputy's lad.' The Constable smiled but said nothing.

'I'll keep my ears open,' she promised. 'And I'll say nowt about this.'

'It's for the best.'

'You ought to go home and rest,' she advised as she stood in the doorway. 'You look like death, Mr Nottingham.'

Rob was the first to come back, just four hours after he'd left. He'd washed and brushed the worst of the dirt off his coat and breeches to smarten himself up, but his drawn face and the dark patches under his eyes told the truth.

'Can't sleep?' the Constable asked.

'I've just been turning over and over.' He drank deep from a mug of ale. 'Any news?'

'Con the fiddler saw James yesterday morning on the bridge. Said he went down by the river.'

'So he wasn't taken?' Rob brightened.

'It looks that way,' Nottingham said with a smile. 'But we still have to find him.' He paused and cocked his head. 'That's not what's been keeping you awake, is it?'

'My father's still talking about arranging a marriage for me.'

'You told him no again?' the Constable asked.

'More than once,' Rob said glumly, 'and he's not happy with me.'

'And what about Emily?'

'She says she doesn't want to marry anyone,' he replied.

Nottingham shook his head. 'That sounds like her, right enough. She has her own ideas about things, does that girl. I can't understand half of them.' He gazed at the lad. 'So what are you going to do?'

'I'm going to keep courting her,' Lister said with certainty.

Nottingham pursed his lips, then said, 'Since you're here, let's get some work from you. That girl, Fanny, definitely lives on the other side of the river. She's most likely with another lass and a man with a limp. Take a couple of the men and ask around.'

'We've tried that,' Rob objected. 'I could help look for James.'

The Constable shook his head. 'I need someone on this. Try again. Someone over there has to know her.'

'What about Wendell?'

'We'll have him sooner or later. The word's out that he killed his sister. No one's going to come to his aid.'

'We should be the ones looking for him.'

'Aye, you're probably right,' the Constable said wearily. 'But we have a child to find, and the child snatcher, as well as Wendell. I don't have enough men for all that.'

Sedgwick opened the door and walked in, his hair wild, looking as though he hadn't rested long.

'Lizzie told me. I wanted to go straight out, but she made me rest a little more.'

'You know she was doing the right thing,' Nottingham told him. 'She's got a good head on her shoulders, that lass.'

'Mebbe. I just felt I should be there, I should be the one to find him.'

'I've had the men searching.'

'Thank you, boss.'

'Go and look for him, John. At least we know now that he wasn't taken.'

'That's one weight lifted.' He looked up, eyes red from tiredness and pain. 'But it still doesn't bring him home though, does it?'

'He's out there and we'll find him,' the Constable assured him. 'Go on, get looking. And Rob, take Holden and one of the others and start asking more questions.'

A little more time, he thought. That was all it would take. Someone was bound to know Fanny, especially if she was with the others. James would turn up when his belly was empty or fear overcame him. And Wendell would find soon enough that he had nowhere to go.

Patience, he told himself. He just needed to let things run their course. Another day, two at most, and all this would be over. He poured more ale, draining the jug. In a few minutes he'd go next door to the White Swan and have them refill it.

As he sat back to drink one of the clerks from the Moot Hall ducked into the jail. 'The mayor wants you,' he said, then left again.

Nottingham sighed, finished the mug and stood. He retied his stock, half-heartedly brushing at the dirt on his coat and his hose. He knew he looked a tatterdemalion, unkempt as any scare-the-crow in the fields, but he was past caring. He'd been working for more hours than he cared to count, with who knew how many more to come. People would have to take him as he was.

At the Moot Hall he knocked on the dark, heavy door and entered. John Douglas was at his desk, his face bleak and unshaven, looking up as the Constable entered.

'Do you have anything good to tell me?' he asked.

'We know my deputy's son wasn't snatched,' Nottingham answered as he sat.

The mayor nodded his approval. 'That's something. Any word on him?'

'We're still looking.'

'People are talking, Richard. Two lads gone in just a few days.'

'They're different cases. You know that.'

'But they don't,' Douglas said with emphasis. 'And I can't tell them.'

'No.' The Constable rubbed at his eyes, trying to push out the gritty feeling behind them.

'What about the other things?'

'Very soon,' he promised.

'You're sure?' the mayor asked.

'Yes.'

'That's good enough for me.' As the Constable stood, Douglas added, 'Richard, go home and sleep.'

'There's too much to do.'

'It's an order,' the mayor said firmly. 'You look like you need rest more than anything, man. You said you trust your men, let them look after things for a few hours.'

'I will.'

Douglas was right, he knew that. He was too tired to think properly, his body ached, but he hated to ask his men to do things he couldn't do himself. Around him, Leeds was busy, the crowds on Briggate, the wheels of the carts pushing up on to the pavements as the axles creaked, the sound of laughter and arguments spilling from the dram shops.

He turned on to Kirkgate and kept walking past the jail. This time he'd give in.

Mary was in the garden, working with her fingers to pull the weeds around the plants. When she looked up and caught him watching her, he saw emotions flicker across her face, fear, joy, surprise.

'I've been sent home to sleep,' he said with a smile.

'About time, too,' she told him. 'Have you eaten?'

'Sleep first,' he said.

But in bed, rest refused to come easily. Even with the shutters closed light still leaked into the room, along with the clacking sounds of the loom, loud and constant next door. He kept thinking of things he should have done, orders he should have given. Finally he drifted away, diving through troublesome dreams.

He woke as Mary opened the door, and rolled on to his back.

'Do you feel any better?' she asked as she sat and rubbed the back of his hand.

'A little.' He ran a hand through his hair, pushing the fringe off his forehead. 'How long did I sleep.'

'Five hours.' She smiled. 'I thought I'd wake you before Emily came home. It'll be all clatter and din then. There's some meat and ale for you downstairs.'

'Thank you,' he said.

She bent and kissed him lightly on the lips. 'Now you'd best get yourself up. You'll be going back to the jail?'

'I have to.'

He took off the shirt and washed himself, the cold water fresh and wonderful on his skin, removing the worst of the dirt and sweat. Once he felt clean he found fresh clothes, old breeches tight on his waist, the jacket and shirt mended often but still too good to sell.

He ate in the kitchen, telling Mary about James, teeth tearing at the old beef and washing it down, hungrier than he'd realized.

'Rob said Emily told him she won't marry anyone.'

Mary raised her eyebrows. 'Maybe she'll change her mind in time.'

'You know what she's like. She might not.'

'What's he going to do?'

'He says he'll keep courting her,' Nottingham said. 'He doesn't want to marry anyone else.'

Mary shook her head. 'I hope it's worth it in the end.'

'So do I.' He wiped the plate clean with some bread. 'I'd better go back.'

'Don't be gone all night, Richard,' she told him.

'I won't unless I have to. If the others are out I will be, too.'

She brushed something invisible from the old, faded material of his waistcoat.

'You've done more than anyone who works for you,' she chided.

'And it needs to stay that way,' he said with a smile. He kissed her forehead. 'I love you.'

John Sedgwick had moved the men out past New Mill and the Upper Tenters, into the woods the spread out from the Aire. The word that James had been seen the morning before had made his heart rise. Just knowing he hadn't been taken by the child snatcher gave him hope.

Now, out here, all that had evaporated like a puddle in the sun. All the terror had returned. Anything could have happened to the boy. He could have slipped into the river and drowned, he could have injured himself somewhere. There were dangers in every step. Time was passing and he was growing more frantic.

'Have you looked over there?' he asked urgently, pointing to a copse just up the hill. The man shook his head. 'Go ahead and search it.' He tramped on through the undergrowth, ignoring the sharp edges of stalk and brambles that sliced at his breeches and hose.

Suddenly he stopped, raising his hand to halt the others.

'Did you hear that?' he asked quietly. Both the men looked at him quizzically. 'Over there.' He nodded to where the riverbank cut away sharply. Slowly he moved towards the area, each step careful and soft.

From the edge he could see how the earth had gone, leaving a tangle of roots under the tree that grew tall above, its leaves casting a shadow. There would be holes down there, he thought, places where a boy could shelter and hide. He'd heard a cry, he was certain of it.

Carefully, the deputy judged the drop and jumped, feeling the shock of cold water rising up his shins. He steadied himself, the river running around him, and looked at the bank.

'Hello, James,' he said with long relief. 'It looks like you've found yourself a good hiding place.'

Twenty

The word had spread quickly. One of the men had run all the way back to the jail, shouting that they'd found the boy.

'Where was he?' Nottingham asked.

'By the river, about half a mile past the New Mill.'

'How was he?'

'Seemed well enough,' the man said with a shrug. 'Dirty and tired. Nowt broken. Probably regretting running away now, mind.'

The Constable grinned. 'Where's Mr Sedgwick?'

'He's taking the lad home.'

'Go and tell him he doesn't need to come back today.'

'Yes, boss.' The man dashed off again.

He sat back in the chair and let out a slow sigh. He could only imagine what the deputy must feel, the flood of relief in his heart. James had been found; that was the important thing. Now he could use the men to look for Fanny and for Peter Wendell.

He wrote a note for the mayor, passing on the news, and paid a boy a farthing to take it to the Moot Hall. Then he locked the door of the jail and set out to find Wendell.

★   ★   ★

James had fallen asleep against his shoulder as he carried him home. The boy had mud plastered against his skin and his clothes, and he'd burst into tears when the deputy held him close, but his bones were whole and he had no bad cuts.

Sedgwick unlocked the door of the house on Lands Lane and pushed it open with his arm.

'John?' Lizzie said, then saw the lad slumped and her face crumpled. 'Is he . . .?'

'He's just sleeping. Don't worry.'

He carried the boy up to his bed and stripped the garments from him, tossing them on the floor. Lizzie hovered close by, holding the baby, rubbing her back tenderly.

'Your brother's home,' she told Isabell quietly. 'We don't want him to go again, do we?'

Quickly and lightly, Sedgwick ran his fingertips over his son, then pulled up the covers. James had barely stirred, his breathing even and deep.

'He'll be fine when he's rested.' He kissed Lizzie then took Isabell from her, taking in the freshness of her and smiling. 'He can wash when he's awake.' He grinned and sighed with pleasure. 'He'll be hungry, too.'

'Just like his father,' Lizzie said, her eyes glistening.

'I could eat,' he said.

'I know you, John Sedgwick, you're always hungry,' she said. 'There's bread and cheese, and a pottage cooking.'

As they sat at the table, Lizzie gently rocked Isabell on her lap and asked, 'What are we going to do about him, John?'

'I don't know,' he admitted soberly. 'Mebbe this will have terrified him.'

'Then why didn't he just come home?'

He considered the question. 'Too scared of what we'd do, perhaps.' He reached across and took her hand. 'I'll talk to him later.'

'We can't go through this again.'

He nodded. 'I don't know what else we can do. We love him, you treat him like he's yours.'

'He doesn't like Isabell.'

'It's not that. He's had us to himself, he liked that. And now she's here he thinks we don't love him any more.'

'But—'

'I know,' he said softly. 'We just need to give him a little time. Let him really see that we still love him.'

'We've tried that,' Lizzie said helplessly.

He sighed. 'Then we've just got to keep on doing it. He's a good lad, you know that.' He yawned and closed his eyes, feeling all the life draining from him.

'Go to bed, John,' she told him. 'James isn't the only one needing his sleep.'

'I need to work. With what happened to that girl when I shot the thief taker . . .'

'Not today, you don't. Mr Nottingham will understand,' she said firmly. 'And if he doesn't, I'll tell him.'

The Constable spent the rest of the day moving between the people he knew who might have seen Wendell. They were the folk who lived like ghosts, the ones unseen at the frayed edges of society.

They were men and women who haunted the market, scavenging for something to sustain them until the next day, rotten fruit and meat too spoiled even for the dogs at the Shambles.

He knew their names, knew where to find them in the shadowed spaces where no one else would go. They seemed to vanish in order to die; their bodies were rarely found, and when they were there was peace on their faces, as if giving up life had been release, not pain.

But none of them had seen the man. They shook their heads to answer Nottingham's question, or pointed fingers to suggest possibilities.

He stayed out until evening was falling, finding his way down to the river, seeking the man Rob had talked to before. Simon Gordonson was there, a face the Constable recognized, the withered right arm close to his chest. Several fires glowed and crackled, people of all ages gathered around them. One girl rocked and suckled her baby while an old man held a small piece of meat in the blaze with a stick.

'Mr Nottingham,' Gordonson said. He worked hard to stay presentable, the worst of the dirt cleaned from his breeches and coat each day, his hose washed, lank hair finger-combed.

'Quite a group, Mr Gordonson,' the Constable said with admiration.

'And more of them every day,' Gordonson said sadly. 'These are hard times.'

'They're always hard times unless you have money. My man said you had Lucy Wendell here for a few days.'

'We did. Maybe if she'd stayed . . .' He shook his head helplessly.

'I'm looking for her brother.'

'He'd find no welcome here.' There was no doubt in his voice. 'I've heard what he did to her.'

'I need your people to keep their eyes open for him. He's out there.'

'And if they see him?'

'Then come and tell me,' Nottingham told him.

'There are plenty of folk here who don't trust the law,' Gordonson said warily. 'They think it's only for those with money.'

'There's law and there's justice, Mr Gordonson. I want justice for Lucy. Tell them that, please.'

The man nodded his agreement.

'I hear they found your deputy's lad.'

'They did, and he's safe now.' Nottingham smiled.

'What about the other boy, the one who went missing on Saturday?'

'We found him, too. I'm surprised you don't know that.'

'It just seemed strange, that's all. People searching all over and suddenly he's there by the Bridge.' Gordonson raised his eyebrows.

'I think people were just glad to have him back,' the Constable said blandly.

'If you say so.' Gordonson looked at him curiously.

'I do.' He kept his eyes firmly on the man. He'd give away nothing on this. The less anyone realized, the better. 'I'd appreciate the help of these people in finding Peter Wendell.'

'I'll ask, but the choice is theirs.'

'Of course,' Nottingham agreed. 'I heard that Robbins is seeking a clerk over at the tannery.'

Gordonson lifted the withered right arm. 'Even with this?'

'If you can write a good hand and you'll work hard I doubt he'll care.'

The man inclined his head towards the groups gathered around the fires. 'And who'd look after them if I left?'

'Maybe they can look after themselves.'

Gordonson smiled. 'I feel a responsibility for them, Mr Nottingham. They're all good people.'

'Most people are, I find.' He reached into the large pocket of his waistcoat and drew out a purse. He'd taken it from a pick-pocket and no one had ever come to claim it. 'This might help them.'

The man's eyes widened as he weighed the money in his palm. 'That's very generous.'

'It's just been sitting at the jail. Someone might as well have the use of it.'

'But it won't buy us, Constable.'

'It's not intended to, Mr Gordonson.' He tipped his hat, turned and walked away.

No one had word of Peter Wendell. Wherever the man was, he was staying out of sight. He hadn't gone home again, according to the man on watch at Queen Charlotte's Court. But he was still in Leeds, the Constable was certain of that; it was the only place he knew.

Rob was at the jail when he returned, hungrily eating a pie before setting off on his rounds.

'Any luck on the other side of the river?' he asked.

'Hints and rumours, that's all. You'd think they were made of air.'

'I'll send Mr Sedgwick over there tomorrow.'

'James is fine?'

'That's what I heard,' Nottingham told him. 'John will be in with the morning.'

'Anything I should look for tonight, boss?'

'Peter Wendell,' he answered after a moment. 'He might well come out at night. Have the men alert for him. Watch out, though, he's dangerous.'

'Yes, boss.'

'Did you see Emily today?'

Rob nodded.

'You'll need your patience with her,' Nottingham told him. 'And I'm saying that as her father.'

'Yes, boss.'

'Now go on, off you go.'

Alone, he finished his report and heard the city slowing with the night. There were shouts and laughter from the White Swan next door and the occasional sound of footsteps, late workers heading to their hearths.

Finally he pushed paper and quill away from him. There was nothing more he could do tonight. With a deep sigh he stood and stretched, locked the door behind him and set off slowly down Kirkgate. On impulse, at the Parish Church he opened the lych gate and made his way over to Rose's grave. The moon was high and bright enough to make out the words on the headstone.

'That sister of yours,' he said quietly. 'I wonder if she'll ever change. She's still bloody contrary.'

He squatted and placed his palm on the grass that had grown over his older daughter.

'We all miss you, love.' He sighed softly. 'I'm not sure God had a plan that let you die, but I'm not sure he looks over this life, either.' He stroked the earth as if it was skin, tenderly and gently. 'You'll always be in our hearts, you know that.'

He stopped again at Timble Bridge, listening to the water burble over the rocks and pebbles, then walked up Marsh Lane, seeing a thin light shining through the shutters at home.

Mary sat in her chair, reading, and he bent over to kiss her. He could hear the footsteps as Emily moved around upstairs in her room.

'I wondered if you'd be home tonight,' she said.

'Nothing more I could do,' he explained, unable to stifle a yawn.

'And more sleep won't hurt you,' she pointed out.

'I know,' he admitted, taking Mary's hand and pulling her to her feet so he could hold her. 'We could have an early night together, if you want.'

'Maybe you should come home and rest in the daytime more often,' she said with a twinkling smile.

'Chance would be a fine thing.'

'Then let the others do more. They're younger than you.'

'I'll be at my best come the morning,' he promised her.

'I hope you'll be at your best before then, Richard,' she told him with a grin.

There'd been no sign or whisper of Peter Wendell during the night. Rob had been out with the men, checking the dark places where someone might hide. There were plenty of folk out there, sleeping in the spaces others ignored, their few belongings on their backs, faces hollow and eyes blank when they were roused, too cowed to complain.

The clock had hardly struck four, with the bare rise of dawn, when the door of the jail opened. Lister looked up from his report, one hand sliding to grab the cudgel. A woman entered, her face as sharp as if someone had planed down the flesh, eyes appraising him carefully.

'Mr Nottingham in yet?' she asked.

'No.'

'You tell him Alice Wendell came by.'

'Lucy's mother?'

'Aye,' she said curtly. 'He came, drunk as owt, needing somewhere to stay.'

Rob stood. 'Is he still there?'

She nodded. 'Sleeping as if God owed him the time.' She pursed her lips. 'Nay, there's no rush, lad, he'll not be waking soon, not the state he was in.' She turned to leave, then added, 'I'll warn you, though, he won't come easy, even in his cups.'

Rob sent men out to fetch Nottingham and the deputy, waiting anxiously for them to arrive. He could feel his heart beating faster with anticipation, flexing his fingers and looking at the cupboard where they kept the weapons.

Within half an hour all of them were there.

'She said he's sleeping?' the Constable asked. He looked calm, his stock neatly tied, clean hose on his legs. Sedgwick seemed distracted, rubbing the sleep away from his eyes.

'But be careful of him.'

'I think we've learned that,' Nottingham said wryly. He drew three swords from the cupboard. 'Don't use these unless you have to. Take your cudgels, too. Rob, get the manacles. I want those on him as soon as possible.'

'Yes, boss.'

'We'll take two of the others. They'll stay outside, just in case we need them. You ready, John?'

'Yes, boss,' the deputy answered.

'How's James?'

'Still sleeping when I left.'

'He'll be fine.'

'Aye, I hope so.' His voice was flat and resigned, the pock marks on his face standing out red and livid in the early light.

'Come on, then,' the Constable said. 'And remember, I want him fit to talk. I want to find out what happened to Lucy Wendell.'

They marched down Briggate, hearing the servants slowly starting their morning work, then along Call Lane. Nottingham was quiet, his jaw set, the deputy striding next to him, long legs covering the distance easily. Rob hung back slightly, walking with the other men, the scabbard banging against his leg as he moved.

At the house on the Calls Nottingham issued his orders.

'The room's in the cellar. Rob, John, you come with me. Alice Wendell will let us in. See if you can get the manacles on Peter before he wakes.' He gestured at the others. 'There's only one door. You two stay out here in case he gets past us. If he comes out, hit him hard and bring him down.'

'Can we trust her?' Sedgwick asked.

'Yes,' the Constable answered without hesitation. Even though it would cost her a great deal, she wanted justice for Lucy. He led the way down the stairs, treading quietly, then tapped lightly on the door, Lister and the deputy so close behind that he could feel their breath on his neck.

She answered quickly, moving aside for them to enter. Peter Wendell lay on the pallet, his skin caked with dirt, the stubble grown heavy enough on his face to make him almost unrecognizable. He was sleeping deeply, the blanket pulled up around his neck.

Nottingham directed them with gestures. Once they were all in position he gave a nod and drew his weapon, holding it close to Wendell's face. Rob threw back the cover and started to put the manacle on the man's wrist.

Wendell sat up with a roar, pushing Lister backwards and slamming him hard into the wall. Nottingham put the point of the sword against the man's neck.

'Don't move,' he ordered, pushing just enough for the point to pierce the skin. Drops of blood trickled down Wendell's skin as the man's eyes burned fire. 'Now hold your arms out.'

Slowly, reluctantly, the man complied.

'Put them on,' the Constable instructed Rob.

Metal clicked on metal, locking in place; Wendell's thick arms didn't sag under the heavy weight.

'Stand up slowly.'

He rose from the bed, the men standing back slightly, three blades facing him.

'Walk to the door. And don't try to run, I have more men outside.'

'I won't,' Wendell said, his voice husky. He glanced over at his mother. 'You told them, didn't you?'

She held her head high.

'Aye, I did.'

'Fucking old bitch.' He spat at her. She let it run down her cheek. The Constable kicked him behind the knee, making the man sprawl on the ground.

'Get up,' Nottingham told him. 'Out. Now.'

He let the others leave and turned to the woman. She was keeping her face hard, looking at nothing and breathing slowly.

'Thank you,' he said.

She shook her head, keeping back the tears he knew were there. 'When you find out why, come and tell me.'

'I will,' he promised.

The Constable had put away his sword but kept the cudgel in his hand, the loop of leather around his wrist. He looked at Sedgwick, walking alongside Wendell, watching the prisoner intently, and knew the memory of the thief taker was uppermost in his mind.

At the jail they added ankle fetters, attaching them with a chain to a heavy staple driven into the flagstone of the cell. Nottingham locked the door, knowing the man was staring at him, but didn't give him a glance. There'd be ample time to talk very soon.

'Good work,' he told the others. 'Rob, you've put in plenty of hours, go home and sleep. John, I want you to take most of the men and look for this Fanny across the river.'

'Yes, boss.'

The Constable smiled and rubbed his hands together. 'I've a good feeling about today, I think we'll find her.'

'What about Wendell?' Lister asked.

'As soon as he's used to his new home I'm going to discover why he killed his sister.'

Rob unlocked the door of the house on Lower Briggate and entered. He could see his father at work, setting type slowly into blocks on the table, preparing the new edition of the *Mercury*. The man looked up briefly and beckoned with an ink-stained finger.

'Who was that you took to the jail?' he asked.

'Someone we've been looking for,' Rob answered. He knew not to pass on information.

'You were all armed.'

'Always better to be safe.'

Lister dug into one of the boxes in front of him, pulling out a piece of type and examining it before adding it to the article then wiping his hand on his dirty apron.

'I hope you've thought more about what I said?' he asked

'Marrying, you mean?'

'Yes, that's exactly what I mean, and you know it.' He stopped and removed his spectacles. 'Well, have you?'

'I gave you my answer the last time,' Rob told him bluntly.

'I'm offering you the chance to reconsider.' There was iron in his voice, his eyes flat and his mouth expressionless. 'You're my son; when you're under my roof I expect you to obey my wishes.'

Bubbles of anger rose through Rob's exhaustion. 'And if I won't?'

Lister regarded his son for a moment, then said, 'Maybe your precious Constable can find you a bed in his house, because I won't have you in mine.' He put his glasses back on and returned to his work. 'I warn you, though, if you choose to leave you'll come to regret it.'

'And if I stay I might regret it even more.'

Rob turned away to the stairs.

'Where are you going?'

'To collect my things and find a room. There are plenty available.'

'Not on what the city pays you. And you'll get nothing from me.'

'I don't need much . . . Father.' He spat the word out viciously. 'You've apparently made your decision, now it's my turn to make mine.'

Twenty-One

The Constable brought two mugs of ale into the cell and offered one to Wendell.

'I daresay you'll be thirsty.'

The man watched him cautiously from under his brows then reached for the cup and drank greedily. Nottingham leaned against the wall.

'I know you killed her,' he said.

'You do, do you?' Something that was almost a smile flickered across Wendell's lips. 'And how do you know that?'

'Why else would you have run when we came to ask you about her?'

The man shrugged. 'Happen I just don't get along with the law,' he answered.

'I'm sure you don't. But in this case I don't believe you.'

'You can believe what you like. You've been telling everyone what you think I did.'

'I know you did it, Peter. I'm just wondering why.' The Constable took a sip of his ale. 'That's what I can't see. Why would anyone kill his sister?'

'You keep saying that. But there's nowt to prove it.'

'You might be surprised.'

Wendell's eyes shone and his mouth twitched slyly. 'Mebbe I would. And mebbe I never killed our Lucy at all.'

'Oh, you did,' Nottingham told him with certainty, watching the man's face closely. 'You did. What was it, you saw she was having a child?'

'Why would I give a bugger if she was going to have a babby?'

'You tell me.'

'I was the one who looked after her. I was the one who loved

her. Don't believe what that old cow tells you, she couldn't wait
to have Lucy out the house.' Wendell had found his voice now
and the Constable wanted to keep him talking.

'She wasn't a bright lass, I heard.'

Wendell shrugged again. 'She'd do owt for anyone, would Lucy.
People didn't want to know her because of her lip, but she were
a lovely girl.'

'She was scared of seeing you. That's why she didn't come to
you or to her mother when she was dismissed.'

'Me? Why'd she be scared of me?' There was an edge of fury
in his tone. 'I told you, I looked after her.'

But Nottingham understood now, it had all come clear.

'You looked after her very well, didn't you, Peter?'

'I made sure nowt bad happened to her.'

'And you loved her like more than a sister.' Wendell leapt
upright, lunging forward as far as he could. The Constable didn't
move. 'Didn't you?'

'You fucking bastard.'

'That was why you killed her. The baby was yours, wasn't it?
And you thought that if she burned in that fire, no one would
ever know.' He could see Wendell's face growing redder, his fists
clenching and knew he was right. 'You killed her, then you ripped
the child out of her and you tried to burn them both.'

The man held up his wrists. 'Take these off me and I'll kill
you. I'll fucking kill you.'

'What was it?' Nottingham continued, pushing and probing.
'Did you think she'd tell someone who the father was? Had you
threatened her, is that why she tried to hide from you?'

The veins stood out on Wendell's neck, the thick, heavy muscles
of his arms straining.

'She trusted you to look after her and that's what you did.
When you saw what had happened you threatened her and then
you killed her.'

'I loved her!' Wendell shouted.

'You loved her so you killed her. Is that the same love you
show that girl of yours when you take your fists to her?' Nottingham
kept his voice contained and even. 'Did she know about you and
Lucy?' The man was silent, breathing heavily, pulling on his chains.
'No, I'm sure she didn't, the same way your mother didn't.'

He waited, letting the silence grow in the room until it became oppressive. He had time. He took another small sip of the ale, seeing the hatred and guilt on Wendell's face.

'She came to me,' the man said finally.

'Lucy?'

He nodded.

'When?'

'Two year back. Someone had said no man would ever love her.'

'And you showed her he was wrong.'

'I was holding her. She was warm, she needed someone to care about her.' Wendell sat down again and looked at the ground.

'But it never stopped.'

'No,' he admitted dully.

'It all changed when she was dismissed, didn't it?' the Constable asked softly.

'She didn't even understand what was going on. She came to find me. I'd just left the Talbot.'

'What did you tell her?'

'I said if she told anyone, if she went to see our mam, I'd kill her. I hit her.'

'So she ran.'

He nodded.

'But you found her again, didn't you?'

'She was up near Town End. I'd been looking for her.'

'What happened then, Peter?'

Wendell remained quiet for a long time. Outside, the Constable could hear voices and carts as they passed. In the cell it was as if time had come to a stop.

'I told her I was sorry and that I'd look after her if she'd come with me.'

'Where did you take her?'

'There's a house on Cripplegate. It's fallen down but you can still get into the cellar. I told her to stay there and locked her in. I took food to her every day.'

'How long did you keep her there?' the Constable asked.

'A while. I had to decide what to do. I thought we could leave together, go somewhere else. But she'd have said summat sooner or later.'

'So you killed her.'

Wendell raised his head to look at Nottingham. His eyes were wet with tears.

'There was nothing else I could do. I couldn't trust her not to say anything. If she had, that would have been the end of us. It was for the best, for her, for me. It was the only way.'

'And then you thought you'd burn her body.'

'If there was nothing left, no one would know,' the man said as if it was obvious. 'They'd have thought she'd left Leeds, gone. Everything would have been all right.'

'But why that house on the Calls? Why so close to where your mother lived?'

'Because those bastards round there had always made fun of her when we went to visit our mam,' he said simply. 'If a few of them died it would be no loss, it would be revenge. Let them fucking suffer.'

'And you ripped the baby out of her.'

'If it hadn't been for the babby, everything would have been all right.' He knitted his fingers together, pushing and squeezing. 'It could all have gone on like it did before. I hated it.'

At his desk, Nottingham sat in silent contemplation. He'd spent weeks imagining the reasons for Lucy Wendell's death, but he'd never suspected the truth of it. It proved to be so much bigger, and so much smaller, than he could have thought.

It made sense to Peter Wendell, as if he'd had no other choice. Everything he did had followed a straight path and he could never have turned from it. In his own mind it all seemed completely logical, so plain and straightforward. He'd never understand how twisted and warped it appeared from the outside.

The Constable pushed the fringe back off his forehead. The man would hang, there was no doubt of it. He'd confessed; everyone would be repulsed by what he'd done. And he deserved it. He'd loved her, but it was love that had grown into a sick, sad thing, one that pulled and ripped at Lucy's innocence, then made her pay the price for his sin.

It would destroy Alice Wendell when she learned it all. But he knew he had to tell her. He'd given his word, and it was better for her to learn it from him before it became public property. She'd blame herself, not the son whose fault it really was.

He poured more ale and drank, barely tasting it as it slipped down his throat. He thought he'd seen every type of inhumanity, more evil than any lifetime should contain. But nothing like this, and all of it in the name of what Wendell deemed love.

The man was mad, not a madness of mind but one that had clawed deep in his soul. It was beyond cure, beyond any help. Only his death on the gallows could end it. He swirled the drink around in the mug, watching the liquid move.

The door opened and Rob walked in and sat down.

'Can't sleep?' Nottingham asked.

'I thought I should tell you, I've taken a room with Widow Foster.'

'Over on the Lower Head Row?'

'Yes.'

The Constable looked at him quizzically.

'My father told me either to do his bidding or leave.'

'I'm sorry,' Nottingham said.

'I'll see Emily after school and tell her. Did Wendell confess?'

'Yes, as much as you can call it that. He thought he did the only thing he could do.'

'What?'

'It doesn't matter, lad. Not now.' The Constable shook his head. 'You walk Emily home later and stay for your supper. You'll be welcome.'

'Thank you, boss.'

Nottingham stood up.

'Where are you going?' Rob asked.

'I have to tell a woman a story that's going to break her heart,' he said.

Twenty-Two

It was an afternoon of frustration. Someone would think they knew Fanny and send the deputy to another street, a different house, but each time it was a chase that led him nowhere.

The men had no better luck, and finally he sent them home

before making his last round of the day. He was eager to be home, to talk to James, caught between thrashing him and loving him, and so fearful of everything the future might bring.

Con was playing his fiddle on the Bridge, and they exchanged a few words before the deputy moved on to check all the usual places. Everything was quiet and he left Leeds to its night, walking up Lands Lane and opening his door.

James was sitting at the table, scooping pottage from an old, cracked bowl with a spoon. Lizzie had scrubbed him clean and put him in fresh clothes, and Sedgwick could feel his heart ache as he looked at his son.

'All rested?' he asked, tousling the boy's hair before kissing Lizzie as she changed Isabell, the baby chuckling softly.

'Yes, Papa.'

He sat across from the boy. 'You had a big adventure.'

James lowered his eyes. 'I'm sorry,' he said.

'Were you scared?' Sedgwick asked.

The boy nodded. 'Sometimes,' he admitted.

The deputy moved as Lizzie settled down next to him on the bench, her hand light on his thigh. She was cradling Isabell, and he noticed the quick look of resentment the lad gave the baby.

'Was it fun?' he asked.

'Yes.' James's eyes brightened. 'Well, it was at first. It's so big outside the city. I wanted to get to Kirkstall Abbey but I didn't know which way to go.'

His father smiled. 'Why didn't you come home?'

'I could hear everyone looking for me and I thought they'd all be angry if they found me.'

'We were worried about you,' Lizzie said.

'Your mam's right, lad. We just wanted you back and safe.'

'I'm sorry,' James repeated, his cheeks reddening.

'You know Isabell's going to look up to you when she's a little older, don't you?' Lizzie asked him.

'But she can't do anything.'

'Not yet. She will. You couldn't when you were her age, either,' the deputy said with a small grin. 'So we did everything for you, like we do for her. You're older now, you can do more for yourself.'

'It doesn't mean we love you any less,' Lizzie said. 'We love you just as much as we ever did.'

'It's true, we do,' Sedgwick agreed.

The boy eyed his sister thoughtfully. 'Will she really look up to me? What will she do?'

'Oh, she'll probably follow you everywhere and want to do all the things you do,' Lizzie told him.

'But she can't do that if you run away,' the deputy pointed out.

'No, Papa.'

'The nights are long when you're out there, aren't they?'

'Yes.'

'And there's no table and no food.'

James shook his head.

'It's better to stay here, you know. You know you have a bed, you have meals. And we love you.'

'I know you do.'

'Even Isabell loves you. She just doesn't know it yet,' Lizzie said, watching as his small face creased into a laugh.

'You go and play upstairs,' Sedgwick told him.

'Yes, Papa.'

'What do you think?' Lizzie asked when they were alone. Isabell whimpered, on the verge of crying, and she took her breast from the dress and put the child's head to her nipple.

'I hope everything will be good again.' He looked at her and raised his eyebrows, then sighed. 'For a little while, at least.' He rubbed the back of her hand. 'He's a good boy. He'll start school very soon. That'll help.'

'I'll try and do more with him.'

'Once he's used to her . . .'

She squeezed his fingers lightly. 'Just give him a little time. You were probably just like him at that age, John Sedgwick.'

'Aye, probably.' He grinned. 'Worse, mebbe. I'll go and put him to bed. He'll still need his sleep.'

'He's growing up very quickly.'

'Sometimes I think it's only the rich who can afford a childhood.'

'He'll grow up to be a fine man,' she assured him. 'Just like his father.'

'But richer,' he told her seriously. 'That's what'll save him in this city.'

The sun had risen, the dawn chorus long past, when they gathered at the jail. The deputy seemed calm and rested, smiling with his mouth and his eyes. Rob was haggard, the strain and the long hours of work telling on his face, his hair flying all over and his clothes unkempt. The Constable looked at the two of them.

'Anything from last night?' he asked.

'Just the usual,' Lister said. 'A few drunks, a couple of scraps. And that letter.' He indicated the unopened note on the desk. 'Someone put it under the door. It's addressed to you.'

Nottingham slid his finger under the seal. It was good, thick paper, the words scribbled quickly on it in dark ink.

'For the lass in a blue dress try a court off Simpson Fold.' There was no signature, but he knew who'd sent it. Joe Buck had paid the price he believed he owed for the thief taker. This would cancel any debt.

'John,' he said, 'go back across the river and ask about our girl in the blue dress over by Simpson Fold. Just do it quietly, I don't want her knowing. She's around there somewhere. When you find out where she is, come and get me.'

'Yes, boss.'

Sedgwick left, the door closing heavily behind him.

'Mary says you're welcome to have your supper with us every night,' Nottingham told Rob.

'I can look after myself, boss,' Lister said.

'I know you can, lad.' He smiled. 'It's an offer, not a demand. And Emily said she'd be glad to have you there, too.'

Rob brightened. 'Thank you.'

'You go and get yourself used to your bed at Widow Foster's. She'll look after you. Any word from your father?'

Lister shook his head.

'Maybe he'll come around in time.'

'I doubt it. He doesn't change his mind easily.'

'Even stubborn men can relent when it comes to family,' the Constable said. 'Keep that in your mind.'

Calmly, he wrote up the report and walked over to the Moot

Hall. A cart had lost a wheel on Briggate, tipping its load into the road. The horse stood dumbly in its traces as two men tried to repair the damage, a line of wagons behind stretching down towards the Bridge.

He moved past the carters yelling at each other, the sense of violence rising, and into the building, leaving the sounds behind him, his heels clattering on the polished boards of the stairs.

The mayor had pushed his work away, sitting back in his chair and smoking a pipe of tobacco.

'We should have the child snatcher today,' Nottingham told him.

Douglas nodded. 'And the rest?'

'Lucy Wendell's brother has confessed to killing her. I'll have him taken to the prison today.'

'Why did he do it?' the mayor asked. 'Who'd kill his own sister?'

'That baby she was carrying was his.'

Douglas grimaced sadly. 'Dear God, Richard.'

He walked up past the bloody butchers' shops the Shambles to the Market Cross, then took the long way down the Head Row and along Vicar Lane back to the jail. The sun kept trying to push through high white clouds and the day was gathering warmth. Another summer was coming, the days becoming longer and longer, the flowers blooming, the crops growing in the fields.

At his desk he sorted through papers, keeping some, discarding others. He heard the clock at the Parish Church striking the quarter hours. Patience, he told himself. Soon Sedgwick would return with the information and they'd be able to finish this business.

Finally he sat back to wait. He could hear Wendell moving around in his cell. His mother had taken the news without a change in her expression, the only reaction one hand gripping the other so tightly that the skin turned white. She'd said nothing when he finished, and flinched when he put a comforting hand on her shoulder. Eventually he'd turned away and left, knowing there was nothing he could do to help her, that words would only weigh like lead on her soul.

He'd brought pottage, bread and ale from the White Swan and finished them by the time the deputy arrived, smiling and rubbing his hands in anticipation.

'There are three courts off the Fold,' he said.

'Have you found her?'

'She's there with another lass and a man. From what folk told me it has to be Davidson and his whores.'

'Then let's go over there and see them.' He unlocked the cupboard and took out a pair of swords.

'Do you think we'll need them, boss?'

'I hope not,' Nottingham answered. 'But we'll take them anyway. Go and find two of the men to come with us.'

They set off in a quiet group, taking their time to stroll down Briggate and across Leeds Bridge. Barges were lined along the bank by the warehouses, loading bales of cloth to take on to Hull and then on across the globe, to Europe and America.

'Do you know exactly where they are?' the Constable asked.

'A room at the top of a house,' Sedgwick said. 'It's right at the back of the court, out of the way. Only one entrance. The place is nigh on falling down, from what I could see. Half the windows are broken.'

'We'll have the men wait below and you and I will go up.'

'Kick down the door?'

Nottingham nodded. 'Take them by surprise.'

'The window up there looks out on the court. They might be able to see us coming.'

'It won't do them much good, John.'

'Treat them harsh?'

'These are the ones who took Morrison's lad. They could have had James.'

'Yes, boss.' He saw the deputy rest his hand on the hilt of the weapon.

Simpson Fold ran off Hunslet Lane, a small street that seemed too quiet and still in the early afternoon. Somewhere in the distance he could hear the urgent call of a magpie and the bleating of sheep.

He let Sedgwick guide them, going into a small ginnel that

led through to the court. They stayed in the shadows, looking at the houses that were lost in their decline, slates gone from roofs, the brown runnels of damp on the old limewash of the walls.

'That one over there.'

The Constable looked. The building was in even worse condition than the rest, lintels sagging, the door jammed open.

'A good place to hide,' he speculated.

'Only a few living back here. Can't afford anywhere better.'

'Right,' Nottingham said. 'I'm not expecting any trouble, but I want everyone prepared.' He waited for their acknowledgements, then told the men, 'You stay down here in case they try to run. If they give you any trouble, you know what to do.'

He advanced across the open ground of the court, hearing Sedgwick just behind him. He glanced up at the window, but saw nothing through the years of dirt accumulated there. Inside the main door he drew the sword from its scabbard.

'Ready?' he asked quietly.

'Yes, boss.'

They climbed the stairs slowly, testing each tread before putting weight on it. He noticed the footprints in the dust, some small, one set larger. There were three flights to the top, the door in front of them tightly closed. The Constable braced himself against the wall with one hand, feeling the plaster damp and crumbling under his fingers. He raised his leg and brought his boot crashing down on the lock. The door flew open and he dashed in, the sword out and ready.

Fanny and Sarah were huddled together, screaming, still in their shifts, a blanket thrown on the floor. Nottingham looked at them.

'Where is he?'

Sarah pointed to the other room, its door still closed.

'Get them dressed and out of here,' he ordered. He looked around the room. It was almost bare, just a chair and a table with a jug of wine and a small bottle. He pulled out the stopper and sniffed it.

'Yes, boss.' The deputy picked up two dresses, one a tired, weak yellow, the other faded blue, and threw them to the women. 'Put them on,' he said brusquely, 'and hurry up.'

The Constable leaned quietly against the wall and stared at the door.

'I'll let the men take them once they're outside,' Sedgwick whispered in his ear, 'then I'll come back up.'

The footsteps were sharp in the air, then fading. He waited until he could hear the muffled sound of voices outside, then said, 'You can come out now, Mr Davidson. It's just you and me.'

He knew the man had heard him, knew he'd come out soon, unable to resist the chance to talk. He waited, breathing slowly and quietly, giving a smile of satisfaction as the knob turned and Davidson emerged, limping slowly into the room.

His face still wore the brash confidence he'd had before but everything else was changed. His skin was sallow, cheeks hollow from a lack of food, fingernails rimed with dirt. His coat and breeches had dark patches of grease on the fabric and he stank of stale sweat and piss.

'All this because we didn't leave Leeds?' he asked.

'All this because you snatched a child.'

'And why would we do that, Mr Nottingham? We're just trying to live, I told you that before.' He gestured around the room. 'But it's harder and harder.'

'Revenge. That's what you wrote, wasn't it?'

'We wouldn't do something like that.'

'I don't believe you, Mr Davidson.'

The man shifted his weight to take it off his bad leg. 'I've no reason to lie,' he said simply.

'I doubt you need any reason to start lying,' the Constable told him. 'And your sisters, if that's what they are, they're just the same.'

'You think you can prove anything?' Davidson asked mockingly. 'There's nothing you'll find here.'

'No?' Nottingham asked. 'That poppy juice over there will make anyone sleep.'

'I take it when my leg's bad,' the man answered smoothly.

'Then there's the lad Fanny took. He remembers more than you might think.' He watched the man's eyes flicker for a moment. 'Whose idea was it, anyway? Yours?'

'We haven't done anything.'

'Then the three of you are going to hang for nothing,' Nottingham said. He kept all the expression from his voice and looked at Davidson flatly. 'And you are going to hang. All of you.'

'We can leave Leeds.'

'It's too late for that now,' he said.

'We've done nowt.'

The Constable shook his head slowly. 'You've done too much, Mr Davidson. You should have gone when I told you.'

The man smiled slyly. 'Do you think you're going to get me to confess to something I haven't done?'

Nottingham shrugged. 'I don't care if you confess or not. The truth will come out in court, and then it'll be a short dance on the gallows.'

'You're making a mistake,' Davidson said. His voice seemed calm enough, but the Constable could see small beads of sweat shining on his brow.

'The only mistake I made was trusting you. You're good, I'll give you that, you must have taken in a few in your time.' The man slapped his bad leg. 'I'd still be a working man if it wasn't for this.'

Nottingham studied him coldly. 'Maybe you would. Maybe not. As far as I can see, there's something died in you.'

'We've done nothing wrong!' Davidson shouted.

'I told you before, I don't believe you.'

'If you hang me you'll be hanging an innocent man.'

'No, I won't,' Nottingham told him. 'Now it's time to go.' He raised the sword and gestured towards the door. Down below he could hear the deputy's footsteps. 'Go.'

The man limped resignedly towards the top of the stairs. From the sound, Sedgwick was just one flight below. Without warning, Davidson's leg seemed to give way and he reached out to the Constable to steady himself. Too late, Nottingham saw the knife in his hand and watched as the blade sliced through his waistcoat into his belly.

He felt the burn in his gut and moved his hand to cover it as he cried out and fell. The blood was warm on his fingers, pouring over them like water.

He saw Sedgwick's face and heard Davidson's scream as the sword cut into him and he tumbled down the stairs. He tried to speak but no words would come from his mouth. His ears roared with noise as the deputy leaned over him, and he closed his eyes.

Afterword

For many years I've considered *Lucy Wan* (also known as *Lizie Wan*, number 51 in Professor Francis Child's *English and Scottish Popular Ballads*) to be one of the most fearful folk songs. It's a tale of incest and death. When Lizie (also known as Lizzy or Lucy Wan) tells her brother that she's having his child, he kills her by beheading her with his sword and cutting her body into three pieces before walking away. His mother drags the truth from him and he decides to leave, saying he'll only return 'when the sun and moon meet on yon hill' – in other words, never.

The words have been honed and worn over the centuries to make it into a work of art, powerful and deadly. It's a song that's stayed with me since I first heard the great Martin Carthy sing it and I've always wanted to use it. Now I've had the chance.

For my knowledge of Leeds in 1733, *The Illustrated History of Leeds* by Steven Burt and Kevin Brady (Breedon Books, 1994) has been invaluable, as have *Leeds: The Story of a City* by David Thornton (Fort, 2002), *The Municipal History of Leeds* by James Wardell (Longman Brown & Co, 1846), *Leeds Describ'd: Eyewitness Accounts of Leeds 1534 – 1905* by Ann Heap & Peter Brears (Breedon Books, 1993) and *The Memoranda Book of John Lucas 1712 – 1750* (Thoresby Society, 2006). Other publications by the Thoresby Society, the excellent Leeds historical association, were helpful on other points.

Simon Heywood was a vital resource on superstition regarding harelips. Penny read the manuscript thoughtfully, correcting errors and offering wonderful suggestions and love. Thom Atkinson, a great friend and excellent writer himself, gave much of his time, applied the yellow highlight and helped to drastically improve the book, as he's done so often before, and he has my eternal gratitude. Please, seek out his books. Thanks, too, to my agent Tina Betts, who patiently reads the bits of books I send her and is always perfectly honest in her assessments. Lynne Patrick, to whom I owe a huge debt, is a wonderful editor, and I'm grateful to Kate Lyall Grant for believing in this book. Leeds Libraries and Leeds Book Club have been great supporters of this series and I value that more than they know. Candace Robb is an inspiration who's become a friend and her wonderful words about these books are a treasured gift. Much of this writing has been fuelled by the excellent baked goods from Botham's of Whitby, whose brack is a joy for the senses. Last, but not least, the supportive friends from all over the world on Facebook and Twitter who cheer me daily. Thank you, all of you.